DARKNESS
IN THE
LIGHT

STELE PROPHECY PENTALOGY
PREQUEL 3

DARKNESS
IN THE
LIGHT

RANDY C. DOCKENS

Carpenter's Son Publishing

Darkness in the Light

©2020 by Randy Dockens

All rights reserved. No part of this book may be reproduced or transmitted in any form or by any means, electronic or mechanical, including photocopying, recording, or by any information storage and retrieval system, without permission in writing from the copyright owner.

Published by Carpenter's Son Publishing, Franklin, Tennessee

Published in association with Larry Carpenter of Christian Book Services, LLC
www.christianbookservices.com

Cover and Interior Design by Suzanne Lawing

Edited by Robert Irvin

Printed in the United States of America

"All Creatures of Our God and King" was written by William Henry Draper and first published as a hymn in 1919. The hymn is based on a poem by St Francis of Assisi.

978-1-946889-72-0

CHAPTER 1

Jubilee Calendar
10:4:2

Sometimes, actions are worth their consequences.

"Me'ira, where are you?" The girl sighed. "Please, My Lady, don't get me in trouble again for losing you."

Me'ira almost giggled but managed to put her hand over her mouth to keep from giving herself away. She ducked deeper into the lemonwood until she heard Lydia's steps get farther away. Maybe she went to check the palace teleporter logs to be sure the teleporter wasn't used. By now, Lydia knew most of her evasive tactics.

She pulled a leaf and inhaled the lemony fragrance. These plants from New Zealand were gifts from her cousin Hadassah. Well, technically, her first cousin once removed, but trying to keep that straight just made her head hurt, so she always said cousin when someone asked. Hadassah was the main priest's wife, and she had given the original plant to Me'ira's father and mother when they first married. Me'ira's father had them planted here along the Sea of Galilee to mark the border of their northern palace grounds. They proliferated over time into a dense grove. The smell brought back memories. When younger, she would hide here while playing hide-and-seek with Lydia. She adored sitting here, smelling the lemony scent and watching the sunlight reflect off the ripples from the sea. Poor Lydia. She still seemed unable to find her here. Me'ira felt a tinge of guilt for the scolding Lydia would receive from her mother. She frowned. Well, she would receive the worse scolding if found out. Still, she believed her mission too important not to follow through.

Once she felt confident Lydia wasn't near, she ran down the hill toward the sea and then took the trail north to the seaside city of Tiberius. She found the designated café next to the shore and scanned the patrons.

There he was, sitting at the table closest to the water, gazing out over the sea watching sea terns squabble with each other as they flew by. She could see his strong jaw silhouetted against the blue-green sea. As he turned, the wind off the sea stirred the curl of hair that naturally drooped over his forehead. She couldn't see his eyes from here, but those hazel eyes with specs of green made them mesmerizing. But the pièce de résistance were his dimples, which formed every time he smiled. Her heart swooned every time he looked at her.

She walked to his table. He was still looking out over the sea. "Hi, Galen."

He looked up. A smile immediately lit up his face displaying those knee-weakening dimples. He stood. "Me'ira. You came." Stepping to her side of the table, he pulled out a chair for her to sit.

She smiled as she sat. "How could I not? You know I wanted to see you just as much as you said you wanted to see me."

The waiter came by. Both ordered tea, and the waiter left complementary hummus and flatbread on the table.

They gazed at each other for several seconds. Galen reached

over and took her hand. "Me'ira, I've missed you. Thanks for coming."

Me'ira smiled. "Seeing you is always the highlight of any day." She repositioned her hand and rubbed her thumb over his index finger. "But do we always have to meet so secretly? I would like my family to get to know you."

Galen seemed mesmerized watching her hand stroking his. He did not respond.

She jiggled his hand and giggled. "Galen, did you hear me?"

He looked up with a sheepish smile. "Yes. I just wasn't sure how to respond."

She turned up her brow. "What do you mean?"

The waiter came with their tea. They released their hold on each other as he set teacups before them. He left the teapot as well, setting it on a trivet on the far side of the table.

Galen poured for both of them. "It's not that I don't want to meet your parents. It's just . . . well, I don't know what they will think of me."

Me'ira cocked her head. "Well, I think they will see how wonderful you are, just as I do."

Galen smiled. "But you're a Ranz. You're royalty. I'm . . . I'm nobody."

Me'ira put her hand over Galen's. "You're a somebody to *me*." She shook her head. "My father isn't snobbish. He cares for all citizens. You'll see—once you get to know him."

Galen took a bite of bread with hummus. He gave a slight chuckle. "Maybe you're right."

"We will celebrate the first new moon of the year next month. Why don't you come? I can introduce you to them then. After all, it's Ephraim's turn to help sponsor the event."

"I'm from Naphtali."

Me'ira's head jerked back slightly. "Oh. I've always met you here, so I assumed you were from here."

"I live in Naphtali, but we have a museum here that I run."

"Why didn't you tell me? I would love to see it sometime."

Galen's eyes lit up. "Really? I thought you would consider it boring."

She leaned closer. "I could consider nothing you do boring."

Galen's cheeks reddened. "Well, maybe next time."

"No more secrets. OK?"

Galen gave a smile, but it seemed awkward—not like him. "Sure."

She took another sip of tea and pushed her cup away slightly.

"All finished?"

She nodded.

He stood and held out his hand. "Shall we go for a walk?"

She smiled, reached for his hand, and stood. After looping her arm through his, they walked along the shoreline with the sea in view but kept the beach at a distance.

Galen looked at the surf and back to Me'ira. "Care to walk along the beach?"

She realized her attire wasn't the best for such a walk. Perhaps an ankle-length maroon taffeta dress hadn't been the best choice for this rendezvous. It allowed for a stroll on solid surfaces, but not in the sand.

She smiled. "Maybe next time. I'll have to plan for that."

He nodded, patted her hand, and smiled back. "Understood."

He led them to a tram as the city extended steeply up the hillside from the sea. Steps allowed those not faint in heart to climb the steep incline, but the tram allowed a more casual venture up to the awaited overlook. Plus, the tram's glass top allowed one to sit and take a 360-degree view. As they traveled to the highest part of the city, they had a great view of the sea. They strolled to one of the overlooks, sat on a bench, and observed the city cascading down before them to the shore below. The pastel walls of the various buildings looked like a mosaic. Ripples within the sea reflected the sunlight, making the entire sea look like a huge blue-green gemstone. Boats with colorful sails were out on the sea creating a spectacular view.

They talked about anything and everything, but nothing substantial, at the same time. Me'ira just wanted to be in Galen's company and enjoy being with him.

"So, will you and your family come next month for the new moon celebration?"

"I'll try. My mother and father travel a lot, so I'm not sure if they will be available."

"Oh, for the museum?"

He nodded. "They're always scouting for artifacts of interest."

"Sounds exciting."

Galen gave a shrug. "I suppose. I've never traveled with them." A smile came to his face. "I like to run their business. That's why I chose to open the museum here. This area is beautiful, not too far from my parents' place, and gives me some stability."

Me'ira smiled. "I think traveling would be exciting."

"Maybe. But I'm content." He looked into her eyes. "What about you, the mysterious Me'ira Ranz?"

Me'ira giggled. "I'm probably anything but mysterious. I think I'm pretty simple."

"I disagree. Ask any young man in the kingdom. Your vision is what fuels their dreams."

Me'ira grimaced. "The thought of everyone thinking about

me is kind of creepy."

Galen pulled her closer. "I'm sorry. All I know is, you fuel mine."

"Well . . . " She gently cupped his face in her hands. "That's not creepy, but actually sweet."

He smiled and kissed her hand.

After a bit more small talk, Me'ira looked up and saw the sun low in the sky. "Oh my, it's getting late. I have to get back."

"I'll walk you back to the café. You can retrace your steps from there."

As they descended in the tram, Me'ira wondered about them and how they could see each other more openly.

She touched Galen's arm as they approached the café. "Galen, you will come to Jerusalem next month, won't you? I want you to meet my family."

Galen stopped. Me'ira turned. "What's wrong, Galen?"

"Do you think that wise? What if they don't accept me?"

Me'ira laughed. "How is that possible?" She put her hand to his cheek. "You're so likeable."

He smiled. "You're sweet. But your father will not see me through the same eyes as you."

"Don't worry. I'll prepare them." Her eyes darted between his. "Just promise me you'll come."

They looked into each other's eyes for several moments.

"OK. I'll come. I promise."

Standing on her toes, she kissed his cheek, turned, and ran back up the trail toward the palace.

She stepped onto the large patio that overlooked the Galilean Sea, hoping she would not be seen until later and that it would seem she had not been out that long. Yet, she knew, Lydia had probably already filled her mother in.

10

She barely got two steps into the room when she saw her mother sitting on the large, plush tan-and-ocher sofa against the wall. Her mother's all-white dress contrasted well with the colors in the sofa. Her light olive skin, dark hair, and hazel eyes made her dress look even brighter. The occasional sequins in her dress and her diamond necklace and earrings enhanced her beauty. Me'ira, as well as countless others, always felt her mother stunning no matter what she wore.

"Hi, Me'ira. Nice of you to join us."

"Hi, Mother. I just went out for a walk."

"I see. Please, have a seat." Her voice contained that awful matter-of-fact tone, which was never a good sign.

It surprised Me'ira to see Lydia standing nearby, her head downcast. As she walked around Lydia to take the matching plush chair opposite her mother, she saw Lydia's cheeks tear-stained. Mother had scolded before, but those sharp talks had never elicited tears. She swallowed hard. This was not going to be mother's typical scolding.

"Explain yourself, Me'ira."

"I just wanted to be alone."

"Do you think your actions have no consequences?"

Me'ira glanced at Lydia. Did that statement have something to do with Lydia crying? Did she cause that?

"Where did you go . . . alone?"

"I went into Tiberius, had some tea, and looked around. It was a pleasant—" Me'ira saw her mother's hard stare and stopped midsentence. "What's . . . what's so bad about that?"

"Unchaperoned?"

She rolled her eyes. "Oh, Mother. That's an old-fashioned custom. Not relevant today." She saw her mother's lips purse. "Besides, what can even happen with the King always watching? What's the concern? The crime rate is zero."

Her mother rubbed her forehead. "Me'ira, you think that is what this is all about? It's about you being selfish and not obeying. Your station in life is different from that of others. Your father is a model for how all are to worship the King. Like it or not, there are elements of protocol that must be maintained. Being chaperoned is one of them."

Me'ira let out a long breath.

"And to show you the seriousness of this, I am firing Lydia."

Me'ira shot to the front of her seat. She looked from her mother to Lydia, who now had tears forming again. "Mother. You . . . you can't."

Her mother's face became stern. "I told you there are consequences to your actions. If Lydia cannot keep up with you, then I will be forced to find someone who can."

Me'ira's eyes watered. She couldn't remember a time when Lydia, only a few years older than she, was not with her. Lydia started out as someone to play with since all her other brothers and sisters were grown by the time she was born. Lydia had grown into a confidant, a friend.

"Mother, Lydia is like a sister to me. She's family. You wouldn't just let *me* go, would you?"

"Oh, Me'ira, of course not. But you have to learn."

"OK, Mother, I get the point. If I had known of such a consequence, I would not have eluded her."

Her mother sighed. "So, you would have forced her to aid and abet in your . . . outing?"

Me'ira nodded.

Me'ira's mother fell back into the sofa and sighed. "I think you're missing the whole point here."

Her mother looked at Lydia. "Thanks, Lydia. I appreciate your help in this matter. Would you please go and check on dinner?"

12

Lydia curtsied. "Yes, ma'am." She smiled. "Thank you, Your Highness."

Me'ira's jaw dropped slightly. Lydia was acting? Me'ira felt relieved—and slightly miffed at the same time. Yet, she had to admit: she deserved it. She had put Lydia in a bad position.

As Lydia walked away, she gave Me'ira a hard stare and pointed her head toward Me'ira's mother. Me'ira knew Lydia was telling her to listen to her mother. Lydia always acted in her best interest.

"Me'ira—"

Me'ira held up her hand. "Mother, before you go further, let me just come clean with everything."

Her mother raised her eyebrows. "Well, this is a first."

Me'ira smiled. Yes, it probably was, but she wanted to show her mother she could be responsible.

"I've met someone."

Her mother's eyes grew wide. "You saw a man . . . alone? In the city?"

Me'ira put her hands to her cheeks and shook her head. "Mother, please let me finish. First of all, nothing happened. No one gave us a second look."

Her mother gave her a grimace.

"Remember the cruise we took on the sea a little over three months ago?"

Her mother nodded.

"Well, I met someone on the ship and we've been seeing each other off and on."

Her mother opened her mouth to say something but then closed it and waited for Me'ira to continue.

"That's who I met today. Three's a crowd in those instances."

Her mother sat up and straightened her dress. "Yes, I don't disagree, but there are protocols to handle those situations."

Me'ira sighed. "Yes, I'm sure there are." She paused. "And . . . I'm willing to abide by them."

Her mother's countenance perked up.

"I've invited him to Jerusalem for the new moon celebration next month. He said he would come. I will introduce you to him then."

"Well, Me'ira, I'm glad you've come to your senses. He will have to be vetted, you know."

Me'ira rolled her eyes. "Surprise, surprise."

"Now, Me'ira. You just said you were willing to abide by protocol."

Me'ira sighed. "Yes, Mother." *Just how many protocols are there for such a simple thing?*

"Being related to the Prince is not an easy task," her mother said.

"Tell me about it."

"Now, Me'ira. Watch your tongue and your tone. Your brothers' and sisters' spouses had to be vetted as well. Their marriages all worked out, didn't they?"

Me'ira shrugged. "I guess."

"Well, they did. There's even protocol about who one can marry and how inheritance can be given. This is all by the King's degree. We must obey."

"Yes, Mother." Her tone exuded that same matter-of-fact tone her mother often used on her.

Her mother raised an eyebrow but didn't retort. "Even I had to be vetted before I could marry the Prince."

"You, mother?"

"Yes, me. My father came out of the Refreshing, married my mother about a decade later, and had me a year after that. Having a glorified half-sister was always a pressure to live up to."

14

Me'ira cocked her head in thought. "How is aunt Adelina glorified? I don't think I've ever asked before. It's just always seemed normal."

"Well, Dad was married before the Refreshing. Adelina was taken at The Receiving before she was born. Her mother died without knowing the Messiah."

Me'ira sat with mouth open. "Mom, that's horrible. Such things like that really happened? It's . . . it's unfathomable."

Her mother nodded. "Yes, we are blessed, Me'ira. We shouldn't take our life today for granted. Grandfather's stories are not just stories, Me'ira. Those things he tells really happened."

Me'ira sat in silence for a moment trying to grasp what her mother told her. "So, when did you marry Father?"

"I didn't marry your father until about thirty-five years after the start of the kingdom. Your father was much older than I, so a lot of things had to be questioned and worked out."

"Well, you both look the same age to me."

Her mother smiled. "That is a blessing of our King. From what I understand, we age more slowly than people did before the Refreshing."

"So, how were you . . . vetted?"

"It was pretty much a formality. Investigations occurred regarding my father's heritage as well as mine. Questions were asked of relatives to be sure all were of great character. However, in my case at least, my father, Lars Isakson, was already well known, being the brother of Edvin and uncle of Ya'akov Isakson, the first priest born into the kingdom. Probably having a glorified half-sister didn't hurt either." She shrugged. "But still, protocol had to be followed."

"OK. Sounds simple enough. Galen comes from Naphtali, so I'm sure there are no issues."

"I would expect not." Her mother smiled. "Let me prepare your father, though."

Me'ira nodded. She gave a sigh of relief on the inside. She was dreading that part and thankful her mother agreed to take on that task.

CHAPTER 2

Well, if vetting is such a simple thing, why is everyone making such a big deal about it?"

Me'ira waited with Adelina, her glorified aunt, outside her father's office. She drummed her fingers on the chair's arm in anticipation. It felt like she had been waiting forever.

Adelina laughed. "Just be patient, Me'ira. It is a big deal, but is usually just formality."

Adelina sat opposite her in front of a large mirror. The reflection of Adelina's glorified body created an aura around her. Me'ira knew Adelina came with the King to set up his kingdom and had lived with a glorified body since that time. Me'ira told herself she should be used to it by now. There were a lot of people like Adelina, but her presence always seemed to awe her. They both looked the same age, yet Adelina was at least five centuries older than she! It didn't really strike her as odd, but her father and grandfather told her stories about life being very different before the Refreshing. Those stories sometimes proved hard to grasp.

One of the large double doors opened. Her great uncle Edvin motioned for them to enter.

Me'ira entered her father's office, which she had done many times before. As a child she liked to sit and look at everything

17

in view as her father worked. The office was a large rectangular room. One side contained floor to ceiling bookcases with rare books—many of a religious nature. She knew he was a serious collector. Maybe that would be a connection Galen could make with him. On the opposite wall hung a large picture of Israel showing the boundaries for each of the nation's twelve tribes. The desk itself appeared large and ornate with emblems of each of the twelve tribes of Israel engraved around its edges. Its legs always reminded her of gnarled olive trees. Behind the desk were large French doors that exited onto a large balcony.

"There's my little light." Me'ira smiled at her grandfather. That was the meaning of her name and the pet name he always used for her. He held out his hands for a hug.

She came over and gave him one. "Hi, Grandfather."

He smiled back and patted the seat next to him for her to sit. She obliged.

She looked around. Why were so many people in this room? She could understand her father and mother being there, but now her grandfather, her great uncle Edvin, her aunt Adelina, and her cousin Ya'akov were also present.

"Am I allowed to say something?" Me'ira looked at each of them.

Her father raised his eyebrows.

"Galen is just coming for a visit. I'm not marrying him. So why all the ado?"

Her mother sighed.

"Now, Kyla, it's a legitimate question," her grandfather quickly said, addressing her mother. "This is the first time she has had to go through this process."

"Yes, Dad, you're right. It is time she better understood protocol," Kyla said, then turned to her husband. "Jeremiah, would you like to proceed?"

18

"Lars, why don't you tell us what you've found out?" Jeremiah said, turning to him.

"Thanks, Your Highness—"

Jeremiah raised his hand. "Lars, we're all family here. We're not in public."

Lars nodded. "As you wish, Jeremiah." He turned to Me'ira. "Sweetie, you said his last name is Shafir?"

Me'ira nodded. "Galen Shafir." She looked around the room. "Is that a problem?"

Lars gestured to Ya'akov. "Ya'akov, do you want to tell of the discrepancy?"

Me'ira looked from her grandfather to Ya'akov, her cousin and priest. "Discrepancy? What discrepancy?"

Ya'akov leaned forward. "Well, Lois and Noah Shafir did have a son, and he should be about the same age as Galen, but . . ."

"But what?"

"We have no record of him ever using a teleporter."

Me'ira looked at Ya'akov as if she expected something more. "And?"

"And . . . that is very unusual. Teleportation is the most common form of transportation these days. There's hardly a person alive who has not used a teleporter—especially someone his age."

"Well, there's one, apparently," Me'ira said, eyes shifting around the room.

Ya'akov sat back in his chair and raised his eyebrows toward her father.

Jeremiah pressed his lips together, looked at Me'ira, and smiled. "Honey, this is all part of the vetting process. It doesn't necessarily mean anything in and of itself, but you have to admit, it is a little odd."

"So, it's a crime not to use a teleporter?"

"Dear, mind your sarcastic tone," her mother said. "He's not just your father. You must remember that. He is the King's chosen."

Me'ira sighed. "Sorry, Mother." She looked at her father. "I'm sorry, Father. But I don't understand the problem."

Lars reached over and patted her arm. "We're not saying it's a problem. Just unusual."

"So, you're allowing him to still visit?"

"Yes, of course, Me'ira," her father said. "We just want you to know what we found."

Me'ira breathed a sigh of relief. "Thanks, Dad."

"There is one complication," Ya'akov said.

Me'ira looked back at her cousin. "What is that?"

"Until he is fully vetted and this . . . discrepancy is better understood, he will not be able to sit with the royal family at the ceremony."

"Well, I know not on stage . . . " She looked at Ya'akov as the true meaning of his words dawned. "Not even in the audience?" Her eyes widened. "But—"

"Don't worry, Me'ira. He can sit with me."

Me'ira's focus turned to Adelina as she gave a forced sigh. "Thanks."

Her mother spoke again. "Honey, I know all of this feels intrusive, but—"

"It's just protocol. I know, Mother."

"I'm sure it will all get cleared up soon."

Me'ira nodded at her father. Lars patted her arm and smiled at her.

"So, when he comes, can I tell any of this to him?" Me'ira asked.

"Just be yourself," Adelina said as she smiled. "The only

thing you *have* to tell him is that he will need to sit with me during the ceremony. Everything else will be normal."

Me'ira nodded.

Her mother spoke up again. "Except, you will need to be chaperoned while he is here."

"Yes, Mother. I know. Protocol."

CHAPTER 3

Me'ira exhibited melancholy mood swings for the rest of the week. Until the vetting meeting with her family, she had looked forward to Galen's coming. Now she didn't feel so positive about it. She didn't want him to feel excluded by her family. If he was made to feel that way, would there be any hope of their relationship blossoming to something more serious? Was that her family's plan all along? Surely not, she had to hope. She couldn't allow herself to believe that would be the case.

* * * * *

The day of Galen's arrival, Me'ira paced in the palace gardens as she waited. Protocol dictated she was not allowed to greet him by herself; Galen would have to be presented to her. She kept looking over the garden walls to view his arrival. To her surprise, she saw an antigravity accelerator pull up at the palace gate. An AGA was not unheard of in Jerusalem, but they were highly uncommon. A man who looked like Galen stepped out. *Is it him?* She saw him talk to someone who ushered him inside. A servant quickly headed out, entered the AGA, and drove it around the palace and out of view.

A short time later, a servant approached Me'ira.

"My Lady, a Master Galen is requesting your presence."

Me'ira smiled and tried to keep the air of decorum expected of her. Still, inside, she felt excited, almost giddy. "Please ask him to come here to the gardens."

The man bowed. "Very good, My Lady."

As Galen entered the garden, Lydia did as well. She stayed at the garden's edge, however, as Galen walked toward Me'ira.

Me'ira practically ran to meet Galen. She smiled. "I'm so glad you decided to come."

Galen took her hands and smiled back. "How could I not?"

She led him around several topiaries, through a wisteria arch, and past some roses to one of the benches next to a corner fountain. Galen seemed to enjoy the stroll with her, but he soon gave a brief nod toward Lydia. "Who's your shadow?"

Me'ira sighed. "She's our chaperone."

Galen's eyebrows raised.

Me'ira rolled her eyes. "I know. It's . . . they tell me . . . *protocol*." She made a grimace. "Sorry."

Galen smirked. "Trying to make sure I'm a gentleman?"

Me'ira giggled. "Something like that, I guess."

He rubbed his fingers over her hand. "I'm looking forward to meeting your family, but nervous at the same time."

"They're just family, Galen. They may have more responsibilities than other families, but deep down, they're just human beings."

Galen laughed. "I guess that's one way to look at it. I'll try to keep that in mind."

After spending about an hour together in light talk, Me'ira saw Lydia approaching them.

"Excuse me, Me'ira. Your family is ready."

"Thank you, Lydia." She turned to Galen. "Are you ready?"

Galen shrugged. "Ready as I'll ever be."

He stood and reached for her hand. Me'ira reached to take it but then saw Lydia give a quick glance, so she kept her hand to herself. Galen gave a slightly confused look but put his hand next to his side. They followed Lydia into the palace.

"We only have time for introductions," Lydia said. "We'll be leaving for the temple shortly. After we come back, we'll have dinner and more time to get acquainted."

Galen nodded.

Me'ira took his arm and stopped. Galen turned her way. "One other thing," she said. "You'll have to sit with my aunt while we're at the temple."

Galen scrunched his brow, then smiled. "Protocol?"

Me'ira nodded as she led Galen into a large living area. Lydia stayed next to the door. A glass chandelier hung in the middle of the room with a sitting area underneath containing twin plush sofas with a leaf print. As Jeremiah and Kyla stood, Galen genuflected and then stood.

"Your Highness. Your Grace. It's my pleasure." He shook both of their hands.

Jeremiah placed his hand on Galen's shoulder. "Galen, we're pleased to have you. I hope you find your stay here enjoyable."

"Thank you, sir."

Kyla smiled, then added, "We'll talk more later, but we need to get to the temple. Did Me'ira explain the seating arrangements?"

"Yes, ma'am. No problem."

Kyla smiled. "Good. Shall we go?"

They traveled back toward the gardens from which they had come, then turned down another hallway to a pair of French doors that opened to a courtyard. Adelina stood next

24

to that doorway.

"Galen, this is my aunt, Adelina," Me'ira said.

He bowed and shook her hand. "My pleasure to meet you." He ran his hand through his hair. "Wow. I've never met anyone glorified up close before."

Adelina laughed. "Well, Me'ira has a lot of glorified and non-glorified members in her family. I promise, we're fun people, too."

Galen laughed, his face turning slightly red. "I'm sure you are."

"Shall we continue?" Kyla gestured toward the door.

A teleporter, situated in the middle of the courtyard, looked like a sculpture in the midst of an ornate garden. Me'ira held Galen's hand, absentmindedly ignoring protocol, while talking with Adelina as they approached. She was surprised to feel a tug on her hand from Galen. She turned and saw his eyes were wide. His hand turned clammy; he looked frightened.

"Galen, are you OK?" Me'ira tilted her head, confused.

"You're going in a . . . " He swallowed. "Teleporter?"

"Yes, of course. The celebration is several kilometers away, and we need to be there shortly."

Galen looked slightly panicked, but his response was immediate. "You go ahead. I'll drive in my AGA and meet you there."

Me'ira laughed. "Galen, don't be silly. By the time you get there, the service would be almost over. Plus, the streets will be crowded. You won't be able to get through anyway."

She saw beads of sweat forming on his forehead. His face looked ashen, as if all the blood had drained away. "Galen, are you OK?"

"It's . . . it's not healthy to use teleporters."

"What? I've never heard of anyone becoming unhealthy

using one."

Kyla turned back to them. "Me'ira, are you and Galen coming? We're going to be late."

Me'ira turned. "Go ahead, Mother. We'll be right behind you."

She observed Galen closely as he watched her mother and father leave the area via the teleporter. Galen's body stiffened. He smacked his lips as if his mouth had gone dry.

Me'ira's tone turned low, concerned. "Galen, have you never used a teleporter?"

He shook his head slowly. "I was told never to do so."

"Why?"

"My parents told me something bad would happen."

"Like what?"

He looked at her with a blank stare. "I don't know. I . . . I never wanted to find out."

Me'ira held his arm. With her hand, she gently turned his face toward her. "Galen, I promise you, nothing bad will happen. It's perfectly safe. I'll go with you, OK?"

He nodded slowly, yet in somewhat of a jerky manner, and walked—unsteadily—with her toward the teleporter.

Me'ira positioned him next to her. He rubbed his palms on the side of his pants in a nervous manner; he was seemingly terrified. She held his hand, but he was shaking all over.

"Are you ready?"

He nodded but didn't seem certain. Me'ira felt so sorry for him. *Why would anyone make him so afraid of a teleporter?*

She pressed the Engage button. Her vision blurred as if looking across a sun-scorched pavement. . . . In a matter of seconds, they were standing in the King's palace courtyard.

She turned to Galen. "See? Everything's fine, right?"

Galen had a strange expression on his face.

"What's wrong, Galen?"

He bent over, hands on his knees. "I . . . I think I'm going to throw up."

Me'ira gave a sheepish grin. "Sorry, Galen." She rubbed her hand on his upper back. "You'll be all right in a few minutes. I forgot about this side effect when a person first uses the teleporter. It's been so long ago since I had that side effect, I forgot about it. It goes away completely after using the teleporter a few times."

Galen's face, already pale, gave a weak smile. "Good to know."

Me'ira noticed only Adelina was near them. "Where's Mom and Dad?"

"They went ahead to get ready," Adelina said. "I told them we'd come shortly." She put her hand on Galen's shoulder. "Galen, are you OK?"

He nodded. "Feeling better already." He cocked his head. "Wait. How did you get here?"

Adelina smiled. "I can teleport myself. I came right before you and Me'ira did."

Galen's eyes narrowed. "Oh. I had heard about that but had never seen anyone glorified do it."

She patted his back, smiled, and gave a slight wink. "We try not to advertise." She nodded toward the courtyard gate. "Let's go."

Once outside, they headed toward the temple. When they arrived, Me'ira kissed Galen on one cheek and headed to the dais in front of the temple's South Gate to join her parents. Adelina took Galen with her to reserved seating near the front.

Me'ira took her seat next to her mother. Her three older brothers and two sisters also sat on the dais. She scanned the crowd and saw Galen sitting next to Adelina. It looked like his color had returned, but he still looked pale in contrast to the glow of Adelina's skin.

Ya'akov walked to the front of the temple steps. He raised his hands. "Shall we all stand?"

As everyone did, he bowed his head but kept his hands raised. "Our Messiah and King, we praise you for all of your blessings toward us. This evening, we give back our praise to you with our offerings and gratitude."

Jeremiah stepped forward. Everyone genuflected and stood once more. "My people, this new moon marks the beginning of another year of our Messiah's Promised Kingdom. Let us rejoice in his blessings."

Applause went through the crowd.

"This year we recognize Ephraim."

More applause rippled through the crowd.

Jeremiah continued. "Your name is fruitful, and your blessing is now all of our blessing, as God has made all of Israel as well as all the earth fruitful. By honoring you, we honor this blessing from our Messiah and King."

Ya'akov again stepped forward. "The Prince will enter the South Gate and make offering at the East Gate of the Inner Court. After the royal family has entered, you may follow and worship in the courtyard. Remember, if you enter the South Gate, you must exit the North Gate."

CHAPTER 4

Jeremiah entered the South Gate. He knew ten priests would follow behind him. One led a young bull, six led a lamb each, one led a ram, one carried grain, and another had olive oil. Behind them would follow the rest of his royal family. Others from the audience would then follow them.

The sacrifices presented were all from Prince Jeremiah's own herds. He led the people in worship and provided sacrifices for the congregational worship of their Messiah and King. He thought back over how many times he had done this same ordinance. This year marked the five hundred and thirtieth year. He recalled doing this alone for the first thirty-five years as the kingdom's Prince in leading the people, not only of Israel, but the world, in worship of his Messiah. The responsibility of these actions never diminished. He was humbled by the proceedings every time.

Jeremiah stopped at the Inner Eastern Gate of the temple as the priests traveled farther to the Inner North Gate and began preparing the animals for sacrifice. Jeremiah walked up the eight steps through the Inner Eastern Gate's vestibule, by its three inner chambers, and stood at the doorjamb of the gate itself, facing the altar. A beautiful palm tree was carved into the doorjamb. Jeremiah couldn't help but run his fingers over its design while standing at a position not quite inside the Inner Court. He waited while Ya'akov offered the sacrifices he had brought. Although he didn't turn, he heard the congregation that had followed him into the courtyard drop to its knees; he knew some would put their heads all the way to the ground while others would assume a completely prostrate posture. All faced the Inner Eastern Gate while the sacrifices were made.

Ya'akov came forward and stood in front of Jeremiah. "The burnt offering is to show how the Messiah gave himself for each of us—and we now give ourselves to him."

Jeremiah led everyone present in saying, "We give him thanks. So be it."

Jeremiah waited as the animals were prepared and sacrificed.

Ya'akov stepped back to the front again. "The grain offering is to show how our Messiah gives us life, and we offer our lives to him."

Jeremiah and everyone said, "We give him thanks. So be it."

Once the sacrifices were over, Jeremiah received a round loaf of unleavened bread from Ya'akov; this had been prepared from the grain provided as part of the offering. He took the bread and exited the gate into the inner courtyard.

He raised the loaf and waved it over his head. "This bread is a symbol of the Messiah sustaining our lives. Just as these sacrifices symbolize what we are saved from, the bread symbolizes what we are given. Our ancestors gave a grain offering out of their want. We give it out of our abundance because the Messiah has fulfilled the promise to our ancestors by giving us peace, abundance of food, and life. I will go and eat this within the presence of Ruach HaKodesh, the Master's Spirit, to symbolize our thankfulness for what he has done for us and how the hope for our future is in him. Please take note. All who do not accept him as their eternal hope cannot enjoy eternal life."

The people parted for Jeremiah as he walked across the courtyard and stood in front of the vestibule of the Outer Eastern Gate. He turned to address the crowd.

"I now enter the vestibule of the Outer Eastern Gate. The gate itself is now forever closed. Our Messiah, our King, entered through it with his Shekinah glory and now dwells in the Holiest Place within the temple to symbolize he is forever with us. I will eat this bread in the path he has walked to symbolize I will follow him wherever he may lead."

Jeremiah turned and walked into the vestibule of the gate. A table stood in the recess of the vestibule, allowing him to sit and eat the bread, a grain offering. This gate appeared a duplicate of the inner gate he had just been in, but in reverse, as the vestibule of each gate faced the inner courtyard. There were multiple windows in the vestibule here and along the gate itself, all allowing light to enter.

He thought back to the temple's beginning. The Messiah entered this gate when the temple was dedicated to him. His Shekinah glory passed through this gate, through the Eastern Inner Gate, through the temple vestibule, and into the Holiest Place. Jeremiah still vividly remembered the brightness of the Messiah as he passed through these gates, a brightness he had never seen before—like a blazing white light. The interior of the gate, even after all these years, still had a faint glow from the penetrating brightness of the Messiah's Shekinah glory. Standing here in this gate's vestibule was a constant reminder of the awesome power of his Messiah.

Sitting here allowed him to think and commune with his Messiah. He would often visit the Messiah in person when called to his palace, but here he communed with the Messiah through Ruach HaKodesh. His time of solitude here helped

Jeremiah reflect on his duties as the kingdom's Prince.

After Jeremiah had nearly finished eating the bread, a calmness washed over him, and he heard that familiar—and appreciated—still small voice.

"Hello, Jeremiah."

"Ah, my Lord. I appreciate your visit."

"I am pleased with your work."

"Thank you, Master."

"Yet, I feel an unsettled nature within you."

"Yes, my Lord. My daughter, Me'ira, has met someone who seems to be a mystery to me."

"He may prove that and much more."

"What do you mean, my Lord?"

"He is the beginning of the key to later prophecy. He is more than he seems, yet less than you think."

Jeremiah pondered these words but had no idea what they meant. Still, he knew the truth of what the Master said always came to light. Just not in the time span he always wished.

Jeremiah chuckled. "Master, sometimes I think you are the greatest mystery of all."

He could almost feel the Messiah smiling. "Once you have me all figured out, eternity will finally become finite."

"Indeed, my Lord."

"Remain faithful. I will always be so."

The calm feeling resided. Now only Jeremiah's own thoughts remained. He bowed his head. "Thank you, my Lord, for your presence. While I don't understand all you have said, I do want to remain faithful and steadfast. Help me to do so."

He finished his last bite, arose, and walked through the gate. The congregation stood.

"Our Messiah has blessed us greatly," Jeremiah said, turning back to the crowd. "All things come from his hand. Let us go and serve him. We will meet here in a similar manner next year to again offer our thanks." He raised his hands and held them wide. "May the Lord bless you and keep you. May he make his face shine upon you, be gracious to you, and give you peace. May his name be praised forever. Amen."

Many in the crowd said, "Amen!", "So be it," or similar words.

Jeremiah's family waited in the courtyard. He walked over to Kyla and extended his arm. As she took it, they walked out the North Gate. His family followed, and the crowd followed them.

As Jeremiah and his family headed back to the palace courtyard to the special teleporter that Professor Tiberius, the head of the Jerusalem Science Center, had erected especially for him, his family, and select guests to travel between his palace and that of the King, he spotted Elsbeth Isakson.

"Kyla, my dear, why don't you go back with the children? I just spotted Elsbeth and remembered I need to speak with her about a matter."

Kyla looked a bit puzzled. "Is anything wrong? Should I come with you?"

"Oh, no. Seeing her just jogged a memory of something to do." He smiled and patted her hand. "After all, we have a guest to take care of."

"OK. Don't take long, though. Dinner will be served soon."

He watched her follow the children into the courtyard and then turned to find Elsbeth. She was Edvin's wife, but she was glorified and he was not. She now held a position as an Administrator at the Jerusalem Science Center, and part of her work dealt with teleportation.

Jeremiah headed down the hallway from the courtyard. As

33

he turned a corner, he and Elsbeth nearly ran headlong into each other.

"Oh, Your Highness, forgive me!" Elsbeth curtsied. "Are you all right?"

Jeremiah laughed. "Yes, I'm fine. I just frightened myself, that's all. I wanted to run into you, but that was more literal than I intended."

Elsbeth laughed. "Did you wish to discuss something?"

"Yes." He gestured toward a settee and two chairs next to a large window. She sat on one end of the settee and he on the nearest chair.

"Anything troubling you?" Elsbeth asked.

Jeremiah squinted. "I'm not sure troubling is the exact word. Perhaps curious is better."

Elsbeth tilted her head to one side and squinted slightly.

Jeremiah smiled. "Me'ira has a boyfriend."

Elsbeth cracked a large smile. "If she chose him, he can't be that bad."

"Oh, no, he is pleasant enough. It's just . . . we found out he has never used a teleporter—until this evening."

Elsbeth raised her eyebrows. "Well, that is very curious. I take it you want me to check something?"

He reached over and placed his hand on her wrist. "Elsbeth, if you don't mind, can you look at the teleporter data for his travel this evening and compare it to that of the son of Noah and Lois Shafir?"

Elsbeth lowered her gaze slightly. "You think something is amiss?"

"I truly can't say. But I would have more comfort knowing that this man and the Shafir's son are one and the same."

Elsbeth nodded. "Of course, Your Highness, but . . . "

"But what, Elsbeth?"

"Well, if truly he has never used a teleporter . . . "

"Oh, well, I'm hopeful his mother at least used it when she was pregnant, or at least before she knew she was pregnant. That would be enough of a genetic comparison, wouldn't it?"

Elsbeth nodded. "It would. I'll check on it right away."

Jeremiah stood, and Elsbeth did the same. "Thank you, Elsbeth."

Elsbeth curtsied. "You're welcome, Your Highness."

Jeremiah put his hand on her shoulder. "Elsbeth, we've known each other much longer than I have been a Prince. It feels awkward for you to give me such deference. Plus, you being glorified . . . "

Elsbeth put her hand over his as he held her shoulder. "Jeremiah, we will always be friends, but the Master has given you your position and me mine. I can do no less than follow his wishes."

Jeremiah nodded.

"Plus, I wouldn't be here at all if it wasn't for you telling me about the Messiah. That alone would be worthy of deference."

Jeremiah gave a chuckle. "If you say so. Good night, Elsbeth." He turned, then turned back. "Oh, can you tell Hadassah we accept her invitation? I'm assuming you will be accepting her dinner invitation as well?"

Elsbeth nodded. "Absolutely, Your Highness." She curtsied again.

Jeremiah smiled and shook his head. "Now you're just playing with me. Please. Saying 'Your Highness' is never needed when we are not in public."

Elsbeth laughed. "Good night, Jeremiah."

He smiled, turned, and headed for the courtyard.

CHAPTER 5

Dinner proved more pleasant than Me'ira expected. Eran, Hyam, and Liam, who sat at the table opposite her and Galen, acted more civil than she expected her brothers to be. Dana and Ayala, her two sisters, thought him cute and egged Me'ira on, especially Ayala, who sat next to her and kept whispering comments in her ear. She could tell Ayala's giggling after each comment made Galen a little uncomfortable knowing they were probably about him. Each of her brothers and sisters were married, but their spouses didn't take part in the sibling banter.

Her father broke into the conversation. "So, Galen, tell us something about your work."

Me'ira felt grateful. Her siblings stopped their banter and looked genuinely interested in Galen's response.

"Well, sir, nothing too elaborate," Galen began. "I run an antique shop and a small museum. My parents travel far and wide to collect the artifacts, and I clean, restore, and sell them."

"What do you sell?" Liam asked.

Galen shrugged. "Oh, about everything. I have vases and dishware that date to pre-Refreshing times, some ancient and rare books—"

"Actual books?" Ayala asked, her eyes widening.

Galen nodded. "Those usually pique a lot of people's interest."

"I can see why. There's something about the printed word, and not just electronic."

"Is that why you have so many old books in your office, Father?" Dana said, teasing.

Jeremiah smiled. "Partly."

"Well, I for one would love to come see your shop and museum, Galen," Dana said.

"Anytime, Dana."

Me'ira looked at Galen and smiled. She was glad her thoughts of his visit turning into a nightmare were proving unfounded. The conversations remained pleasant.

Shortly after the dessert course was served, Azariah, Me'ira's father's personal assistant, approached the table.

He bowed. "Excuse me, Your Highness, but Mrs. Isakson is here to see you."

Kyla looked from Jeremiah to Azariah. "Which one?"

"Mrs. Elsbeth, Your Grace."

Kyla's eyebrows turned up as she looked at Jeremiah.

Jeremiah smiled and patted her hand. "No worries, my dear. She was checking on something for me."

"At this hour?"

Jeremiah chuckled. "My dear, you know those who are glorified do not have to sleep." He gave her a wink. "That's why the kingdom runs so efficiently."

He glanced around the table at everyone. "Excuse me, please."

From her vantage point at the dining table, Me'ira could see Elsbeth and her father talking in the next room. She saw them look their way every now and then. *Curious. What are they discussing? Does it have anything to do with Galen?*

Jeremiah came back to the table after only a few minutes and acted as if there had been no interruption at all. He apparently wasn't bothered by anything. Or he was very good at hiding any concern. After five hundred years serving as the Prince, likely he had grown accustomed to hiding his true feelings at times.

After dinner, everyone said their goodbyes.

"No one's staying over?" Kyla asked, looking disappointed.

"Sorry, Mother, we all have to get back home," Ayala said, giving her a sympathetic look and hug.

All the siblings kissed their mother and father good night. Me'ira knew they each had a teleporter not far from their home, so it wouldn't take long to return. With the teleporter in the courtyard, visiting the palace, and returning, proved quite easy.

"Galen, I need to talk to father for a short while, but I could then take you to a nearby guest house if you haven't made arrangements yet," Liam offered.

Galen nodded. "Thank you, Your Highness, I appreciate that."

Liam smiled. "Liam, please."

Galen smiled and bowed slightly.

Liam continued. "It's just around the corner. With no large feasts on the calendar at the moment, they should have plenty of rooms even without advanced notice. Give me about half an hour?"

Galen nodded.

Everyone else headed for the courtyard to take the teleporter home. Liam and Jeremiah headed to Jeremiah's office. Me'ira took Galen's arm and led him back out to the gardens. Lydia stayed toward the sidelines but kept them in view.

38

Galen looked up at the stars and took a deep breath. "Your family is wonderful." He chuckled. "I was so nervous about meeting them. They were really great, though."

Me'ira laughed. "I think that was because you were new to them. Don't expect the same next time. They can be . . . quite obnoxious."

Galen smiled. "You want there to be a next time?"

Me'ira sat on one of the oversized planters and pulled Galen down for a seat. "Of course I do. Why wouldn't I?"

He smiled. "Just checking. It may be a little while. I'll likely be busy for the next couple of weeks getting inventory in order."

Me'ira nodded. "Let's just take it one visit at a time."

A pregnant pause filled the air. Me'ira sat up straight. "Why not come for Passover?" She looked at Galen with anticipation. "Would your inventory work be done by then?"

Galen looked in thought. "Maybe. I can't say for sure."

"What all do you have to do?"

Galen spent the next several minutes explaining all that goes into running an antique shop and museum.

"You think you'll take the teleporter next time you visit?"

He smiled. "Maybe. It wasn't so bad the second time. I only got a little nauseous."

"That side effect goes away pretty quickly." She turned and looked at him, holding his gaze. "Why do you think your parents told you to never use a teleporter?"

Galen shrugged. "I have no idea." He laughed. "I thought I would pass out this afternoon when I went with you."

Me'ira checked to see where Lydia was standing. She was within view but not where she could see both of them fully. Me'ira took Galen's hand and rubbed hers over the back of his. "I could tell you were very frightened. I'm sorry you felt that way. You were very brave in going through with it, though."

"Others may see that differently." He smiled. "Being with you made it not so scary."

She looked into his eyes and scooted a little closer. "I'm glad."

Lydia walked up. "Galen, Liam is ready."

Galen laughed. "Lydia, you have such perfect timing."

She exhibited a forced smile. "I know."

He looked at her and smiled a bit himself. "It wasn't exactly a compliment."

She continued to produce her forced smile. "I know."

He looked at her and laughed harder. "You take your job very seriously, don't you?"

"Shall we go?"

He stood and kissed Me'ira's hand. "See you tomorrow?"

"Absolutely. Good night."

He followed Lydia back inside the house.

Me'ira sighed. Were things happening too quickly between them? *Maybe.* She didn't care. Galen seemed so perfect. Maybe it was the dimples, but she couldn't stop thinking about him. He did get along well with her family. *That had to count for something positive, didn't it?*

She walked to the side of the garden, looked over the edge, and saw Galen and Liam walking down the street. In only a matter of minutes they turned the corner and were out of view. Maybe she would ask to ride in Galen's AGA tomorrow. She smiled. Never having ridden in one, it should be fun. As quickly as the thought came over her, though, her smile vanished. Most AGAs were two-seaters. How would a chaperone fit in one? The thought of tying Lydia onto the roof of the AGA, however, made her chuckle.

She sighed. It seemed an AGA trip would not be an adventure for her. Not soon, anyway. She headed toward the house and then to bed.

Who made all these rules of protocol anyway?

CHAPTER 6

Me'ira looked at Galen and smiled. He smiled back displaying those awesome dimples. They were so hard to resist. "Are you getting hungry?"

Galen nodded. "A little. All this walking and sightseeing builds up an appetite."

He turned back toward Lydia, who was walking a short distance behind them. "Hungry, Lydia?"

Me'ira glanced back to see Lydia's response. She gave a slight smile and nodded.

Galen looked back at Me'ira. "Keep the chaperone happy, and all is right with the world."

Me'ira laughed. "That's very practical of you."

He smiled and gave a slight shrug. "Where to?"

"I know a great falafel place."

Galen looked pleased. "That sounds promising."

"It's not far from the Overlook, which is where I want to take you next anyway."

Galen gestured for Me'ira to lead the way.

She felt Galen's hand on the small of her back as he guided her to lead, but then heard a loud "ahem!" from Lydia.

Galen's hand immediately dropped. He turned and did a fake curtsy in Lydia's direction. "Apologies, My Lady."

Me'ira saw Lydia give Galen a cold, hard stare.

Galen sighed. "Lydia, I'm sorry. That was rude. I know you're only doing your job."

Lydia nodded.

Galen gave Me'ira a grimace as they walked to the local teleporter. "I may have made an enemy with that little moment."

Me'ira giggled. "She'll get over it, I'm sure." She leaned toward Galen and whispered, "She also thinks you're cute."

Galen chuckled. "Well, that look said the opposite. I'll have to try and make it up to her."

While in line at the teleporter, Galen bounced on his toes.

"Are you OK?" Me'ira asked. "You're not still anxious about using the teleporter, are you?"

He gave a sheepish smile and held up a hand with his index finger and thumb a short distance apart. "A little." He gave a short laugh as he shook his head. "I know it's ridiculous. I guess not using a teleporter became so engrained in me that it will take some time for it not to feel strange using one."

Me'ira gave a sympathetic look. "Don't worry. By the end of today, you'll be so used to it you won't give it a second thought."

Galen smiled and nodded.

The line in front of them cleared quickly and they stepped onto the platform. Galen let out a long breath.

She looked at him. "Ready?"

He had a nervous look on his face but nodded.

Before Me'ira could press the Engage button, however, Lydia stepped onto the platform.

Me'ira's eyes went wide. "Lydia, what are you doing?"

"Sorry, Me'ira, but I must travel with you."

"But—"

Galen touched Me'ira's arm and stepped from the platform. "I get it." He looked at Lydia. "Protocol, right?"

Lydia nodded.

Mei'ra sighed and mouthed a silent "sorry" to Galen. "Will you be OK?"

He nodded and smiled. To Me'ira, though, it looked forced.

She pressed Engage. Her vision blurred and, when it returned to focus, they were close to the temple complex. They stepped off the pad and waited for Galen.

In a few minutes Galen appeared and stepped from the teleporter pad, this time smiling. He looked far more confident this time.

"Hey, I think I'm getting the hang of this thing," he said.

Me'ira laughed and pointed in the direction of the temple. "The falafel place is just up the street here."

As they walked, Me'ira noticed Galen looking at various people they passed. "What are you thinking?" she asked.

Galen shook his head. "Everyone seems so happy. Almost everyone smiles and nods at me as they pass." He paused briefly, in thought. "A genuine smile, you know? Not a fake one. It's like they have a settled peace within themselves."

Me'ira nodded. "That's because they're happy with their King, and with what they do."

Galen nodded, but he didn't appear confident of Me'ira's statement.

When they reached the restaurant, they chose a bistro table that overlooked the city cascading downward before them. Lydia sat at a table next to theirs. As Mei'ra ordered for them, Galen glanced around, apparently taking in the view.

"Me'ira, this view is spectacular. I never knew the city had so many parks in it. They add so much color."

She smiled. "I just love sitting here so high in the city. You can see the water flow from the temple toward the escarpment. You can't see the waterfall from where we sit, but we will later. The river continues into the valley you see in the distance, and it ends up flowing into the Jordan River. You can see it in the far distance."

Galen nodded. "It's quite beautiful." He looked around. "There are so many people here. No one seems to be in a hurry. Everyone seems courteous and happy." He shrugged. "I guess living in such a beautiful city has a positive impact on people."

Me'ira smiled but thought that an odd statement. Galen didn't seem to acknowledge—or even understand—the fact that Ruach HaKadosh, or the King's Spirit in people's lives, made all the difference.

In a few minutes the waiter brought coffee, and the falafels came shortly after.

"Me'ira, these smell incredible." Galen breathed in the aroma. "The smell of coriander and cumin—it just leaves your mouth watering." He took a bite. "Wow." He pointed at the falafel with his fork. "This is the best I've ever eaten."

Me'ira smiled. "I told you."

Galen leaned in and whispered. "Don't you dare tell my mom I said that."

Me'ira giggled and waved her fork as she chewed. "Don't worry. Your indiscretion is safe with me."

Galen smiled. "Everyone in Naphtali says Mom is a wonderful cook. I often have plates of goodies in my shop that she bakes—when she's actually there."

Me'ira saw a tinge of regret in Galen's face. She knew Galen's parents traveled to various places looking for artifacts for their shop, often leaving him to run things by himself. "You're left alone a lot? Must be kind of lonely."

Galen shrugged. "Yeah, my parents travel a lot. I run the

shop and museum pretty much by myself most of the time." He produced a weak smile. "I have a few friends and we do things together every now and then."

Me'ira nodded. "Ever consider opening a shop here in Jerusalem?"

Galen stopped chewing and looked at her. "No, actually." He chuckled. "I'll tell you, though, seeing everyone here and how happy everyone seems to be, it may not be a bad idea." Again he looked out at people walking by, then back to Me'ira. "Why are they so happy?"

Me'ira tilted her head. It struck her as an odd question. "The King makes everyone feel special." She reached out to touch his hand, then glanced at Lydia and pulled it back. "Don't you feel special?"

He smiled. "I do when I'm with you."

She smiled back. "Well, that's good to hear."

Galen sat back in his chair. "You mean that goes for everyone? Feeling special?"

She nodded. "Why? Why wouldn't it?"

He gestured toward Lydia. "That goes for Lydia, too?"

Me'ira scrunched her brow. "Yes, of course. Why wouldn't Lydia be happy?"

Galen shrugged. "I mean no disrespect, Me'ira, but she is, after all, a servant."

Me'ira set her fork on her plate and leaned forward, interlocking her fingers with her elbows on the table. "Galen, she's a very respected part of our family. She's treated with dignity and respect. It's a job just like your job."

"Really?"

"Yes, really." Me'ira got Lydia's attention and waved her over to their table.

Lydia had a puzzled look on her face as she stood and came

over. "Yes, My Lady. Anything wrong?"

Me'ira shook her head. "Would you please sit with us for a few minutes?"

"My Lady?"

Me'ira sighed. "Surely, that's not against protocol?"

Lydia shook her head.

"Then, please sit."

Lydia sat and looked from Me'ira to Galen.

Me'ira gestured toward Galen. "He has some . . . questions for you."

Lydia looked at Galen with a blank expression.

Galen smiled. "I just want to know if you're happy with your position as a servant."

Lydia's eyes widened. "Servant?" She shook her head. "No, I'm an attendant."

Galen scrunched his brow. "Is that not the same thing?"

Lydia shook her head. "No, of course not."

Galen tilted his head but allowed Lydia to continue.

Lydia produced a smile, though it was a weak one. "I have to admit, I may have been envious of Me'ira in the beginning."

Lydia gave a sheepish smile to Me'ira, who put her hand on Lydia's arm and smiled back.

Lydia shook her head and turned back to Galen. "But no more. After my talk with the King at my sacrificing ceremony, he put everything in its proper perspective. Everyone has a place in his kingdom, and he respects every position. While certain positions have more responsibility than others, all are important. As long as I do my job for him and his approval, that is all that's important. I help Me'ira reflect her father in a favorable light so he is respected by the people; her father reflects the King in a favorable light so he is respected by everyone. So, in a way, I help all members of the Royal Family reflect the King in a favorable light so the world will worship the King properly." She shook her head. "What better way could I serve the King and give him honor? I am truly blessed."

Me'ira rubbed Lydia's arm. She looked at Galen. "Lydia is like a sister to me." She smiled. "And just as sisters sometimes get annoyed with each other, we do too." She patted Lydia's arm. "But the love is always there and remains after the spat is over."

Lydia chuckled. "That is very true, My Lady."

Me'ira looked at Galen. "Does that make sense?"

Galen nodded. "It does. It sheds light on all the happiness I see in this city. It's a very different perspective than I had thought of before." He took another sip of coffee. "So, why is your family so far from the temple?"

Me'ira squinted. "Do you not understand the purpose of this part of the city?"

Galen shook his head slightly. "What do you mean?"

"You've visited Jerusalem in the past, right? For festivals, honoring ceremonies?"

Galen gave a small shrug. "I remember being here at least once or twice. With my parents traveling so much and me banned from the teleporter, coming here was not that easy."

Me'ira nodded but didn't really understand. Galen was a bigger mystery than she had thought. Still, she knew his heart was in the right place.

"This section of the city we are in now belongs to the descendants of Zadok."

She saw Galen turn up his brow, confused.

"You know, the famous priest who assisted King David before he became glorified?"

Galen continued to give a blank stare. Her T-band vibrated, revealing a text from her mother. After sending a quick reply, she returned her focus to Galen.

"Anyway, these are the priests who help make the sacrifices for all the people. My cousin Ya'akov was the first of these descendants born in the King's Promised Kingdom. He's now the head priest."

Galen nodded his head but still looked as though he didn't grasp what Me'ira was saying.

"Then, north of the temple, between it and Judah, is the area for the Levites, the ones who take care of the temple. They live there and work here. Many people from around the globe come here to worship at the temple, and they help the priests oversee it. My great uncle Edvin and his friend Mik'kel are descendants from Levi, and this allows them to live there and work here to assist the priests."

A small grin found its way across Galen's face. "You seem to be related to everyone."

Me'ira giggled. "Yeah, I guess it does appear that way. That's mainly because my grandfather is Uncle Edvin's brother. It sort of makes many of the non-glorified—as well as many of the glorified—related to me." She gave a shrug. "I think that's the way the King designed it so all the subjects in his kingdom understand they are important to him."

"That idea seems to be important to him."

Me'ira nodded. "It is." She gestured toward Lydia. "It's like what Lydia said. Every person and every position are important to him."

"So why do you and your parents live so far from him?"

"We aren't, really. As you saw, the teleporters only leave us a few minutes away."

Lydia leaned in. "The Prince is the one who is the inspiration for both Israel and the world to worship the King. It's important he live within the city to identify with his people, the Israelites, as they lead the world in worship. He officiates over all the celebrations for the world to worship the King under Israel's example and guidance."

Me'ira nodded. "Is it all making sense?"

Galen tilted his head side to side just slightly. "Somewhat." He paused, still quite obviously in deep thought. "And King David is in the heart of the city because he is the king of Israel with Jerusalem its capital?"

Me'ira smiled and nodded. "That's right. Just like there are other kings around the world, King David is our king."

Lydia jumped in. "And our Messiah is their king—the King of kings."

"Seems pretty well thought out," Galen said with a nod.

Me'ira laughed. "You'd expect anything less from the King?"

Galen gave a light chuckle. "I guess not."

Me'ira put her palms on the table. "Enough geography for now." She looked at Galen. "Ready to go to the Overlook?"

Galen smiled, displaying his dimples. "I can't wait."

They walked east, with Lydia again following behind, until they came to the Overlook. They sat on one of the benches nearest the Overlook itself, and it provided an exceptional view.

Galen shook his head. "I had no idea this was here. This view is . . . it just takes your breath away. The color, the texture . . . " He pointed. "And the spray from the waterfall—wow, that makes lots of rainbows with butterflies and humming-birds everywhere . . . " He shook his head. "I never thought something so beautiful could exist."

"And they keep adding to it each year," Me'ira said.

Her T-band vibrated; again, it was her mother. She texted a reply.

She turned to Galen. "I think we may need to head back. Mom keeps texting me the same question. I'm not sure she's getting my reply."

Galen nodded and stood. "It's getting late anyway. I don't want to make a bad impression on my first chaperoned trip out with you."

Me'ira laughed. "Very strategic of you."

CHAPTER 7

"Me'ira, where have you and Galen been?"

"Don't worry, Mother. Lydia stayed close."

Kyla shook her head. "No, that wasn't my concern. You were supposed to be back an hour ago."

Me'ira gave her mother a blank stare as Lydia untied and took her cloak. "Mother, you didn't say it was an ultimatum. Besides, I sent you three texts telling you where we were and when we'd be back."

"Texts? I didn't get any! I became worried."

Me'ira walked over to her mother and held up her wrist. She pressed the T-band on her mother's wrist and then pressed Display Texts. "Mother, they're right here."

Kyla sighed. "I thought this thing would alert me automatically. Why do I have to go fishing for them?"

Me'ira sighed, took her mother's wrist in her hands, and pressed a few more selections on her mother's T-band. "There. Now you'll be alerted automatically."

"Thank you," her mother said. To Me'ira, though, it sounded more like, "It's about time."

Me'ira bit the inside of her cheek while trying to remain calm and not irritated. "Sorry, Mother. I should have set it before I gave it to you as a gift."

Kyla took a deep breath. "And I'm sorry for getting so upset. Go to your father's office. He needs to see both of you."

"About what?"

"He didn't say. But he said it was important."

As Me'ira and Galen headed down the hallway, she got a bad feeling. *Did this have something to do with Aunt Elsbeth coming to the house at dinnertime last night?*

She glanced at Galen. "You OK? Any idea what's going on?"

He looked at her, his face somewhat pale, and shook his head. "No idea, but it doesn't sound good."

When they arrived at her father's office, Adelina was waiting outside.

Me'ira threw her arms out and gave a shrug. "What's going on?"

Adelina gestured to some chairs just outside the office door. "Have a seat for a few minutes. Your dad is finishing a conversation."

"With whom?"

"All in good time."

"What's with all the cloak and dagger?"

"It's just—"

"Protocol. I know." Me'ira folded her arms across her midsection. "If I hear that word one more time, I may just scream."

Galen took her hand in his and gently rubbed the top of it. "It's OK, Me'ira. Just be patient."

After a short pause, Adelina broke the silence.

"So, where did you guys go today?"

Me'ira gave a smirk; Galen responded as though this was a very normal question.

"Oh, it was a great day. We spent most of the morning walking through the city. Then, after lunch, Me'ira took me to the Overlook."

"Nice. I love the Overlook."

"Me too," Galen said. "I didn't expect so many plants, and so many colors and textures—it takes your breath away. I love how the spray from the waterfall makes rainbows as the sunlight hits it . . . just right. All the butterflies and hummingbirds—I've never seen so many."

Adelina nodded. "I'm glad you had a great time."

Jeremiah's office door opened, and he stepped outside to ask everyone in. This time, Elsbeth and Liam were in the office as well. Adelina stood to one side.

Jeremiah gestured for Me'ira and Galen to have a seat. They found the two empty chairs in front of the floor to ceiling bookcases. Me'ira felt like this was an inquisition; everyone else took seats to face them.

Galen had a worried look on his face. Beads of sweat formed on his forehead and Me'ira felt his hands getting clammy. She patted his forearm to give him assurance, as if to say she was on his side.

"Dad, what's going on? Are we in trouble or something?"

"No, Me'ira. We just have some questions to clear up."

Galen glanced from Me'ira to each of the others. "What type of questions? What did I do?"

Elsbeth responded. "Galen, I don't know that you did anything, but . . . "

"But what?"

Elsbeth crossed her legs, placing her hands on her knee. "Let me explain some things about the teleporter."

Me'ira felt Galen's hand start to tremble just a bit. She rubbed it to help him remain calm.

"The teleporter reads your genetic makeup as it dematerializes you and then rematerializes you. It needs to do that to ensure the machine does its job correctly on the other end.

That gives a type of blueprint of the person traveling through it. Now, the teleportation department does several things with all of those data."

"Aunt Elsbeth, surely you don't use that information against people?" Me'ira asked.

Elsbeth shook her head. "Quite the contrary, I assure you. We compare each blueprint over time to ensure there is no tissue or genetic damage." She smiled. "I can assure you, I have never seen a single case where harm came to anyone using a teleporter."

Me'ira heard a small sigh come from Galen. She whispered in his direction, "See, I told you."

Elsbeth turned to face Galen directly. "Because you and Me'ira used the teleporter several times today, we were able to verify your genetic patterns and compare them to the only other time you had ever been in the teleporter."

Galen's head jerked back slightly. He looked at Me'ira and back to Elsbeth. "But . . . I've never used the teleporter before yesterday."

Elsbeth smiled. "Yes, I know. But your mother did before you were born—likely before she even knew she was pregnant."

"I guess that makes sense." He shook his head. "But I don't understand. What's the issue?"

Elsbeth looked at Jeremiah and Adelina and then back to Galen. "Galen, the genetic pattern produced by the fetus your mother carried . . . was not you."

Galen sat stonelike for several seconds. Me'ira couldn't tell if he was even breathing.

"What?" he said in a hushed tone, shaking his head. "That's . . . that's impossible. What are you implying? Are you trying to say I'm . . . I'm . . . " He choked up. His eyes began to tear. "So, what *are* you really saying?"

Me'ira interlocked her fingers in his and held tight.

Elsbeth continued. "Galen, I know this doesn't make sense. We're still trying to understand it ourselves. But it seems the truth of the matter is, you are not your parents' biological son. As crazy as that sounds, that is what the evidence suggests."

Galen wiped his free hand down across his face in shock.

"Aunt Elsbeth, has this ever happened before?" Me'ira asked.

Elsbeth shook her head. "No. Never."

Me'ira let go of Galen's hand and quickly held it with her other; she rubbed his back gently with her just-freed hand. She turned to face him directly. "Do you have any siblings?"

Galen shook his head as his eyes glistened. "Me'ira, I'm an only child." He looked at Elsbeth. "My parents love me." Galen sat up straighter and wiped a few tears away. "They do," he said, nodding as if to convince himself.

Elsbeth put her hand on his knee. "Galen, we're not imply-ing they don't. I'm sure they do. But there is a mystery here that seems . . . unexplainable at the moment."

Liam walked over and knelt next to Galen. "Hey, buddy, do you mind staying with us a few more days?"

Galen looked up, puzzled.

"I have some friends looking for your mom and dad," Liam said. "We want to bring them here so we can get all of this straightened out. OK? There's probably some logical explana-tion, and if anyone can explain it, it would be your mom and dad. Don't you agree?"

Galen nodded slightly. "Yeah, I guess." He began to fidget. "Uh, I really need to get some air. I feel . . . kind of sick. Even worse than the first teleporter ride."

Me'ira rubbed his back. "Come on, Galen. I'll take you out to the gardens."

They stood. Adelina held out her hand. "Me'ira, here, let me take him."

She looked at her dad, who nodded. "OK. I'll be right out. OK, Galen?"

He nodded but didn't really seem to comprehend. He and Adelina left the office.

Me'ira sat with a thud. Liam sat next to her. He put his arm around her shoulders and then rubbed her back.

She looked at all three of them. "Can someone tell me what's going on?" She stood and paced the length of the office. "None of this is making any sense."

"Sis, it's not making any sense to us either. We won't know anything until we find his parents. Maybe they can shed some light on this."

"Me'ira, please sit, sweetie," her dad said, speaking for the first time in several minutes. "Your pacing is giving me motion sickness."

She returned a weak smile knowing her dad was trying to add a little levity to the situation. She returned to sit next to Liam.

Her eyes were wet. "I just want everyone to like him," she said softly.

"We do, sis. We do," Liam said.

Elsbeth gave Me'ira a handkerchief. She wiped her eyes.

She leaned back, sighed, and looked at her father. "Are there any protocols for this?"

CHAPTER 8

It took several days for Galen's parents to be located. Me'ira met with Liam every morning to find out what he knew. He was open with everything, confirming Galen had been truthful: his parents traveled frequently. Elsbeth kept track of their teleportation travel, but a number of times Galen's parents would travel to a new location before Liam's men could find them.

Me'ira spent almost every waking hour with Galen. This pensive time drew them closer as they went on many walks together, with Lydia still in tow. Galen held nothing back from her, but he also had no real answers to the dilemma. He seemed as anxious as everyone else to solve this mystery. When not on a walk, they spent a great deal of time in the palace gardens.

One afternoon, Lydia brought them lemonade while they sat on a bench in one of the garden corners near a water fountain. They sat in silence for several minutes with their drinks.

Me'ira decided to embrace the moment and ask Galen an important question. "Galen, have you asked the King for his help in all of this?" Some of his previous statements the other evening had seemed a little odd to her, and they bothered her the more she thought about them. She needed to understand how connected he was to the King.

Galen tilted his head. "What do you mean? I can't just go to the King and ask for an audience." He shrugged. "Besides, I'm sure he has many more important things to take care of than the concerns of one insignificant person."

Me'ira turned on the bench to face him more directly. "Galen, is that what you think? You think the King feels you are insignificant?"

Galen shrugged. "Why wouldn't he?"

She sat her glass down and took his hand. "Galen, the King believes each and every one of his subjects is important and significant. Ruach HaKodesh doesn't help you feel and understand that?"

"Me'ira, I have no idea what you're talking about."

Me'ira sat even more upright, and looked stunned. "You don't have a connection to the King through Ruach HaKodesh?"

Galen shook his head. "How on earth does one do that? Is it important?"

She ran her hand through his hair above his ear. "Galen, it's the most important thing in the world. You receive Ruach HaKodesh as a gift when you accept the King as the hope for your eternal future."

She looked at his eyes and face to see his response, but his expression seemed blank.

"You've never considered needing to know the King? Feeling something was missing?"

Galen shook his head. "I've been pretty content with my life. Well, until now. I'm doing what I love to do, and now I've met you." He gave a big smile. "That's looking pretty good to me."

"But Galen, there is more—"

Lydia seemed to appear suddenly in front of them. "Me'ira, I'm sorry, but Liam is asking to see both of you."

Me'ira took his hand and stood. "Can we continue this later?"

Galen nodded and stood with her. Lydia gave Me'ira a raised-eyebrow look. Me'ira rolled her eyes and let go of Galen's hand.

They followed Lydia back to her father's office in silence.

Lydia stayed outside as Me'ira and Galen entered. Sitting in the chairs where Me'ira and Galen had sat earlier were Galen's parents! Both stood as soon as they saw Galen.

Galen hurried over and hugged them both. His mother, Lois, hugged him, eyes moistening.

Jeremiah waited a moment, then spoke. "Why don't we all have a seat?"

Liam sat on the corner of Jeremiah's desk.

Jeremiah looked at Elsbeth. "Mrs. Isakson, please explain to Mr. and Mrs. Shafir what you have found."

Elsbeth nodded and looked at Galen's parents. "I don't want this to feel so formal. Please call me Elsbeth. May I call you Noah and Lois?"

Both nodded.

"Thank you. Well, Lois, as you may know, the teleporter keeps something like a blueprint of one's genetic pattern when one uses the teleporter."

Lois nodded. Noah reached over and took his wife's hand. She looked visibly shaken.

"There is a record of your unborn son when you used the teleporter. You were probably less than two months pregnant."

Lois used her other hand to grasp Noah even more tightly. Her bottom lip trembled slightly.

"Well, we found out something this week. The genetic pattern of your natural son does not match that of Galen. We have been trying to understand that discrepancy."

Lois quickly turned toward Galen. "You . . . you used the teleporter?"

Galen nodded. He looked down as if ashamed, but then back up at his mother. "You said something bad would happen, but it didn't. I feel fine. Mrs. Isakson here said nothing bad has ever happened to someone using a teleporter."

Tears trickled down Lois's cheeks. She shook her head. "That wasn't the bad we were talking about."

Puzzled, Galen twisted his face. "What? I don't understand."

"Son, this conversation is the bad your mom and I were talking about," Noah said. "We never wanted to have this conversation."

Galen glanced from his parents to Elsbeth. He shook his head.

Elsbeth continued. "Lois. Noah. Is Galen your only child?"

Lois squeezed her husband's hand. Her tears now were coming more rapidly. She shook her head slowly—barely a discernible motion.

"Mom?" Galen's tone was filled with disbelief. His eyes widened. "I . . . I have a sibling? Where . . . how?"

Lois let go of her husband's hand and put her face in her hands and wept. Her whole body shook. Noah rubbed her back as his eyes now began to get wet.

"Dad, how is this even possible?"

Noah sighed. He looked at each of them. "I guess it was naïve to believe we could keep this a secret forever. Galen, left on our doorstep as an infant, had instructions left with him."

"What?" Galen's tone was barely a whisper.

Lois, now only sniffling, looked at Galen. "None of this changes how we feel about you. We love you just like you are ours. We feel you are."

Noah nodded. "Absolutely."

"Noah, please continue," Jeremiah said.

"Yes, Your Highness." Noah cleared his throat. "The instructions were somewhat simple, yet puzzling. We were given his name, instructions that we had to have him stay in Israel, and that he could never use a teleporter."

Lois continued. "We were also told he had to be treated as an only child. The two boys were roughly the same age. Afraid to use the teleporter, I took our son by various non-teleporter modes of travel to Australia. We had been doing some excavating there at the time, so I created a second home."

Noah nodded. "Because we traveled so much, we had a nanny at both homes to help out. No one gave our absences a second thought."

Lois gave a weak smile toward Galen. "Galen never wanted to go with us on our trips, and he became a great asset to us by running our business while we were away. We never had to worry about him."

Every so often, Galen would simply shake his head. "But, why, Dad? Why did you and Mom do it? And why *you*? Why was I left with *you*?"

Noah shook his head. "Galen, I don't know why we were chosen. The instructions stated we would regret it if we didn't comply. That frightened us, so we went along. Yet after a while, we came to love you as our own and really never thought anything more about it. We really loved having you as our son."

Lois nodded. "Galen, you have to believe us. We love you as if you are our own."

"But what about . . . my . . . your son?" Galen's eyes moistened.

Me'ira took his hand as she understood Galen was realizing

this other man wasn't his brother at all.

Lois gave a slight chuckle through some sniffles. "Caleb has been a little more . . . difficult."

Noah nodded. "We've had a hard time keeping him from using the teleporter. This last month, he has been challenging us more than usual. We were wondering what we would do since he recently took a job with an agricultural department that will require him to travel throughout Australia." He looked at Jeremiah. "I guess you finding this out takes that pressure off of us."

"So, who are my parents?"

Noah shook his head. "We still don't know."

"Periodically, we get notes stating we are still being watched," Lois said.

Noah nodded. "I guess just to be sure we don't let our guard down."

Lois's voice wavered. "I don't know what this means for us now that you know."

Elsbeth put her hand on her knee. "Lois, I don't know what these people could do now. Both Galen and Caleb are grown. They have the right to make their own decisions. I think your crisis is over."

Lois's eyes teared up again. She looked at Noah and then back at Elsbeth. "Do you really think that's true?"

Noah rubbed Lois's back. "We're free, Lois. I think we're finally free."

"Free?" Galen's eyes got wet and tears now started down his cheeks.

"Oh, sweetie." Lois went over, knelt, and hugged him. "Not of you. I never want to be free of you. We're free from the secrets and the fear. I would do it all over again to have you in our lives."

She looked at Noah, who was nodding. "Absolutely. Galen, we truly love you and have always thought of you as our son."

Galen nodded.

"Dad, why don't we let Galen and his parents have some time alone?" Liam asked.

Jeremiah nodded. "Good idea. Lois. Noah. Why don't you two stay here and talk with Galen a while. Take your time. Just open the French doors to the balcony when you're done."

Lois smiled.

Noah nodded. "Thank you, Your Highness."

Everyone exited to the balcony except for Galen and his parents. Me'ira patted Galen's hand and gave him a smile before she stepped outside. She closed the door behind her.

"Well, I guess that solves the mystery," Me'ira said as she took a seat next to Elsbeth on the edge of an oversized planter.

Liam leaned back on the edge of the balcony, his hands behind him. "Yeah, but that opens up a whole new mystery."

Jeremiah, pacing, nodded. "Yes. Who are Galen's parents?"

Elsbeth shrugged. "I'm sure that's the main question on Galen's mind."

"Dad, any idea who would give up their child like that?" Me'ira asked. Her eyes were tearing up again. *How could anyone do something like this to their own child?*

Jeremiah shook his head. "If we were living pre-Refreshing, I could imagine something like this. But now it's . . . it's unimaginable."

Elsbeth spoke up. "I think Ya'akov may have some perspective on all this."

"How is that, Elsbeth?" Jeremiah asked.

"It's just a hunch, Your Highness. Let's talk to him at dinner tomorrow night."

CHAPTER 9

Liam approached and sat on the sofa next to Me'ira as she completed some embroidery. "Where's Galen?" He chuckled. "This is the first time I haven't seen you two together."

She smiled. "He's in the garden. He wanted some time to himself." She set her work aside. "I can't blame him. All of this probably came as a bigger shock to him than even to us."

"Hmm. Why don't we take him out to dinner? Maybe that will take his mind off it for a while. What do you say?"

"We?"

Liam sat up straighter. "What, I'm not good enough to be a chaperone?"

Me'ira grabbed his arm. "Really? I'd love that."

He smiled and kissed his sister on the forehead. "Great. I'll go tell Nyssa. I promised her a night out to take her mind off Sarit's wedding planning."

"How's that going, anyway?"

Liam scrunched his brow. "OK, I think." He chuckled. "You'd have to ask Nyssa. I'm only there for moral support."

"And don't forget financial support," Me'ira called to him.

Liam turned and pointed at her with raised eyebrows.

Before he could say anything, she replied, "You know you'd do anything for your daughter."

Liam smiled and nodded. "Very true." Liam shrugged. "And I even like her fiancée."

Mei'ra laughed as Liam turned and went to get Nyssa. She then looked around for Lydia.

With excitement, Me'ira waved Lydia over. "Please ask Galen to come back in. I have a surprise for him."

Lydia gave a stare as if wanting more information, but Me'ira didn't supply it. Lydia gave a hushed sigh and turned to fulfill Me'ira's request. Mei'ra stood and looked at herself in a nearby mirror. She needed to freshen up, so she rushed off before Galen got back with Lydia.

Me'ira had never felt closer to her older brother. So he and his wife, Nyssa, would serve as their chaperones. That would be such a welcome change.

She expected a dinner for four, but once they arrived at the restaurant, Liam asked for separate tables. While Liam helped Nyssa into her chair at their table, he looked over and gave Me'ira a wink. She grinned back.

After the waiter took their order, he left pita bread and spiced pickles for snacks.

Me'ira figured she should dive into some of the tough stuff. "So, Galen. Did your parents leave on a good note?"

Galen nodded. "They're going back to Australia to tell Caleb about me. I'm going to go there in a couple of weeks to meet him."

Me'ira smiled and grabbed Galen's hand. "I'm so happy for you, Galen. It sounds like you're on the road to happier times."

Galen shrugged. "Different times, anyway. I thought I was already happy. Even more so when I met you." He smiled and plopped a pickle in his mouth. "I have no idea how Caleb will accept me. After all, I'm the odd man out. I still have no idea who my mother and father are."

Me'ira patted his hand. "I'm sure everything will work out."

The waiter soon brought their entrées. After a few minutes of silence as they began to eat, Me'ira went on. "How long will you be gone?" She smiled. "I'm going to miss you terribly."

"I'm hoping not too long. I have to go back to Naphtali and get the business in order and manned while I'm away. That will take a couple of weeks. Then . . . " He shrugged. "I'm assuming I'll be gone for about two more weeks."

Me'ira remained quiet for another minute .

"What's wrong, Me'ira?"

"Oh, I was just thinking a month is a very long time."

"Well, we can talk often. You have a T-band, right?"

She nodded. "I know we can talk often with our holo-coms." She smiled. "I'll miss the personal touch, though."

"It's only for a short time."

Me'ira nodded. "When are you leaving?"

"I need to get back to Naphtali tomorrow." He squeezed her hand. "I'm going to miss you."

"Me too."

* * * * *

Me'ira didn't sleep well that night. She had grown accustomed to having Galen around, and she knew she would miss him terribly. After breakfast, she walked outside with him to his AGA, which had been brought to the front of the palace.

"Galen, please don't forget about the discussion we had the other day about the King. Your acceptance of him for your future is really important. Think about what my father said at the temple the other night. Just . . . think about it. OK?"

Galen nodded. He kissed her hand, got into the AGA, and

drove away.

Me'ira stood in place looking at Galen and then waving until he was out of sight.

Liam came up to her, wrapped his arm around her shoulders, and wiped a tear from her cheek. "Don't worry, sis. He'll be back. He's smitten. I can tell."

She looked up at her big brother and smiled. He walked her back inside as she placed her head between his chest and shoulder.

CHAPTER 10

M e'ira walked back to the garden where she and Galen spent much of their time. She missed him already. She chuckled to herself. *I guess this is evidence enough that this is not just a fling.*

She walked back to the corner of the garden near the bubbling fountain, folded her arms, and propped her chin on them as she looked over the balcony ledge. Although out of sight, she still stared in the direction Galen had left. How long would she have to wait to see his AGA coming back down that road? She turned and leaned against the balcony ledge. That wouldn't be for a while. She sighed again.

She thought about their conversation about the Messiah. It dumbfounded her that Galen had not yet accepted the King as the hope for his future. Yet, with the way he had been raised, he had so many strikes against any real attempt to know the King. How was he supposed to understand the King thought him special if no one had ever told *him* that before? But she had told him. He trusted her, she knew, so hopefully he would take her words to heart. If he never took that step, she knew, there was no hope of them being together. Putting her arms out, she took a deep breath. *Slow down, Me'ira. He'll come around.* She nodded to herself. Yes, there was no reason to think he wouldn't.

She ran her hand through the fountain and turned. Something on the large planter where she and Galen often sat and had their conversations caused her to pause. Getting closer, she smiled. Several flowers had been tied together with a bright multi-colored ribbon. Picking them up and bringing the small bouquet to her nose, she giggled. Galen seemed quite the romantic. She would take the bouquet to her room, press it, and dry it as a keepsake to remind her of this special time with him. Her eyes darted around as she held the flowers close. The gardener couldn't see this; he would be upset that perfectly good flowers were picked for no good reason. Still, as she twirled and smelled them again, she thought she could justify that they had been picked for a *very* good reason.

As Me'ira headed back inside the palace, she meandered through the garden area smelling the flowers while she twisted and twirled thinking about herself and Galen. She tried not to think that it would be an entire month before he returned. That put a damper on her feelings, so she kept looking at and smelling the flowers to think of little but him.

Once Me'ira got close to the palace doorway, she stopped. There was Lydia with a wry smile on her face. Me'ira suddenly felt foolish, but she was determined not to let Lydia know that.

Me'ira raised her eyebrows. "Yes?"

Lydia chuckled. "I think you have been bitten—very hard."

Me'ira flicked her wrist. "Oh, what do you know?"

As Me'ira walked past, Lydia put her hand on Me'ira's arm. "Don't be that way. I think he's cute, too."

Me'ira looked at Lydia for a few seconds, stone-faced, then burst into laughter. "He is, isn't he?"

Lydia nodded. "Especially the dimples."

Me'ira giggled. "I know, right?" She turned serious. "He has other wonderful qualities too, though."

Lydia stopped laughing and nodded, giving a serious look. "Absolutely."

They looked at each other and burst into laughter once more. Finally Me'ira said, "But his dimples are truly knee-weakening."

Lydia laughed again. "Like I said. You've been bitten . . . hard."

Me'ira laughed with her. "I guess I have."

As they entered the living area, Me'ira looked around. "Where's Mom and Dad?"

"They're getting ready. They're having dinner with Priest Ya'akov and his wife tonight."

Me'ira nodded, then perked up. "Want to go shopping?"

"Shopping?"

"I want to get something new for Passover."

Lydia laughed. "You mean something new for Galen."

Me'ira bobbled her head. "Well, it can be for both, can't it?"

"Me'ira, Passover isn't for another month."

Me'ira nodded. "Yes, but it may take that long to find just the right dress."

Lydia shook her head. "You are impossible."

"We can go to dinner first," Me'ira said. She snapped her fingers. "I know. I'll take you to that new restaurant that just opened."

Lydia perked up. "You mean the one that creates unique desserts using liquid nitrogen?"

Me'ira nodded.

Lydia squinted. "I hear they're booked for months in advance."

Me'ira smiled. "They sent me tickets to a special dessert showing tonight."

"Well, now you have my attention."

"Good. I wonder if Sarit would want to join us?"

Lydia shrugged. "Well, you could tell her she could get ideas for her wedding dinner."

Me'ira smiled and locked arms with Lydia. "Good thinking. Now, let's get dressed."

"Get dressed to go buy a dress."

Me'ira laughed. "Absolutely."

CHAPTER 11

"Your Highness. Your Grace. Please come in."

Hadassah curtsied and opened the door wider so her guests could enter. Jeremiah, Kyla, and Liam stepped inside.

Everyone else was present. All either curtsied or genuflected to the Royal Family.

Jeremiah bowed. These were all his friends—several from before the Refreshing, like Edvin, Elsbeth, and Mik'kel. Edvin had married Elsbeth a few years before the Messiah came to set up his Kingdom. She became pregnant with Ya'akov and died in childbirth just before the Messiah came. That was why she was now glorified, but Edvin—alive at the time of the Messiah's return—was not. Ya'akov had become the first priest of the Kingdom and married Hadassah about the time Jeremiah met Kyla. They were all important in the King's kingdom and wonderful friends. Plus, he reminded himself, almost all were related to him after his marriage with Kyla. He really needed an informal night.

"Ya'akov, Hadassah, Edvin, Elsbeth, and Mik'kel, there is a time for official protocol and a time to be ourselves. Tonight, we are Jeremiah, Kyla, and Liam. Can we do that?"

All remained quiet for several seconds.

73

"Well, don't just stand there, Jeremiah. Come on in," said Ya'akov, who then laughed.

Jeremiah smiled. They each settled into a seat, and Hadassah brought out hors d'oeuvres and drinks.

"Liam, I'm sorry Nyssa couldn't join us," Hadassah said.

Liam smiled. "Me too, Hadassah. Although Sarit is going out with Me'ira tonight, Nyssa felt she should get back so as not to get behind with Sarit's wedding plans."

"Yes, we received her invitation. Congratulations," Hadassah said. "My, I can't believe she's that old already. Where does the time go?"

"Thank you. I can't either. I can still remember her being just a baby."

"Think how I feel," Kyla said, laughing.

"Now, mother, let's not get sentimental," Liam said. "I'm sorry I brought the subject up."

Hadassah laughed.

"But you were such a cute baby, Liam," Jeremiah said.

Liam rolled his eyes. "Dad, don't encourage her." He looked at Mik'kel. "Care to tell some stories on Dad? I'm sure you have some pre-Refreshing tales you could tell."

Jeremiah pointed his finger and shook it at Mik'kel. "Now see here. I think I have a story on you for every one you tell on me."

Mik'kel laughed. "Unfortunately, that's probably true. What about some stories on Edvin instead?"

Edvin had been talking with Kyla. He turned when he heard his name. "What? How did I get into your conversation?"

Mik'kel chuckled. "You're in all my stories."

"Yeah, that's what I'm afraid of." There were lots of laughs as this banter went on for a bit.

"Sorry to do this, but I need to turn the conversation seri-

74

ous for a little while," Jeremiah said, turning to Ya'akov. "You've probably heard about the issue with Galen, Me'ira's friend."

"Dad, you might as well say it as it is," Liam said, jumping in. "He's her boyfriend. They're getting pretty serious."

Ya'akov smiled and nodded. "Mom did mention it to me."

"Do you think this is tied to your experience from many years ago?" Jeremiah asked.

Ya'akov rubbed the back of his neck. "Well, it's hard to say. That was so long ago. Yet, I wouldn't put it past him in the least. To me, the leader of The Order seemed . . . well, there's no other way to say it: very, very cold. I can't think of anyone else who would even consider doing such a thing with their son—or anyone's son for that matter."

"But to what purpose?" Liam looked from his dad to Ya'akov. "What have they accomplished with this deceit? They had to know it couldn't last forever. I mean, once a person is grown, it's very hard to control their actions or their decisions."

Ya'akov shook his head. "I don't know. But whatever the purpose, rest assured, it was calculated."

"Has their plan already been fulfilled, or is it still in the future?" Liam asked.

"That is the question," Mik'kel said as his gaze panned the room. "But if Galen is the son of the person Ya'akov encountered, do we know his heritage?"

Jeremiah lgave a blank stare and then shook his head. "We never fully vetted Galen. This . . . discrepancy took precedence."

"What is your point, Mik'kel?" Liam asked.

"Liam, you said Galen and Me'ira may be getting serious."

Liam nodded.

"Think back to when you and Nyssa got married," Mik'kel said. "Was heritage important?"

"Well, she had to be . . . an Israelite." Liam's eyes widened, a light bulb moment happening for him. "We don't know if Galen is or not."

Mik'kel nodded.

Edvin jumped in. "When he said he was from Naphtali, it meant his parents were from there. We have no idea where he is from."

"What about the teleporter?" Kyla looked at Elsbeth. "It creates a genetic blueprint, right?"

"Well, yes, but not the kind you're thinking of," Elsbeth said. "It compares patterns but doesn't identify actual DNA sequences. We can't identify heritage from teleporter data alone. The fastest way is from a DNA sample."

"Maybe he'd be willing to give a blood or hair sample," Kyla said.

"Maybe, dear." Jeremiah patted Kyla's arm. "And we may have a sample at home."

Kyla's eyes widened. "An unauthorized sample? I . . . I don't think we should do that." She looked at the others as if looking for support.

"What percentage are you going to deem acceptable?" Mik'kel asked.

Jeremiah turned to Mik'kel. "What do you mean?"

"Well, after five centuries of Israeli marrying Israeli, the percentage of an Israeli's DNA being identified as Israeli has increased dramatically. But if you recall, it wasn't that way in the beginning. Are you going to require him to meet today's standards?"

Jeremiah, thinking, said nothing.

"Because, if you do, the odds of Me'ira being able to marry him will be almost nonexistent if Galen's parents are not already identified as Israeli or Jewish," Mik'kel said.

"Dad, Mik'kel makes a good point," Liam said. "Not being

able to marry him will break Me'ira's heart if he decides to propose. He shouldn't be punished for something his parents did to him."

"Jeremiah," Mik'kel continued, "If you think back to pre-Refreshing times, President Hatim considered five percent the tipping point."

"But Mik'kel," Edvin interjected, "there's another matter Jeremiah has to consider."

Liam looked perplexed. "What is that, Edvin?"

"Liam, if he hasn't accepted the Messiah as the hope for his future, that's another mark against his passing the vetting process."

Liam nodded. "I know Me'ira talked to him about that, and to my knowledge he hasn't as yet accepted him."

Jeremiah sighed. "Well, it seems he may have two strikes against him already. Maybe I need to prepare Me'ira for not being able to marry Galen before their time together makes her heartache too great."

Kyla touched Jeremiah's arm. "Probably the earlier we do that . . . the better."

Jeremiah sighed and nodded.

"Well, if I dare change the subject, dinner is ready," Hadassah said. "Shall we dine together?"

Jeremiah smiled and nodded. "Thanks, Hadassah. A change in subject is entirely in order."

To dine, Jeremiah and Kyla were seated at each head of the table. Elsbeth, Edvin, and Mik'kel were seated on one side with Hadassah, Ya'akov, and Liam on the other.

The conversation turned less serious and, within minutes, much laughter filled the room. Jeremiah enjoyed the evening immensely. It had been so long since he had such a lighthearted evening, one in which he was able to relax with friends without having to worry about what he said or how he said it. He hoped such an evening could happen again soon.

After dessert and still more light talk, Jeremiah announced his family had to leave.

As Jeremiah stood, so did everyone. "Hadassah, Ya'akov, I have truly enjoyed tonight. Thank you so much for taking the time and trouble to put this together. I do hope we can do this again sometime."

Hadassah smiled. "Thank you, Jeremiah. I hope we can as well."

"Edvin, Elsbeth, Mik'kel, thank you for your friendship. I am truly glad it has continued since our pre-Refreshing days."

"That goes for all of us," Edvin said.

There were handshakes and hugs just before Jeremiah, Kyla, and Liam left.

As they walked back to the palace, Jeremiah couldn't help but think about what the Messiah had said about Galen:

He is the beginning of the key to later prophecy. He is more than he seems, yet less than you think.

Although Jeremiah didn't understand the Messiah's point, he knew he didn't want his daughter part of it.

Yet, was she already? He couldn't help but feel that, in the end, heartache would be an unfortunate part of this saga.

CHAPTER 12

"What makes you think he won't?"

"I'm not saying that at all." Liam got up from his chair and sat next to Me'ira on the sofa. "I'm on your side here."

Me'ira sighed. It certainly didn't feel like her brother was on her side as he kept telling her reasons why she and Galen shouldn't, or couldn't, get married.

Liam put his hand on her shoulder. "I really do like the guy, sis. I also don't want to see you hurt."

"Well, I appreciate that." Her sarcastic tone came through more than she intended. She took a breath and tried to be less so. "But we don't even know his heritage yet, and I've been talking to him about accepting the King. Don't count him out before he's even given a chance."

Liam gave her a sympathetic look. "I know this is hard. I'm sorry. But his name doesn't necessarily support an Israeli or Jewish heritage."

Me'ira plopped her hands in her lap and forced out a sigh. She gave an incredulous stare to her brother. "And what does that have to do with anything? I can point out many people without a Jewish-sounding name who we now consider very Jewish or Israeli. Look at Uncle Edvin. You can't tell me his name is Jewish or Israeli. Yet the King has used his family for

79

centuries to show how he cares for all people—both glorified and non-glorified alike. And then there's Shepherd Franklin. His name is certainly not—"

Liam held up his hands. "OK, OK. Point well taken." He laughed. "You should be on a debate team."

Me'ira's stare softened and she eventually laughed with him. "Well . . . " She bumped her shoulder into his. "Try to make sense next time you start such an argument."

"Speaking of Shepherd Franklin. It might not be a bad idea if I talk to him about this," Liam said.

"Why?"

Liam raised an eyebrow. "Well, Shepherds do more than just teach Scripture. He travels throughout Israel. Maybe he's heard something or knows something."

"Would you try Shepherd Benjamin as well, then?" Me'ira asked. "I think he travels more in the north while Shepherd Franklin is more in the south." She shrugged. "They're both stationed here in Jerusalem, so you could talk to both of them without much trouble."

Liam nodded. "I'll do that." He sat in thought for a few minutes. "Has Galen left for Australia yet?"

Me'ira shrugged. "I don't know. We haven't been in contact since he left."

Liam turned up his brow. "Really?" He smiled. "I thought the two of you were going to be in contact every day?" He leaned over and gave kissing sounds near her face. "The two of you were so lovey-dovey when he was here."

She pushed him away, and he broke out in laughter. Me'ira didn't laugh, however. Her eyes were beginning to tear up.

Liam put his hand on her shoulder. "I'm sorry. I was just joking."

She nodded. "I know. It's not that." She smirked, just a bit.

"Although you are obnoxious." She looked into his eyes. "Liam, that's just it. We were supposed to talk to each other every day. I'm concerned. I haven't heard from him at all since he left."

"You've tried calling him?"

She nodded.

"Maybe he's just taking time to think things over about his parents . . . guardians . . . whatever they actually are."

"Maybe. But there's no answer and no voice or video recording. I can't even leave a message."

"Hmm. That is rather curious."

Me'ira looked down at her lap for a few moments watching her hands. She looked back at Liam. "I've been thinking about what you said, you know, about needing a DNA sample."

Liam's eyebrows went up.

"Would that . . . help? I mean, would that help in identifying his real parents?"

Liam gave a small shrug. "If I understood Aunt Elsbeth correctly, one can't get a DNA read from a teleporter blueprint."

"What about the reverse?"

Liam shook his head slowly. "What do you mean?"

"Well, although you can't get a DNA read from a teleporter blueprint, can you get a teleporter blueprint from a DNA sample?"

Liam cocked his head in thought. "Hmm. Maybe you aren't just a pretty face."

She smirked and shoved him again.

He laughed. "Let's find out." He took his T-band off his wrist, set it on the coffee table in front of them, had it dial, and scooted closer to Me'ira.

In a few seconds, a hologram of Elsbeth hovered over the T-band. "This is Elsbeth Isakson."

"Hi, Aunt Elsbeth. Me'ira and I have a question for you. Do

you have a few minutes?"

"Oh. Hi, Liam. Hi, Me'ira. Sure. What's your question?"

"I told Me'ira what you said the other night about not being able to get a DNA imprint from a teleporter blueprint."

Elsbeth nodded. "Yes, the teleporter recognizes patterns only."

"But, can the reverse work?" Me'ira asked, jumping in. "Liam was unsure."

"Actually . . . " They could see Elsbeth in thought. "Me'ira, I never thought about that, but yes, I think so. At least in theory. If we know the DNA sequence, we could likely reconstruct what the teleporter pattern would look like—or at least some of it."

"Would it be enough to find Galen's true parents?"

Elsbeth shrugged. "I think so, Me'ira. Assuming, that is, they've been using the teleporter recently."

Liam looked from Me'ira to Elsbeth. "Why is that?"

"It could still be done, I suppose, no matter when they've used the teleporter. But it could take quite some time to find. The longer back they've used the teleporter, the more data we'd have to go through, so the longer it would take. Since it's pattern recognition, there could be a lot of false positives."

"Thanks, Aunt Elsbeth. That's very helpful. We'll be in touch." Liam reached for his T-band and disconnected the call. He slapped it back around his wrist.

Me'ira looked at Liam. "I understand Mom's concern about doing this without his consent, but I'm afraid something has happened to him. I think he would have called me by now. Plus, who doesn't allow anyone to leave a message?"

Liam nodded. "So, that begs the question. Do you have a hair sample from Galen?"

Me'ira grimaced. "I don't know. I must, though, somewhere." She thought a few seconds. "Let me check my clothes. I don't think Lydia has gathered them yet."

"OK. You check on that. Call me if you find it. I'll go get Dad's permission, I'll talk to Shepherds Franklin and Benjamin, and I'll have someone stop by his place in both Naphtali and Ephraim."

Me'ira smiled and gave Liam a hug. "Thanks, Liam. I really appreciate you helping me like this."

He kissed her forehead. "Sure. You're family."

Me'ira went to her bedroom while Liam headed to their father's office. Nervousness and excitement overtook her at the same time. Something, she reasoned, was not right. Galen would never just leave and not contact her. She knew that.

Once in her bedroom, Me'ira took one of the dresses she had worn when Galen visited and spread it across her bed. Using a magnifying glass and a pair of tweezers from her embroidery basket, she kept combing—and felt a bit like a real detective.

She searched slowly and methodically. While it was tedious work, she pressed on, determined to find a hair. There were many of her own, but none were short enough to have been Galen's. She searched her entire dress—to no avail.

Me'ira plopped onto her bed, disappointed. Crying should not be something she turned to, she told herself, but her eyes were moistening. Shaking her head, she told herself not to get emotional, but instead to think. Her mind played back every moment she had been with Galen. A thought suddenly came: her hairpin! Once, when she hugged him close, her hairpin had pulled his hair. They laughed about it at the time. She went to her vanity and looked for the hairpin she wore that day, the one with a red rose on it. The small leaves of the rose were composed of some type of stiff mesh material. This was where she hoped to find her prize.

The hairpin was still laying separate from her other things. Carefully lifting it, she held it under the magnifying glass. Two hairs were visible. One was definitely hers. The other looked caught in the mesh material, just as she suspected. Taking the tweezers, she carefully pulled it from its entanglement. As she examined it more closely, it still had the root ball intact. She smiled, then slightly cringed. No wonder Galen had rubbed his scalp and mockingly complained how dangerous it was to hug her.

She placed the sample in an empty vial then held it up, studying it closely. Amazing something so tiny could—potentially—solve such a huge mystery.

She hurried from the room to find Liam.

CHAPTER 13

M e'ira didn't find Liam anywhere, so she assumed he was still in her father's office. She hesitated, then knocked. She heard some shuffling of feet, and the door opened.

Liam smiled. "I assumed it would be you."

"Come on in, Me'ira," her father said. "Liam was telling me about your plans."

She glanced at Liam, who gave her a half shrug. *Oh wow. This means he hasn't convinced Dad to go through with it.*

She held up the vial. "Found it."

Liam walked over and took it from her. He held it to eye level. "Nice, sis." He glanced at her. "To be honest, I had doubts." He looked more closely. "Look. It even has a root ball." He glanced back at her. "Well done. Aren't you quite the detective?"

"Well, thanks for your vote of confidence."

He laughed and turned to their father. "Well, Dad. It just went from hypothetical to real."

Jeremiah sat back and sighed. "It's like your mother said, though. It seems like such an invasion of privacy."

Me'ira opened her mouth to speak up, but Liam's holo-com sounded.

He looked at the caller ID. "Excuse me. I need to take this."

He went behind Jeremiah's desk and exited the French doors onto the balcony. Through the door's glass pane, Me'ira saw Liam activate his holo-com's holographic projection.

Me'ira turned back to her father. "Dad, it's not an invasion of privacy if it's what Galen would want."

"But he isn't here to tell us that."

Me'ira was having a hard time understanding her father's hesitancy. "But he *did* say that when he was here."

Jeremiah turned up his brow. "When? I never heard him say that specifically."

Me'ira sighed. She wanted to remain respectful. "Dad, when he asked Mr. and Mrs. Shafir who his real parents were, they didn't know. It's obvious he wants to know who his real parents are. Shouldn't we do this for him?"

"Well, I think there's more ethics involved here—"

Liam reentered through the French doors. He looked solemn; his lips were pursed.

His gaze met Me'ira's. "What's wrong, Liam?" she asked.

He walked to the front of the desk shaking his head. "There's no sign of him in either Naphtali or Ephraim."

Me'ira put her hand to her mouth, which let out a small gasp.

Jeremiah looked from Me'ira to Liam. "But couldn't he have already left for Australia?"

Liam shook his head. "Doubtful."

"Why?" Me'ira asked.

Liam turned her way. "You said he was going to have someone man his shop and museum before he left for Australia, right?"

Me'ira nodded. "Yes. Why?"

Liam glanced from her to their father. "Well, both places are closed. No one is manning them. Also, no one is at their home in Naphtali or where he stayed in Ephraim."

Tears welled over Me'ira's bottom eyelids and fell to her cheeks. Liam gave her a sympathetic look. He walked her way and gave her a big hug. "Don't jump to conclusions, sis."

She looked into his eyes. "But you already have. I can tell."

Liam gave a grimace to their father, who sat back in his chair and sighed. "Well, I think this tips the scale. It's not about ethics anymore. It's about finding a missing person."

Me'ira buried her head in Liam's chest and wept. He wrapped his arms around her and kissed her on top of her head. "I'm sorry, sis." He turned to his father. "So, we have your permission, Dad?"

Jeremiah nodded. "Yes, you have it. This has turned into quite a mystery."

Me'ira pulled back from Liam. Her weeping had stopped, but she was still sniffling. "I . . . I want to go with you when you give the hair to Aunt Elsbeth."

It looked as if Liam was going to object. She put her hand on his chest. "Liam, please. I need to *do* something. I think understanding what she will be doing will be helpful."

Liam glanced at their dad. He gave a reluctant nod. "OK, sis. Let's go."

Liam opened the door and Me'ira stepped out. Jeremiah called, "Liam?" He turned.

"Keep me informed."

Liam nodded. "Absolutely, Dad."

Since the Jerusalem Science Center sat close to the temple, they took the teleporter from their palace to the King's. They only had to travel a few blocks from there to where Elsbeth worked.

Once they reached their aunt's office, Elsbeth's administrative assistant paged her. The assistant motioned for them to enter her office and have a seat. Elsbeth's desk had a type of frosted glass with a smooth top. Several monitors were on the wall, as well as a large map of teleporter locations around the globe.

Elsbeth entered in about one minute, and before they even sat down, Liam gave her the vial with the hair sample.

Elsbeth held it up and did a quick study. "Well, it looks like a very good, viable sample." She looked at Me'ira. "Are you sure this is Galen's?"

Me'ira nodded. "Yes, Aunt Elsbeth. I'm positive."

"OK." She looked at Liam. "Just checking. Your father has deemed that we do this?"

Liam nodded. "He feels it's now a necessity. I had some people go check on Galen. He can't be found. He's not at either home, and both his shop and museum are closed. It's like he's just disappeared."

Elsbeth furrowed her brow. "I see. He either left in more of a hurry than he let on when he left here, or . . . "

Liam nodded. Me'ira glanced between the two. Her eyes were watering again, but she worked hard to hold back the tears.

Me'ira pointed to the vial. "So what now?"

Elsbeth sat at her desk and motioned for them to have a seat. "Well, don't expect a fast answer here." She shrugged. "We can get his DNA sequenced in relatively short order. Likely, sometime tomorrow I can tell you his heritage, but that's not the main question." She tapped her fingers on her desk. "That still won't tell us who his parents are."

Me'ira leaned forward. "But I thought you said you can use his hair to find out."

"Oh, yes. We will." Elsbeth put her elbows on her desk

and interlocked her fingers. "I'll be honest with both of you, though. While, theoretically, this can work, we've never done anything like this before." She gave a small shrug. "We've never needed to before."

Liam looked from Me'ira to Elsbeth. "So, you don't know how long this will take?"

Elsbeth grimaced and gave a slight shake of her head. "I wish I did. We have software for pattern recognition, but it's not like plugging something into an equation for an answer to spit out. But we do have some experts in fuzzy logic, so I don't think you could be in more capable hands."

Liam nodded. Me'ira sighed.

"All I can tell you is to be patient. I'll contact you as soon as we know anything. I'll make this a high priority. I wish I could make it go faster, but some things take time. This is one of them."

Elsbeth stood and gave each of them a hug. "I'm sorry, Me'ira."

"Aunt Elsbeth, let me know even of the false positives," Liam said. "I have resources who can help us sift through them and narrow the search."

Elsbeth gave a small smile to Liam. "Sure thing."

When they had left the Science Center, Me'ira took in a long breath and let it out slowly. "I'm so wound up. I want to do something."

"What about getting a falafel?"

Me'ira laughed and shook her head. "That wasn't exactly what I meant."

Liam smiled. "I know, but I'm hungry. I don't get a chance to go to that great falafel place around the corner very often. Let's go."

Me'ira shrugged. "Sure. Why not? Just letting you know: I'm not very hungry at the moment."

"No problem. I'll finish yours for you."

Me'ira laughed. "Yeah, I bet you will." She gave a slight slap on his arm. "This time, wait until I tell you I'm done before you decide I'm done."

Liam gave a mock hurt look. "When have I ever?"

"Yeah, *when*? When have you not?"

"Snooze you lose."

She smirked. Even while he wrapped his arm around her shoulders, she said, "I warn you: my fork-stabbing skills have improved."

Liam looked at her and broke out laughing. "Duly noted, My Lady. Duly noted."

Once they ordered, Me'ira turned to Liam and made a pronouncement: "I'm going to Australia."

Liam's eyes widened. "What? Where did that come from?"

"Well, I can't just stay here and do nothing."

Liam leaned in. "But you don't know if he's even *in* Australia. Even if he is, you don't know where to look."

Me'ira leaned back and crossed her arms. "Well, finding Caleb can't be *that* hard."

"You think finding one hair makes you a great detective?"

"Oh, don't be condescending. Of course not. But how hard can it be to find a Caleb Shafir?"

"How do you know he even has the same last name?"

Me'ira unfolded her arms and scooted in. "Now who's not using their brain? Noah and Lois were not the ones trying to deceive. Plus, they had a life in each place, and they would have to be very meticulous not to get their stories mixed up between the two places."

"You don't think they could pull that off?"

Me'ira turned up a corner of her mouth with a half chuckle. "Did they strike you as capable of that?"

Liam shook his head. "No, not really."

Me'ira put her arms and elbows on the table. "After Passover, I'm going to Australia." She gave Liam a very determined look.

Liam locked gazes with her for a few moments. "Then I'm going with you."

"What? Really? You have obligations here."

"Part of that is ensuring the well-being of our citizens. I think this falls into that category."

"What about Sarit's wedding? Don't you have an obligation there?"

"The wedding is still several months away." He grinned. "Besides, I've already answered my question and received my instructions."

"What were those?"

"'Where's your wallet?' . . . And: 'Show up.'"

Me'ira gave a hard laugh. Being with her older brother was enjoyable. She couldn't remember spending this much time with him. All her brothers and sisters were married by the time she was born. Their age difference always seemed like such an impediment to getting to know them better. Now she had a chance to change that.

They had an enjoyable lunch together. The thought of spending more time with Liam made Me'ira glad. After celebrating Passover next week, they would be off on an adventure—together.

Me'ira's last bite caught in her throat. Realization was hitting her. This was not an adventure; it was her trying to find Galen.

Still, having Liam to lean on would be comforting.

CHAPTER 14

"Have you seen my cuff links?" Jeremiah opened several jewelry boxes on the dresser. He had a noon meeting with King David in just half an hour followed by the Passover ceremony later this night. Kyla had asked him to start getting ready earlier and he had ignored her. He didn't want to admit his sense of timing was off, but he couldn't go to the meeting without his cuff links.

"Are you going to admit I was right?" Kyla asked, a gleam in her eye.

"Did you hide my cuff links just so you could win our little argument?" He gave her a sly smile.

She put her hand to her chest. "Why, Jeremiah, I'm shocked you would accuse me of such a thing."

He laughed. "You're far feistier than anyone gives you credit for."

"I am but a lamb with my only desire to do the bidding of my shepherd," Kyla said, batting her eyes.

Jeremiah laughed so hard he had a coughing attack. "Ah, your words sound innocent, but they will do me in."

She came over and kissed his cheek. "Arguments are easily won if you know how."

Jeremiah looked at the clock on his dresser and sighed.

"All right, my dear. I concede. You were correct. I should have started dressing earlier."

She smiled. "Let me see if I can help you. I don't want you to be late."

He rolled his eyes but couldn't help smiling at her. This type of banter was one of the things he loved about his wife. Kyla was truly a treasure.

She walked over to the dresser and lifted a figurine. "Ah, here they are." She held them up like a winner's trophy. "Almost hiding in plain sight."

He held out his hands and gave her a smirk. "Yes, how could I have forgotten I put them *under* a figurine so I wouldn't forget where to look? What was I thinking?"

She smiled as she pushed his Star of David cufflinks through the buttonholes of his cuffs and secured them. "Exactly."

Jeremiah looked at them and smiled. Each point had a gemstone representing each tribe of Israel—six on one, six on the other. It was the first gift given him by King David. He wore them every time he met with the king in formal attire. They were one of his prized possessions.

"Thank you, my dear. I will listen to your words of wisdom next time."

She smiled and kissed him. "Time to go. You'll be right on time."

Before he left, she secured his golden sash and sea blue cape to his gold-trimmed shoulder epaulets and placed his crown upon his head. He only wore it on special occasions, and this was certainly one of those times. He looked at himself in the mirror and ensured the crimson pinstriped seams in his trousers, which matched his cape, were straight. He checked to ensure the two rows of gold filigree buttons down the front of his pure white shirt, attached with additional small crimson-colored epaulets, were secure.

He turned and smiled at Kyla. She smiled back and patted him on his chest.

Thankfully, he didn't have far to go. The palace, built somewhat like a duplex, looked like a single building, but internally it functioned as two separate residences. The large balcony upon which they would stand to greet the people was the point where the two buildings joined. Both men could exit onto it from their respective receiving rooms.

Jeremiah went to his receiving room and stood at the door that opened to the large outdoor balcony. Azariah stood with him. As soon as they heard the first noon chime, Azariah opened the door and Jeremiah and the king stepped onto the balcony simultaneously. Jeremiah turned to the king and genuflected. King David gave a bow. He was a good-looking and muscular man with a neatly trimmed, reddish-colored beard and mustache. He was also glorified. Each man turned and walked to the edge of the balcony.

A large crowd, which had increased in number all morning, waited below. Many of them clapped, yelled, or whistled as the two men stepped forward. Both Jeremiah and King David, dressed even more regally than Jeremiah, waved. The dominant colors in the king's ensemble were gold and crimson while gold and blue dominated his attire. Each man's dominant color was the less dominant color in the other's outfit. Each of their crowns were of pure gold and lattice-patterned in similar style, but the king's sat higher and thicker than Jeremiah's. Gemstones similar to those in Jeremiah's cufflinks, but larger, were strategically placed around David's crown; Jeremiah's, although gold, had no gemstones.

King David raised his hands to quiet the crowd. "Thank you, my friends. Another Passover is upon us. This evening we pay homage to what our great King and Messiah has done for us."

Applause echoed off the surrounding buildings. Since this assembly was held in the heart of the city, most of those here were from Israel. There would be many more people from around the world at the temple this evening when the Passover lamb would be sacrificed. There were many kings from around the globe representing various nations. David reigned as the king of Israel—just as he did millennia ago. The only difference now was he had a glorified body. The glow of his skin complemented the gold in his clothing and made his crown shine even brighter.

"As your king, I am proud of how you are always so welcoming to those of all the other nations of the world who come to worship our Messiah, the King of kings. We are honored to have him reside in our great city, and I am proud we get to share him with the rest of the world."

Jeremiah raised his hands to speak. "This night you will observe the Passover sacrifice as a symbol of what our great Messiah did for us so we can know future punishment can also pass over us if we accept him as the hope of our eternal future. We will eat unleavened bread for seven days to symbolize that we dedicate ourselves to him, we will listen to angels sing, and we will revel in the joys of our Messiah."

More applause rose to a crescendo, then to complete silence when King David raised his hands to speak again.

"When I reigned as Israel's king millennia ago, we celebrated God's miracle of bringing his children out of Egypt into the Promised Land he had bestowed to us. Yet our God has done an even greater miracle, and we revel in it today. Our nation, once divided, has been reunited through our King's great wisdom and might. Israeli and Jew are again together from every nation of the globe, and we are now one nation before him within his Promised Kingdom. Let us celebrate and remember this miracle tonight."

A thunderous applause rose up from the crowd. King David and Prince Jeremiah stood motionless for several moments as the crowd cheered. Both waved, turned, and walked back to the door of their receiving chambers.

Before they reentered, however, Jeremiah asked, "Your Majesty, could I have a few moments of your time?"

King David nodded. "Certainly, Jeremiah."

After entering, Jeremiah opened the door that joined their two receiving rooms. David's was much more elaborate than Jeremiah's, but that was as it should be. While Jeremiah's receiving room was his large office, David's was truly a throne room. It was set up to be reminiscent of the throne room he had when he was king over all Israel many millennia ago. His throne sat on top of six marble steps. The throne itself had two armrests, each composed of lions made of gold. Similar golden lions were on each end of each step, one for each tribe of Israel. Also, flanking the throne, displayed on each opposing wall, were large wall hangings, also of gold, showing the emblems of each tribe with six on each wall. Jeremiah always found this room extremely impressive.

David sat on his throne, and a seat was brought in for Jeremiah to sit next to him.

"Thank you, Your Majesty."

"What is troubling you, Jeremiah?"

"I've been somewhat surprised to learn there is likely some discontent brewing, and I'm at a loss to know how to address it."

David smiled. "Well, that is one of the burdens of royalty, I'm afraid."

96

"But don't you find it odd, especially in the time in which we live?"

David's eyebrows went up. "And you thought your appointment by the Messiah would be an easy one?"

Jeremiah gave a short sigh. "Well, sort of. I mean, who would have thought anyone would have trouble with a utopian world? We have a Messiah and King who loves us, has removed the curse on the world by removing all disease and malady—even death has given us peace between all animals and man, and has given us a ground that provides crops in abundance without harmful pestilence."

"Jeremiah, what is ordinary?"

"Sir?"

"Ordinary. Please define it."

"Well, ordinary is what is experienced and expected on a day-to-day basis. It has been, and is always, expected."

"Is our current world ordinary to you?"

"Oh no, of course not, sir. It's absolutely wonderful. I appreciate all the Master has given us. Truly, I do not take it for granted."

"I'm sure you don't. What is ordinary for Me'ira?"

"Well . . . " He had never thought of that.

"And what is ordinary for so many of earth's citizens today?"

"The world today as they experience it." Jeremiah wasn't yet sure the point King David was trying to make.

"Can they appreciate the world today as you and I do?"

"Well, yes, if they heed the teaching of the Shepherds who help them see how great our Messiah is."

"True. They appreciate their world because they accept, by faith, what our Messiah has given to us is wonderful and cannot be better."

Jeremiah nodded. "That's right."

97

"But will they ever appreciate it as much as you and I? Without experiencing hardship, disease, war, famine, or death, will they truly know what they have been given?"

"Probably not, my lord."

"That is why there is unrest in such a utopian society, as you have called it. People are experiencing their ordinary and do not understand *their* ordinary is actually extraordinary."

"What do we do?" Jeremiah looked at the king intently.

"We can teach, but we cannot make them learn. We can provide opportunities but cannot make them accept. Truth comes from knowledge and acceptance of the One who truly defines it. That is why the Shepherds teach 'you shall know the truth and the truth shall set you free'—because their truth is from the One who is the source of all truth. False truth, lies disguised as half-truths, only leads to enslavement. There are those who cannot discern the difference and thereby fall into discontent."

Jeremiah sat in thought for several moments. He knew David spoke truth. He had never really thought about it in this way before. He could only point to the truth but could not make people accept it.

"Thank you, my king. I see why God chose you to be king—twice. We all benefit from your wise counsel."

David smiled. "I can only counsel what the Master has taught me as well. We are all students under his tutelage."

Jeremiah nodded. "Indeed, my lord." He rose and bowed. "Goodbye for now, your Majesty."

"I'll see you at the temple," King David said.

Jeremiah bowed and headed back to his office.

CHAPTER 15

M e'ira studied herself in the mirror. She should be happy, but discontentment filled her instead. The dress wasn't the culprit. She turned back and forth admiring it, happy with her selection. The bodice had white, blue, green, and lavender all intertwined together in a tight weave pattern. It then blossomed out from the waist with large blue and green flowers, with the colors intermingling with just a hint of purple throughout—just enough to add contrast. The material from the waist down had a green-colored tulle over it, giving all an ethereal look and feel. A bright blue fabric acting like a belt with a silver star of David in its center became the crowning touch for this dress.

The purpose of the purchase had been to wow Galen. He would have loved it; Me'ira was sure of that. Yet that would now not happen. At least not tonight. He should be here to celebrate Passover with her, she told herself. And yet she had no idea where he was. It wasn't possible that he wasn't here because he didn't want to be here. Something had gone wrong, and she had to get to the bottom of it. She knew, though, that she could do nothing until after Passover. But even if against protest, she was not going to simply remain here and wait. That wasn't her. Protocol or no protocol, she would go to Australia.

99

She heard a knock on her bedroom door. "Come in," Me'ira called.

The door opened and a familiar face appeared.

"Sarit! Hi." She motioned. "Come on in."

"Hi, Me'ira." Sarit stopped. "Wow, your dress is gorgeous."

Me'ira gave a slight smile. She looked down at it and then back to Sarit. "Thank you." She shook her head. "But I'm not sure why I'm even wearing it."

Sarit turned up her brow. "Why? It's so . . . you. I just love the style. It's elegant and simple at the same time."

"Galen's not coming."

Sarit sat on Me'ira's bed. "I know. I heard. I'm so sorry. That's one of the reasons we're meeting you here rather than at the temple. Dad needed to talk to Grandpa about something."

Me'ira's eyes widened. "Did he hear anything?"

Sarit shook her head. "I don't think so. I think he just wanted to talk to Grandfather about you going with him." Sarit grimaced. "I think everyone is against it—except for Dad." She raised her eyebrows. "I'm on your side, though."

Me'ira sat next to her. "Thanks, Sarit." She sighed. "It seems I've done everything backward. I don't think my parents are very happy with me."

Sarit took her hand. "Me'ira, they love you. They just want the best for you."

She nodded. "I know. But I don't think they believe Galen is the best for me."

"And you do?"

It was a penetrating question. Me'ira looked into Sarit's eyes. "I really do, Sarit. I really do." She shook her head. "I know it doesn't make sense to anyone else, but I just know he is."

Sarit gave her a smile and hug. "I'm praying for you, Me'ira.

If this is the best for you, I'm sure the King will make that happen."

Me'ira nodded and gave a weak smile. She tried to perk up. "So, what about you? How are your wedding plans going?"

Sarit smiled and her eyes twinkled. "Really well. Oh, Me'ira, it's so exciting." She patted Me'ira's hand. "You'll get there one day. I'm sure of it."

"So what colors did you finally choose?"

"Yellow and white."

Me'ira laughed. "I told you that when you first began choosing. Didn't I?"

Sarit chuckled. "Yes you did. There were just so many options presented."

Me'ira shook her head. "Sarit, you've loved yellow ever since I've known you. I knew you couldn't have a wedding without yellow being a main color theme."

"Well . . . " She shrugged. "At least that part is settled." She smiled. "Now Mom can get decorations ordered."

Nyssa appeared in the doorway. "Sarit. Me'ira. Time to go to the temple."

Sarit stood. "Yes, Mother."

Nyssa turned to head back downstairs, but Me'ira called her back. "Nyssa, can I ask you something?"

Nyssa nodded. "Sure. Your mother will be calling us down at any minute, though."

"What if Sarit had fallen in love with someone who was not yet vetted?"

Nyssa's expression softened, and she walked over to Me'ira and put her hands on Me'ira's shoulders. "Me'ira, that's a hypothetical question. I'm not sure I can give a simple answer to that."

Sarit chuckled. "Very hypothetical, considering my father."

Nyssa gave Sarit a hard look.

Sarit's face flushed. "I'm sorry, Me'ira. I didn't mean to be insensitive." She shrugged. "Our experiences were just totally different, that's all."

Me'ira nodded.

Nyssa smiled. "OK. Come on, let's go." She gave Me'ira a hug while being extremely careful not to crush her dress. "I'm sure the King will work everything out. Let's just give him time to do that."

Me'ira gave a weak smile and nodded. "I'm sure you're right."

Nyssa and Sarit walked down the stairs together. Me'ira followed. So, what Nyssa didn't say, but had implied, was that Sarit was the compliant one and she the rebellious one. She couldn't really deny that she had always balked at rules, regulations, and, yes, protocol. Maybe she should take some tips from Sarit.

Maybe some of Liam's traits would rub off on her when she traveled with him next week to Australia.

CHAPTER 16

"Dad, we waited until after Passover. I fear we've already wasted too much time." Me'ira didn't want to be difficult, but she deeply felt Galen was in danger, and everyone seemed to be taking too much time for definitive action.

"Me'ira, this is crazy. I don't think one of my daughters should be traipsing off into the unknown in Australia." Jeremiah shook his head. "Who will look after you there? Plus, it's just . . . I mean . . . "

Me'ira's lips pursed and her hands went to her hips. Liam, standing behind her, put his hands on her shoulders. She knew he was preventing her from saying something she would regret. Yet if her dad mentioned protocol, she would likely lose it.

"I'll go with her."

Jeremiah's gaze shot to Liam. Before he could say anything, Liam held up a hand.

"Dad, this is what I tried to tell you before Passover. If this was Mom, what would you do? Me'ira loves Galen and is willing to do anything for him. I'm willing to go with her. I'll watch after her."

Jeremiah's hands flew into the air in exasperation. He turned to his right. "Ya'akov, this is why I had you come.

103

Maybe you can talk some sense into them." Jeremiah plopped into his desk chair and shook his head.

"This so-called 'Leader of The Order' is not anyone to be taken lightly," Ya'akov said. "He's very crafty and knows how to go to the limit of rebellion and not get classified as rebellious. Also, he's very good at manipulation. He may manipulate you to do something you wouldn't otherwise do or manipulate someone else to do something that may or may not be rebellious. I've seen him convince others to do rebellious acts so they get taken. This could be a very dangerous trip."

"Ya'akov, I appreciate your words of wisdom. I know you have encountered this person before," Me'ira said while trying to remain calm. She turned to look at both her father and Ya'akov. "But that doesn't change what we need to do now. If either of your wives were in this position, you would not hesitate to go. This is no different."

Me'ira couldn't understand why both Ya'akov and her dad were so resistant.

"Me'ira, there is a big difference," Jeremiah said. "You are not married."

Me'ira folded her bottom lip under and bit it with her teeth to let her anger pass before she said something. "OK, Dad. If you want to get technical. You loved Mom before you married her, right? So I'm sure you would have gone to look for her even before she became your wife. That's what you do when you love someone."

Jeremiah ran his hand over his mouth and readjusted in his chair. "All right, Me'ira. You've made your case, and I can't say you're not right." He scooted closer. "Let me at least send someone else to look for him."

She put her hands on the edge of his desk. "Dad, I can't sit here idly and do nothing. You just said you would do the same."

Jeremiah rubbed his forehead. He looked at Ya'akov as if seeking support.

Ya'akov just raised his eyebrows as if to say: She has a point.

Jeremiah sighed. "OK, OK. You win, Me'ira." He looked at Liam. "But you must keep a watchful eye on her, and . . . " His gaze turned back to Me'ira. "You must obey your brother."

Both looked at each other, then back to their father, and nodded.

"I have some additional information from my mother," Ya'akov said.

All eyes turned his way.

"She said Caleb recently used a local teleporter to go from Perth to Sydney. A firm just hired him to design farm equipment, and he's attending a conference in Sydney. The conference ends tonight. It's likely he will travel back sometime tomorrow."

Me'ira looked at Liam. "So, to Perth then."

"It may not be that easy," Ya'akov interjected. "We know he owns an AGA, which likely means he lives farther inland from Perth." Ya'akov nodded to Jeremiah. "If you please, Your Highness."

Jeremiah pressed a remote. A large monitor on the opposite wall came to life and a large map of Australia was displayed.

Ya'akov walked near the screen. "It's likely he traveled to Perth because the closest teleporter is there."

He pointed to Perth. The others came forward for a closer look.

Liam turned to Ya'akov. "So what's your best guess as to where he lives?"

Ya'akov pointed to a small town a few hundred kilometers east of Perth. "My guess would be Hyden. It's fairly small and out of the way. A place where not too many questions would likely get asked. But a place from which Noah and Lois could easily get to a teleporter for any necessary travel."

"Correction." Me'ira smiled as she looked at Liam. "To Hyden—that's where we'll go."

"When will you go?" Jeremiah's eyes looked sad.

Me'ira glanced at Liam and back to her father. "Tomorrow."

Liam nodded. "Best chance to get to Caleb before this Leader fellow does."

Jeremiah rounded his desk and grabbed both Me'ira and Liam in a hug. "Me'ira, you come back safe . . . and soon. Your mother may not speak to me until she sees you back safe and sound." As he released the hug, he looked both in the eyes. "You two keep each other safe."

Both nodded and turned to leave.

"And keep in touch on your holo-com."

* * * * *

The next morning, despite Me'ira asking her not to, Kyla met them at the teleporter to see her son and daughter off.

"Your dad has a business meeting, so I thought someone should see you off."

Both Me'ira and Liam gave their mother a hug.

"Where's Nyssa? I thought she would see you off as well," Kyla asked.

"I went home last night and said my goodbyes there," Liam said.

Kyla nodded. Her eyes were wet.

Me'ira knew getting through the teleporter was going to take longer than they wanted—or planned.

Kyla turned to her daughter once more. "Me'ira, dear. I

hate to see you going out like that in public. What will people think?"

Me'ira glanced at Liam, who suppressed a laugh. She gave him a hard stare and turned back to her mother.

"Mom, I'm going to a fairly remote place. I'm not sure what all I will have to do. I can't go in a fine dress and fancy shoes."

Kyla raised her hands and shook her head. "But trousers? They're so . . . so . . . out of character."

Me'ira gave her mother another hug. "It's fine, Mom. It's out of character here, but not where I'm going. I'm sure there will be plenty of women dressed like this."

Kyla turned to Liam. "If what she says is not true, you get her some respectable clothes immediately, all right?"

"Yes, ma'am. Absolutely." He glanced at Me'ira and smiled.

She rolled her eyes at him, careful not to let her mother see.

Me'ira couldn't take much more of this. She stepped onto the teleporter pad. "Liam, it's time to go."

Liam gave his mom a final hug, stood next to Me'ira, and pressed the Engage button.

They exited the teleporter at the palace and headed for the long-range teleporter, which was a few blocks south of the palace.

"Do you want to shop for something here before we go, or wait until we get there?" Liam looked serious, but his eyes gave him away.

Me'ira slapped his arm.

He gave a hearty laugh. "It shows she cares, Me'ira."

"I know, but you don't have to milk it."

Liam laughed again.

In only a matter of minutes after they stepped on the long-range teleporter, they found themselves in Sydney.

As they walked to find the local teleporter, Me'ira looked around. The city looked beautiful but very different from Jerusalem. Here, nothing looked old. They passed a few parks with colorful shrubs and plant life as they walked toward the teleporter. Likely, other parks were scattered around the city just as they were in Jerusalem. Me'ira had to admit, however, that she still thought Jerusalem was prettier.

"Very different from Jerusalem, huh?" she asked her brother.

Liam nodded. "From what I've been told, the original port city got destroyed before the Refreshing due to the Great Earthquake that took place at the Messiah's coming, and due to the rise in the water table at the time."

"So they rebuilt?"

Liam nodded. "It's beautiful, though. Being near the ocean reminds me a bit of home on the Mediterranean Sea. I love the smell of the salty air."

Me'ira pointed to a sign. "It looks like the teleporter is down this street."

There were several people in line ahead of them, so they had to wait. The line moved fairly quickly, however. When their turn came, they stepped on the pad, Liam pressed Perth as the destination, and he hit Engage. Again, their vision blurred . . . and when it came clear, they were on the opposite side of Australia.

The city didn't look much different from Sydney.

"I'm not sure I would know this is a different city if I didn't know we just teleported here," Me'ira said. She looked at one of the parks as they passed. "Although the flowers here look different." She had to admit that the sea of color of the wildflowers around the park looked lovely.

Liam nodded. "It's probably because they had to rebuild

this city as well. What happened to Sydney is what happened to many coastal cities around the world. They either rebuilt them or moved on to a different city to live."

"So, what now?" Me'ira asked.

Liam looked at her and smiled. "Now? Now your wish comes true."

"And which one would that be? I do have more than one, you know."

Liam chuckled. "You get to ride in an AGA."

"Well, that fulfills only half the wish."

He glanced at her while scrunching his face. "Oh?"

"I want to ride in an AGA with Galen."

Liam stared at her and laughed. "Sorry. I guess I'll have to do in a pinch."

She shrugged. "It could be worse."

"Ah, always the optimist, huh?" He wrapped his arm around her shoulders and gave a squeeze.

Me'ira looked at her brother and smiled. She loved this banter with him. He always took it in stride.

They soon found a business with a sign stating AGAs could be rented by the week. Me'ira looked down the street to see if there were places with better options, but she didn't see any.

Liam shrugged. "Maybe we should rent for a week anyway since we don't really know how long we'll need to be here."

Me'ira nodded. "Good point."

Liam took the necessary steps to rent the AGA. The owner gave a few instructions and pointed out how to switch from manual to autopilot and the advantages of each transmission setting. After a short time, both got in.

"Since we're in a bit of a hurry, I'll just input the destination and let it do the driving," Liam said.

Me'ira nodded. "That's probably best. No sense putting our

lives in more danger than necessary."

Liam looked at her, head tilted. She smiled. He shook his head and smiled back. "I could take offense at that."

The AGA propelled forward with barely a sound.

She looked at Liam with another smile. "Truth is truth."

"Ah, but that one will come back to haunt you."

She laughed. "Probably."

When they reached the town of Hyden, Liam took over the controls. He found a restaurant and parked the AGA.

"Why here?" Me'ira asked.

"Let's cover two agendas at the same time. I'm hungry, and we need directions to the Shafirs' house."

Me'ira nodded. "Sounds like a plan."

As they ate, Liam casually asked their waiter if he knew Noah, Lois, or Caleb Shafir.

"Oh, sure. I know Caleb," the waiter said. "We went to school together. Although I hear he got a job that may take him outta here."

Liam smiled, then asked, "So where's their house?"

"Oh, drive past Wave Rock and it's just on the other side of that." He briefly described their house.

Liam furrowed his brow. "Wave Rock?"

"Is that a metaphor for something?" Me'ira asked.

The waiter looked at Me'ira and laughed. "No. It's just a rock that looks like a gigantic wave. You'll see. Just continue down that road. You can't miss it."

"Thanks." Me'ira looked at Liam and shrugged.

The waiter nodded and headed to another table.

As they walked back to the AGA, Me'ira hoped they would find Caleb and that he would help them make sense of all this.

She was having deep thoughts, though. Maybe her dad was right. Was she really out of her league? Probably.

She said a quick prayer as they got back in the AGA and Liam drove off.

CHAPTER 17

In only a few minutes they reached Wave Rock. Me'ira's jaw dropped. She had never seen anything like it.

"Sorry, Me'ira. I have to stop to look at this."

"No, no. Please do. It's . . . it's unbelievable."

Before them loomed what, indeed, looked like a gigantic wave rolling into shore, but one trapped in suspended animation—but it was a massive rock instead.

They stepped from the AGA to take a closer look.

"It must be about ten meters high," Me'ira said, looking nearly straight up in disbelief.

Liam nodded. "And at least one hundred meters in length." He shook his head. "Incredible."

They looked for several minutes. Liam turned. "We need to get going."

Me'ira nodded. She wanted to stay longer but knew they didn't have the luxury.

After driving for another ten minutes, they came upon a farmhouse—or at least a house on a farm. The house looked very modern. It had many sides and many of the walls were composed of tinted glass. Nearly the entire roof looked to be tiled, but upon closer look, Me'ira could tell the "tiles" were actually solar panels.

Liam whistled. "I've seen modern before, but this outdoes them all."

"Pretty impressive." Me'ira got out of the AGA and looked around. "No sign of another AGA."

"Could be in that barn structure." Liam pointed to a building several meters behind the house. It had a silo next to it—but it still looked more like a house than a barn.

Me'ira looked where Liam pointed and did a double take. "That's a barn?"

Liam shrugged. "Must be. What else could it be with that silo attached?"

Me'ira shrugged. "A good question for Caleb—if he's home."

They walked to the front door and rang the doorbell. They heard a melodic chime, and then a smooth mechanical voice said, "No one is home at present. Care to leave a message?"

Liam raised his eyebrows. "No. Thank you."

"Very well. Enjoy the rest of your day. Goodbye."

Liam laughed. "Well, that was different."

Me'ira gave a half chuckle. "One of the most pleasant versions of 'bug off' I've ever heard."

"So," asked Liam. "Does that mean Caleb hasn't gotten back home yet, or that he's already encountered Galen's real parents?"

Me'ira shrugged. "Let's see if Aunt Elsbeth can tell us if he used the teleporter today. If he did, it's likely he's just late getting home."

"Good idea." Liam took off his T-band, set it on the hood of the AGA, and punched in his aunt's code. Elsbeth's holographic image displayed in short order.

"Liam." Her eyes squinted. "Where are you?"

"We're in Hyden, Australia, looking for Caleb." Liam pulled

Me'ira closer so she would be in view.

Elsbeth nodded. "Ya'akov told me you would be heading there. Hello, Me'ira."

"Hi, Aunt Elsbeth. We were wondering if you could tell us if Caleb used the teleporter today."

Liam jumped in. "We were expecting him home, but he's not here—at least not yet."

"Well, let me check." Elsbeth moved partially offscreen for several minutes. "It says here he arrived in Perth shortly before the two of you." She came back into full screen. "Do you think something's wrong?"

Liam shook his head. "Probably not. I'm surprised we got here first, but he could have made a stop for something on his way home. We'll wait a while and see."

"OK. You two be careful." She reached to disconnect, then hesitated. "And keep in touch."

Liam nodded and the communication ended. He slapped the T-band around his wrist. They got back into the AGA to sit and wait . . .

In less than ten minutes, another AGA pulled up. It slowed as it drove by theirs. It then pulled closer to the house and stopped. A young man stepped out. He looked to be in his early twenties, about the same age as Galen, though a little taller. His hair and skin were slightly darker than Galen's. Me'ira thought to herself that he was cute, but he didn't have Galen's dimples. That put him in second place in her mind. She could see them as brothers, though. Too bad they had never met.

"You think he's going to freak out with our news?" she asked Liam.

Liam shrugged. "Only one way to find out."

He stepped from the AGA and Me'ira followed. Caleb stood next to his AGA until they reached him.

"Can I help you folks? You lost or something?"

Liam shook his head. "Not if you're Caleb Shafir."

Caleb cocked his head. "And who are you?"

Liam smiled and held out his hand. "I'm Liam, Liam Ranz. And this is my sister, Me'ira."

Caleb shook both of their hands. As he shook Me'ira's, he said, "Pretty name, by the way."

She blushed in spite of herself but managed to say, "Thanks."

"Wait." His eyes darted between them. "You said *Ranz*?"

Liam nodded.

"Of the Royal Family?" His voice nearly cracked. His eyes widened.

Liam nodded again.

"Wh . . . What . . . I mean . . . why . . . why are you here?"

Liam smiled. "If you invite us in, we'll tell you all about it."

"Oh, yes." He bowed. "By all means. Come in."

Liam went to the door; a pad next to it read his thumb-print, and the door opened.

The house was beautiful on the inside. It didn't feel large, but it felt spacious, likely due to most of the outside walls being glass. Caleb gestured for them to have a seat. There were two plush tan- and copper-colored oversized chairs facing a large tan sofa, so Liam and Me'ira each took one.

"Care for some tea?" Caleb asked.

Both nodded. In a matter of minutes, Caleb brought it out and placed some nuts, hummus, and flatbread on the table in front of them. "Just in case you're hungry." He smiled.

Though she wasn't hungry, Me'ira made a small plate of food to munch on while they talked. She pointed to a large picture of Wave Rock over the sofa. "That is quite an impressive structure," she said.

Caleb looked at the picture and then back at them. "Yes it

is, isn't it? From what I've been told by Shepherd Malcolm, it survived the Great Earthquake. Apparently, this area used to be very arid and desert-like. Now, as you can see, it's a farming area, but there are still remnants of those large structures dating back to pre-Refreshing times."

Me'ira swallowed a bite of hummus. "So, you support the King?"

Caleb nodded. "Absolutely. About a year ago I became intrigued with what Shepherd Malcolm taught, and I went to see him more regularly. About a month ago I believed the King to be who he claims to be and became connected to him by Ruach HaKodesh." He smiled. "That was pretty awesome."

Me'ira smiled and nodded.

Caleb's smile vanished. "I just wish I could get my parents to see the truth of the King." He looked in thought for a moment and then looked back at them. "They've always acted a little funny when others talk about the King." He shrugged. "I've never understood why."

"Have you had your sacrificing ceremony?" Liam asked.

Caleb shook his head. "Not yet. I haven't gotten my parents on board with the whole thing yet."

Me'ira jumped in. "Because of them not wanting you to use the teleporter?"

Caleb looked her way, puzzled. "How did you know that?"

Me'ira wondered if she should have said that, but pressed on. "Well, we met them a few days ago in Jerusalem."

Caleb nodded but still looked confused. "Yes, they always told me it was dangerous for children to use the teleporter. I didn't think too much of it until I got older. I read almost everything Professor Tiberius wrote about the teleporters. I couldn't find anything bad about them. I began to talk with Shepherd Malcolm about the sacrificing ceremony, and then

I got this job that requires me to travel to Sydney. My parents sort of . . . freaked out." He turned quiet and got lost in thought again.

"What happened, Caleb?" Me'ira asked quietly.

He looked back at her. "We had this big falling out right before they left this last time. I told them I was going to take the job and use the teleporter. And when I told them I was going to set a sacrificing ceremony date with Shepherd Malcolm, they totally lost it. We, uh, unfortunately . . . didn't part on very good terms."

"How did you get your job, if you don't mind me asking?" Liam said.

He smiled. "Serendipitously, actually." He shrugged. "I guess I've always been technically savvy. I've worked on our farm equipment and that of our neighbors: fixed things, improved them, even made a few small things myself. I designed our house here."

Liam raised his eyebrows. "Impressive."

Galen's cheeks turned slightly red. "Anyway, one thing led to another. One of our neighbors invited a friend of his from Sydney here, showed him some of the things I had done for him. The guy seemed impressed and offered me the job."

Liam nodded. "Congratulations, Caleb."

"Thanks. I think I'm really going to like it." He looked at his T-band. "I thought my parents would be back by now. Actually, I thought they would be back before I got home."

Me'ira looked at Liam and then back to Caleb. "Caleb, about your parents. I think we need to tell you something."

Caleb looked from one to the other. "Has something happened?"

"Well, sort of." Me'ira swallowed hard. "Let me try and explain." She leaned forward. "I've been seeing a guy recently

117

named Galen Shafir. We've become somewhat serious."

Caleb shook his head. "Sorry. I'm not following you. Who is he, some distant cousin or something?"

Me'ira shook her head. She glanced at Liam; she wasn't sure how to break the news to Caleb.

Liam picked up the account. "Caleb, your parents had instructed Galen to also not use the teleporter. When he came to visit Me'ira, he used the teleporter for the first time. We first thought it odd for someone in their twenties to never have used a teleporter. Then, we discovered his teleporter signature did not match that of their son. This Galen thought . . . he was their only son."

"What?" Once again, Caleb looked from one to the other. "Who is this Galen person? Why did he claim to be me?"

"Caleb, Galen didn't think he was you. He just thought he was their son," Me'ira said, jumping in. "They had told him he was their only son."

Caleb's sat up straighter, head jerking to attention. "Me'ira, I don't understand what you're saying at all. My parents have never told me about this Galen person. Why would they do something like that? Nothing you're saying makes any sense."

Liam placed his elbows on his knees, leaning in. "Caleb that was our feeling as well. It didn't make sense. Your parents were out in the field, so I had some men find them and bring them to Jerusalem. We had a conversation with them, and they confessed to the whole thing. Someone forced them to be parents to Galen and keep him separated from you. That's why you are here in Australia—and why Galen lived in Israel."

Caleb ran his hands through his hair and leaned back. "I can't picture my parents functioning like spies. That's just not them at all." He rubbed his hand across his mouth and shook his head. "How could they keep something like that from me?"

He sat forward again. "What would it matter if the two of us ever met?"

"Well, your parents didn't know why this unidentified couple selected them to raise Galen," Liam said. "We don't know either, but one reason may have been you and Galen were born near the same time. Questions would be raised if your parents suddenly had another child. Apparently this other couple didn't want to, or couldn't, raise Galen and looked for another way to have him raised without questions."

"Liam, that seems pretty flimsy," Caleb said, scratching his head. "But it is at least an explanation. But why would my parents go along with that?"

"It may have been an empty threat, but your parents felt something bad would happen if they didn't comply with these instructions forced on them."

Caleb squinted. "Do you think this couple forced my parents to find something for them?"

Me'ira sat back. "Well, I've never thought about that. Maybe. What makes you think that?"

"They never involved me with their antique finds, but the last time they were home, Dad asked me to store something for him. And . . . he didn't want me to tell him where I put it."

Me'ira scrunched her brow. "That didn't strike you as odd?"

Caleb shrugged. "At the time, I just assumed it was a secret gift for Mom. But after hearing all this mystery you've been talking about, it makes me wonder."

Liam sat his cup down. "So, what is it?"

Caleb lifted his index finger. "Let me get it."

As he left, Me'ira turned to Liam. "Do you think this could be the key to the whole mystery?"

Liam shrugged. "Maybe. But I assumed it would be something more complicated."

CHAPTER 18

Caleb came back with a small box and handed it to Me'ira. "This is what Dad gave me to keep for him."

"Do you know what it is?"

Caleb shook his head and chuckled. "No. He called it the Prophecy Plaque."

"And that didn't pique your interest to even look at it?" Me'ira asked.

"Oh, I looked at it. But that still didn't help me know what it was."

Me'ira opened the box and pulled out a piece of stone roughly in the shape of a rectangle. The edges were rough, but the front felt smooth. It had rose-colored striations throughout.

"Caleb, this is a beautiful piece of stone."

Liam leaned in for a closer look. "What is the lettering? It definitely looks Hebrew."

"What does it say?" Caleb asked.

Me'ira looked at Caleb with raised eyebrows. "You mean you don't know?"

He shook his head. "I can't read Hebrew."

"Well, let me see if I can decipher," she said. "Do you have pen and paper?"

As Caleb got up to grab something to write with, Liam looked over Me'ira's shoulder and they began working on the stone together. They disagreed on several words at first but soon came up with an interpretation they agreed on. Me'ira wrote it down.

Caleb came over and looked at what they had written. "You mean it's a poem?"

"Well, not exactly," Me'ira said. "But it seemed obvious that was the intent, so we made the lines rhyme by arranging the words in the correct order and still maintaining their meaning."

Caleb leaned over and read out loud:

> He will overtake, the morning star.
> Wished by many. Driven by two.
> One near the prince. One through afar.
> His power they ignite, renew.

Caleb looked up. "Nice poem, but what does it even mean?"

Me'ira shook her head. "I have no idea. Liam?"

"I'm sure that's the correct interpretation, but its meaning is a mystery. Maybe Ya'akov will have a better idea."

Caleb's holo-com beeped. He looked excited. "I think it's Dad." He answered, his hologram off. "Dad, is that you?"

Caleb's face went from a smile to concern to a frown. "Yes, Dad. Understood. Coming now." He closed his holo-com and gave a big sigh.

Liam turned to Caleb. "Anything wrong?"

"Dad said to come to Mulka's Cave and bring the Prophecy Plaque."

"What's Mulka's Cave?" Me'ira asked. "And where is it?"

"It's a cave not far from here. Shepherd Malcolm told me

it used to be a tourist attraction, but the Great Earthquake turned it into a deep cavern." Caleb turned to start packing a backpack.

"Did he say anything else?" Me'ira raised her eyebrows, wanting more information.

Caleb shook his head. "Just that it was important I come quickly and bring the plaque."

Me'ira and Liam glanced at each other. Me'ira nodded.

Liam patted Caleb on his shoulder. "Mind if we come with you?"

Caleb's eyebrows raised as he glanced between the two of them. "I suppose. I warn you, though. It's very dangerous— not a tourist attraction anymore. My parents always warned me to stay away." He turned to pick up his backpack, but then turned back. "Why do you even want to come?"

Me'ira locked gazes with Caleb. "Because I feel sure Galen is with them."

"Why do you think that?" asked Caleb.

"He's gone missing. He was to come here with your parents for them to talk to you."

"And you think they took him to the cave? Why?"

Me'ira shrugged. "Don't know. But I'd like to find out."

Caleb returned a slight shrug. "Fine, but we need to be quick."

"OK," said Liam. "You go in your AGA and we'll follow."

Caleb nodded. "Let's go. It's only about fifteen kilometers. Pull your AGA up to the barn. I'll get some rope, gloves, and lanterns."

Liam nodded.

"Uh, why does your barn look so much like a house?" Me'ira asked, then shrugged. "Just curious."

Caleb laughed. "Oh, that used to be our house before I

designed and had this one built."

Me'ira laughed as well. "You're pretty amazing, Caleb."

He smiled, turned, and went toward the barn. Liam pulled their AGA up to the barn; Caleb brought out gloves and two lanterns for them. He put similar equipment, plus rope, into his AGA.

As they pulled out and followed Caleb, Me'ira looked at Liam. "What do you think all of this is about?"

Liam shrugged. "I don't know. But it's beginning to sound like this so-called Prophecy Plaque is the key to everything."

"So, this other couple needed someone to watch their son and then threatened them to do that and find this Prophecy Plaque?" Me'ira shook her head. "I think it's beginning to sound complicated."

*****

After driving for about twenty minutes, Me'ira noticed a large rock formation with a split down its middle. "Is this the place?"

Liam looked at the view before them. "Must be. Looks like Caleb is heading toward it."

Caleb pulled close to the cave entrance and Liam parked next to him.

Me'ira got her lantern and a pair of gloves, handing the other pair to Liam. "Caleb, the way you described the cave made it sound massive. If that's the case, how will you know where to find your parents?"

Caleb got his backpack and hoisted the rope over his shoulder. "We'll descend until we see their light shining."

As they entered the cave, each turned on their lantern. Me'ira noticed faint handprints. "Liam, look at this."

Liam looked where Me'ira pointed. "That's awesome. Who did that?"

"Shepherd Malcolm said these were original Aboriginal hand stencils made many millennia ago," Caleb said. "Apparently, before the Refreshing, people would visit to see this type of cave art."

Liam looked at Caleb. "It's amazing they're still so clear after all this time."

Caleb nodded. "Let's get going. There's a narrow path here that goes around a massive hole in the middle. Stay very close to the wall of the cave and you'll be OK. After a few meters of heading down, the hole will turn into a type of tunnel."

"If you were supposed to stay away, how do you know so much about this cave?" Liam asked.

Caleb grinned. "I said it was dangerous and we were told to stay away. I didn't say I did."

Liam laughed. "Well, this is likely one time your parents will be glad you disobeyed."

The path became serpentine in nature and the cave walls turned increasingly rough and inconsistent. The path was strewn with rock debris. The walls were jagged, and several low overhangs caused Me'ira to repeatedly hit her head. A muffled *umph!* from Liam could be heard now and then.

Although Me'ira felt badly for the difficulty she was putting Liam through, she knew Galen was here somewhere. He just had to be. If they found him, the difficulty would be worth it.

It was nearly half an hour before the trail went from winding around the hole to a more linear path that followed the tunnel. They walked over and around a good deal of debris in their way. At times they had to crawl through narrow openings to stay on the trail.

"Just be careful!" Caleb called. "Some of the walls are really brittle and unstable."

Me'ira had noticed. Several times she went to steady herself against the wall and some of it crumbled from her touch. Debris fell, but nothing went substantially wrong. Unsure how long her luck would hold out, Me'ira tried her best not to touch the cave walls.

They worked their way forward for another twenty minutes. Me'ira's whole body became sore from all the climbing over boulders, squeezing through narrow openings, debris falling on her feet, and every so often hitting her head on an unexpected low overhang. She wasn't sure how much more she could take.

Finally, they heard Caleb yell. "There! I see my parents!"

Me'ira lowered her lantern for a better look. In the distance, she saw a light and movement. Caleb started running toward the light. She and Liam jogged along behind him. Still, that proved difficult as they had a lot of rock debris to maneuver around. The debris didn't seem to bother Caleb as he flew around the rocks like they weren't there. The distance between Caleb and them widened.

"Caleb, wait for us!" Me'ira's words went unanswered as Caleb kept running.

Liam passed her and ran after Caleb. She was glad. Her muscles were getting weaker and she was getting slower. As she watched their lanterns, she saw Liam gaining on Caleb.

She heard Liam yell. "Caleb, wait! It may be—"

Me'ira heard a loud crash and felt the ground shake. Her eyes widened. Had there been a cave-in? Were Liam and Caleb OK?

She heard Liam finish his sentence. " . . . a trap."

She heard nothing from Caleb and only saw one lantern ahead of her. She ran harder to catch up to Liam but tripped over something. Putting the lantern near her feet to see what she tripped over, she saw Caleb's rope, which he must have dropped so he could run faster. Picking it up, she placed it over her shoulder. No wonder he dropped it; the thing was heavy.

When she reached him, Liam was pounding on a large boulder and repeatedly calling Caleb's name.

"Liam . . . what . . . happened?" She had to slow her talking to take a few needed breaths. "Where's Caleb?"

Liam hit the boulder one last time and yelled in frustration. "He's behind this boulder." He paused, worry clearly on his face. "It was a trap."

Me'ira ran her hands over the boulder. It felt massive—and thick. They would not be able to move it.

"What do we do, Liam?"

He shook his head. "I don't know." He picked up his lantern. "Let's see if there's a way around this. Maybe there's another path."

Me'ira held up her lantern. The area her light was illuminating widened quite a bit from where they had just been.

As they looked around, Liam called. "I think I see an opening."

Me'ira came over and lifted her lantern. "Well, we've gone through smaller openings in this cave."

She followed Liam. They had to nearly double over to make it through an open space. After a short distance the passage opened into a cave. It felt massive. They couldn't see far, but their echoes seemed to indicate a very large cave.

Me'ira pointed to a faint glow to their right. Liam nodded. As they traveled farther into the massive cave, they saw Caleb standing on a ledge. In front of him lay a pit—just as the cave had appeared when they first entered it. Here, though, there did not seem to be any trail around the opening for Caleb to step off. He seemed stuck on his ledge.

Liam called, "Caleb are you all right?"

"Yeah, it was just a hologram." The disappointment was evident in his voice. "My parents aren't here."

Suddenly, a stray voice spoke up. "Oh, let's not jump to conclusions."

Me'ira dropped the rope and looked at Liam, her eyes wide. The voice had come from somewhere above them.

"Who's there?" Liam held up his lantern, as if that would illuminate something worth seeing.

Again, the voice. "Oh, let's just say a *friend* of the family."

Liam whispered. "That must be the Leader Ya'akov talked about."

Me'ira nodded. That had already been her thought.

Suddenly, the entire cavern was lit with glowing orbs. Their light cast a greenish-yellow glow over everything as several floated at eye height, and others allowed sight to a depth of several meters below. Me'ira then saw that, indeed, there was a deep hole in the middle where the cave continued straight down. Opposite Caleb, on the other side of the cave, were his parents.

It was then that she noticed another person between them and opposite her position. Galen.

"Galen, are you all right?" Me'ira realized she didn't need to shout as the place echoed whatever was said. Her eyes were watering.

"Me'ira. It's good to hear your voice. Yes, I'm OK."

"Now, now. Let's not get ahead of ourselves." That voice again. Then it began laughing.

Me'ira shivered. The laugh was maniacal.

"Let's not forget why we're here." The voice was condescending in tone. Now it became more purposeful. "Caleb, you brought the plaque?"

Caleb unzipped his pack and held up the stone. "I have it right here. But if you don't let my parents go, I'll throw it into this abyss."

The man laughed again, but the laugh now had a bit of a wary tone to it. "It's hardly an abyss, it has—"

"A bottom. I know," Caleb said, cutting him off. "But did you know there is a river at the bottom with a strong current? It may not be that easy to find your precious piece of stone if I throw it down there."

"Oh, threats do not become you, Caleb." Disdain now filled the man's voice.

"Oh, really? Well, it's obvious you're somewhere above me, so how are you going to stop me?"

The man laughed again—and now that maniacal quality was returning.

Me'ira nearly had enough of this deranged man. "Anything you do to anyone here will get you a front row seat with the King. Is that what you want?"

The man laughed even harder. "Oh, Galen, you really captured a feisty one, didn't you?"

Liam touched Me'ira's shoulder. He pulled her close and whispered as low as he could: "You keep him busy. I'm going to see if I can climb up and find him."

She nodded, but as Liam turned to go, she grabbed his arm. He turned slowly. She whispered, "Be careful." He nodded and slipped off.

"You leave Galen out of this," Me'ira said, turning back to the voice.

"Oh, my dear." He laughed once more. "Galen has been in it since birth."

"The King won't let you get away with this," Me'ira said.

"Away with what?" Now his condescending tone returned. "No one was forced here. Everyone came of their own free will. Not that it was likely their original idea, but no arms were twisted." Again, that laugh. "You came to find your loving Galen. He came to find his loving parents, as did Caleb. They came . . . Noah? Lois? Should I spoil your big surprise?"

"What are you talking about?" Caleb held up the stone. "If you want this, you had better start explaining."

"Oh, my." The man laughed still harder. "Ignorant to the end, eh?" The man laughed a few more seconds. "I'm laughing so much, I should have brought tissues."

"I'm glad you're enjoying yourself," Caleb answered, trying to remain calm. "I still have the plaque, you know. I can throw this in there at any second."

"Oh no, don't." The man sounded panicked. Then he burst into laughter again. "Oh, sorry. I just couldn't resist." The laughter suddenly stopped. "But if you throw it away, you throw your parents away with it."

Suddenly Noah spoke up. "What are you talking about? That was never part of the deal."

"Oh, Noah," the voice said. "Neither was it 'part of the deal,' as you put it, for you to betray me." He gave a half-hearted laugh. "You thought you could find the plaque and hide it from me? When did *that* ever become part of the deal?"

"We just wanted in. That was our bargaining chip," Noah answered.

Lois also responded, but her voice was cracking. "We didn't want to be pawns any longer. We wanted . . . to be players."

"Dad? You called me here voluntarily?" Caleb's voice had a tone of disbelief. "Why . . . why would you do that?"

"Mom?" Galen said. "What you said in Jerusalem was an

129

act?" His voice sounded full of hurt.

"No, no." Lois began to cry. "You've both got it wrong. We love both of you. There's . . . there's just more at stake here."

Me'ira couldn't believe what she was hearing. "Mrs. Shafir, you mean you were willing to put your personal agenda ahead of your children?"

"Not at first, but . . . "

Noah broke in, his voice becoming more hardened as he spoke. "As the kids got older, what the Leader was doing made more and more sense. We were risking so much; we wanted the respect that came with our sacrifice."

"*Your* sacrifice?" Me'ira couldn't believe these words were coming from the same people she met and talked with in Jerusalem. "What about the sacrifice of Galen and Caleb? It seems they've sacrificed the most."

"Children, children, children." The Leader chuckled. "I know it's therapeutic to get all of this off your chests. But let's not get too far off topic, shall we?"

"What do you really want?" Caleb asked.

The Leader paused for a moment. "Caleb, surely you're not as dense as you look. Were you not paying attention? I want that plaque you're holding."

"Oh, you mean this plaque?" Caleb was now trembling, full of anger. He held it over his head. "Well, you're not going to get it."

Before anyone knew what was happening, Caleb tossed the plaque into the middle of the cavern.

Me'ira watched it fall. She had no idea what that decision would lead to.

CHAPTER 19

The cavern narrowed the farther it descended. Me'ira watched the plaque fall toward the blackness below. To her surprise, before it descended below the level of the light of the orbs, she saw someone jump from the side of the cavern, grab the stone, do a flip in midair, and land on the other side of the cavern.

Everyone gasped at the sight.

"I knew I probably shouldn't have told you about your parents until I got the plaque," the Leader said, laughing once more. "But you have to admit, that was a great backup plan. No? It gave Isabelle a chance to show off her incredible acrobatic skills, didn't it? Isn't she impressive?"

Me'ira had to admit the feat was impressive, but it angered her at the same time. "You won't get away with this," she said.

The Leader was now cackling with laughter. "My dear, that's what everyone says when they know they are defeated." He laughed some more, then cleared his throat. "To show you I'm not totally heartless, I'm going to free Noah and Lois. If they leave in time, they can either catch me or join me. But . . . " This last word was spoken in a singsong fashion; clearly, he was toying with them.

"But what?" Noah yelled. "What did you do?"

"Oh come on, Noah. You know games must have a twist to make them interesting."

"Like what?"

"Let me explain the rules. That always helps with new games, doesn't it? Each of you are on a ledge." He laughed. "That's stating the obvious, I know. But what you may not know is each ledge is held up by a boulder beneath it. Each boulder is calibrated to your weight. Any extra weight, or less weight, causes the boulder to give way and the ledge will collapse. Each of these boulders is tied to each of the other boulders under each of the other ledges." He paused. "Now for the fun part."

Me'ira couldn't believe what she was hearing. "You're insane. If one falls, all fall?"

"Oh, my dear, you're hurting my feelings. But, yes, you've captured the concept quite well." He paused as if to let that sink in.

"Now, where was I? Oh yes, the fun part. The rock trapping Noah and Lois will be removed. That will trigger a motion detector. If it detects no motion within five seconds, another boulder hits the ledge and the whole ledge collapses. So you must not forget to move for your motion detector."

"This is premeditated," Me'ira said. "You can't get away with it."

"My dear, each of these people voluntarily put themselves where they are. I'm simply offering a way out and stating their choices. One, you can exit and join me. Of course, in five seconds the ledge will collapse along with those under Galen and Caleb. Maybe that's of no consequence to you. If so . . . I guess I shall see you outside." He laughed again. "Or, maybe that will get you taken by the King. After all, your leaving is what causes them harm. Actually, I'm very curious to see if that scenario will play out. However, if you decide to stay . . . "

Me'ira heard an *umph!* followed by scuffling and what sounded like fist blows. Then she heard something hurtling in her direction. To her shock she realized it was Liam's body falling next to her, but the momentum of his fall propelled him just over the edge of her ledge.

She screamed. "Liam!"

Diving for his arm, she latched onto it with her hand just before he went completely over. The momentum of his body going over the edge pulled her down and nearly pulled her over as well, but she managed to hook her arm around a boulder to anchor both of them momentarily. She heard Liam's body hit the side of the cave with a thud. She cringed, then felt a sharp pain in her shoulder. Stopping the momentum of his fall had likely pulled her arm out of socket.

Trying to ignore the pain, she focused on Liam. "Liam, are you OK? Can you hear me?"

All was quiet for several seconds. *Is he unconscious?* She pulled hard to get to a sitting position, then scooted over to brace her feet against a boulder that seemed secure. Pulling with all her might, she got his torso over the lip of the ledge and then grabbed the top of his pants with her other hand, finally pulling him fully onto the ledge. She laid back and collapsed.

After a couple of moments, Liam groaned.

Me'ira tried to sit up but yelled in pain. Attempting to prop herself with her left hand proved impossible due to the excruciating pain shooting into her shoulder; she was seeing stars. Somehow, she shifted to her right hand and sat up. "Liam, are you OK?"

Liam groaned some more and slowly sat up. "I think I'm OK. Just bruised up a bit."

"What happened? Did he throw you off? Did he disappear?" Me'ira was hoping the Leader had been charged with rebellion by the King and was now standing before him for judgment.

Liam shook his head. "No. My foot slipped and I fell. He just didn't try to help."

Liam slowly got to his feet and limped toward his sister. He tried to help her up, but again she yelled in pain. Never had she experienced pain like this. The throbbing literally took her breath away and made her eyes water.

Liam quickly knelt next to her. "Me'ira, what's wrong?"

"There's something wrong with my shoulder. I can't move it at all without severe pain." She looked up at him and gave a small smile. "You're pretty lunky, you know."

He chuckled just a bit. "Here, let me check." He gingerly eased her to a sitting position and began checking her shoulder. "Sis, I hate to tell you this, but it's a dislocated shoulder. The way to make it heal the fastest is to put it back in place."

She nodded. "Do it."

"It's . . . it's going to really hurt."

"I know, but it has to be done. Besides, it already hurts. I don't think it could hurt more than it does." She glanced up at him. "Have you done this before?"

He smiled and held her arm out carefully. "Didn't I tell you of the time—" Without warning, he pulled on her arm—hard.

She felt it snap back into place, but the pain made her grit her teeth and almost lose consciousness. She yelled and then panted. "I was wrong. It *can* hurt more."

"Is it better now?"

She nodded, now amazed at how much better it felt. The way Liam had pulled on her shoulder, though, made Me'ira mad. "You could have warned me."

134

"No, it's better when you don't," he said. "That way, you don't have time to tense up. Moves back into place better when relaxed."

She nodded a bit. It was the suddenness of his actions that took her off guard. She rubbed her shoulder. It still hurt, but now she was able to move it. "How are *you*?"

"I'll be OK. I think my scrapes are already starting to heal. They're not burning like they were a little bit ago."

She could feel her pain slowly subsiding as well, and this made her even more thankful for her Master's gift of healing. Never had she experienced pain that bad before. This made her realize she could never again underappreciate the goodness of her King.

"How many times have you done that before?" Me'ira asked Liam.

He looked at her and smiled. "Including yours?"

She nodded.

"One."

Her eyes bulged, but before she could respond, she heard, "Me'ira, are you OK?"

"Yes, Galen, I'm fine. I had a dislocated shoulder and Liam put it back in place. I'm good now."

Me'ira pointed to Lois and Noah. "They're still there. I guess they love their sons after all."

Liam nodded and said, loud enough for the couple to hear from their ledge, "Good to see you're still there, Noah."

"My wife and I are not as heartless as the Leader made us out to be," he said. "We've made some wrong choices, but never at the expense of our love for our sons."

"Any ideas of how to get out of this mess?" Liam asked.

Noah shook his head. "No. You?"

Liam cocked his head and raised an eyebrow. "Maybe. I'm

not sure anyone is going to like it very much."

"Any idea is better than none at this point," Noah said.

"How much do you weigh, Noah?"

"About eighty kilos. Why?"

"I'll explain in a moment." Liam turned to Me'ira. "How much do you weigh? I'm guessing about sixty-five kilos?"

She nodded. "What are you thinking, Liam?"

"I know this sounds crazy, but if I put fifteen kilos of rocks in my shirt, give it to you, and you and Noah swap places quickly while you hold the additional weight, that should allow the weight to be the same on the ledge. Then he and I can work out a plan to rescue Galen and Caleb. It's going to take some heavy lifting to do that, I think."

Me'ira swallowed hard. "You want me to go out on that ledge?"

Liam took her arm. "Me'ira, I know it's dangerous, and I know it's crazy. If you have any other ideas, I'm more than willing to hear them."

Looking over the ledge, she shut her eyes, then looked at Galen; she knew she had to do whatever was necessary. "OK," she said to Liam. "I'll do it."

He held her arm and smiled. "You're very brave, sis."

She gave a short laugh. "Or very stupid."

He smiled. "If it works, we'll call it very brave."

CHAPTER 20

Me'ira and Liam worked their way over the rocks and boulders that formed the wall of the cave. While no serpentine trail lay in front of them as before, there did seem to be enough large boulders to provide secure footing as they moved forward. Smaller rocks proved too unsecure and would cause their feet to slip from under them. They had to go slow to first ensure their footing was secure before they could trust it with their entire weight.

They were able to get behind the ledge on which Noah and Lois stood. Once they arrived, they found the two of them pacing back and forth across the ledge so the motion detector would read their movement.

Noah paused briefly before he began pacing again. "What's the plan, Liam?"

"It's kind of crazy, but I can't think of a better one. You said you weigh eighty kilograms. Are you pretty sure about that?"

Noah nodded. "Yes, why?"

"Well, I'm going to have you and Me'ira exchange places."

"What? There's no way she weighs as much as I do."

Liam took off his shirt. "Exactly. That's why I'm going to put fifteen kilos of rocks in my shirt—so her weight will match yours."

Liam tied off the sleeves and buttoned the front. Me'ira helped him pick up stones to put inside the shirt. After a few minutes, he stood. "I think we have about fifteen kilos here."

Me'ira came over to the threshold of the ledge. She took the shirt from Liam, careful not to drop any of the stones. They were heavier than she anticipated, especially with her muscles already sore. Still, determined not to drop anything, she took small steps to keep the stones stable in her hands. "Let's do this before my arms give out," she said.

Noah came over to the entrance to the ledge, but not so close it would not feel his weight. Lois kept pacing to ensure the motion detector would read her movement.

Liam lined Me'ira and Noah up to face each other, but with Me'ira on the outside of the threshold and Noah on the inside. "OK now. Go slowly. But you each need to take steps matching pace and breadth."

Me'ira looked at Noah. "Make them small, but quick," she said. He nodded. As Noah picked up his right foot, she did the same, and she worked to mimic his stride and rhythm. They took steps as quickly as they dared, but in synchronous movement. Sweat beaded on her brow from both the tenseness of the situation and the stones becoming so heavy. Her arms began to quiver. She tried to will them to become steady.

Once Me'ira stood completely on the ledge, she stepped out to its middle. Everything seemed to be OK. She let out a long breath; she realized she had been holding it. Lois came over and helped her set the shirt of rocks down slowly so no rocks would spill over the side and lower their total weight. It felt good to finally lay those rocks down. Me'ira shook her arms; they felt like they would float over her head after being released from their burden.

Me'ira looked at Lois and gave a thin smile. Lois wrapped

her arms around her. "Me'ira, please forgive me. I'm so, so sorry for all of this."

Me'ira wasn't sure she was in a forgiving mood just yet. "Let's first get out of this and then we can deal with our emotions."

Lois nodded as she tried to hold back her tears—then resumed her pacing.

Mc'ira looked back at Liam. "What do you plan to do now?"

"Well, my thought is, I will go above Galen and Noah will be above Caleb. If we can get this rope cut in half, we'll pull them up to safety."

"What about us?" Lois had a wide-eyed expression.

Me'ira nodded. "My thought as well."

Liam smiled. "That's why I let you do this, sis. It was the safer option. Once we're in place and both Galen and Caleb have the rope tied around them, you two will jump through this opening together. The ledges will crumble, but we'll pull them up to safety."

"OK. That sounds like a plan. Only . . . "

"What, Me'ira?"

"Well, the Leader said a boulder will fall to cause the other ledges to crumble. You may want to tell Galen and Caleb to plaster themselves against the boulder blocking their opening so the falling boulder doesn't hit them."

Liam nodded. "Good point."

"And you two had better force yourselves against the side of the cave for the same reason."

Liam smiled. "See, sis? I knew you were more than just a pretty face."

She smirked. "Careful or I'll throw one of these rocks at you."

"Uh, you might want to wait until after you're rescued, though," he answered. Me'ira smiled.

They went back to work. Liam found the midway point of the rope but had no knife for cutting. Noah had a trowel, so they made do. Liam put the point of the trowel on the rope and then used a rock to drive the trowel through it. It was not very efficient work, but eventually it got the job done. Liam then tied loops with a slip knot in each.

Me'ira saw the two of them go back the way she and Liam had come. That likely allowed Noah to travel the least distance with Liam traveling the farthest to reach Galen. She looked at Galen and Caleb, who were both still pacing on their narrow ledges.

Once they reached Caleb, she saw them lower the rope, which had plenty of slack, to go over Caleb and be placed under his arms. They figured that would keep him from falling if his feet lost their grip on the side of the cave wall as Noah hoisted him up.

As Liam headed toward Galen, she saw Caleb and Noah talking quietly. She could only imagine what the two of them were saying.

She became concerned as she watched Liam climb higher and higher the closer he got to Galen.

"Liam, you're getting too high," Me'ira said. She was probably stating the obvious, but she didn't see how he could rescue Galen from that height.

"I know, Me'ira. The rocks won't let me go lower. They don't seem to be stable any farther down."

Me'ira paced with Lois but kept an eye on Liam's progress while biting her nails from worry and anticipation. Liam finally positioned himself over Galen. She looked from Noah to him. Liam looked so much higher than Noah. *Will the rope be long enough?* Me'ira wondered to herself.

Liam lowered the rope, but it only reached the top of Galen's head. *How will they make this work?* She saw the two of them talking for a long while. She saw Galen nod. He put the rope around his arm as he raised it over his head. *Oh, that's so risky,* Me'ira thought. Galen wouldn't be able to help Liam. Liam would have to raise Galen the entire way by himself.

"OK. You girls ready?" Liam called back their way.

"Are you sure, Liam?" Me'ira had to ask the question. "Can't you find a better position?"

"It's now or never, Me'ira."

She nodded and paced with Lois as near to the threshold as they felt reasonable. She wrapped her right arm around Lois's waist, and Lois wrapped her left arm around Me'ira's.

Me'ira looked at Lois. "Ready?"

She nodded.

"Ready, Liam."

"OK, everyone. On three. One . . . two . . . three!"

Me'ira ran as fast as she could through the threshold while holding to Lois. Once through, they turned and waited. It felt like the longest five seconds of her life. She heard a cracking sound followed by a huge boulder falling onto the ledge. Lois screamed. Me'ira held her in a tight hug. The falling ledge pulled the rocks out from under the other two ledges, and they collapsed as well.

Once the dust cleared, Me'ira saw Caleb climbing up to his father, and this was going well. There were a couple of stumbles, but Caleb made it without any significant problems. Father and son hugged when Caleb reached his position. This left Me'ira smiling.

When she looked over at Galen, however, her heart nearly stopped. He looked like a rag doll being pulled up by Liam by one hand. Galen tried to get his other hand on the rope, but that seemed to make him sway. Every so often his body would bang into the side of the cave. *That has to hurt.* She hoped and prayed he would hold on and not slip. As Liam continued to pull, his foot slipped, and he went down to one knee. Galen fell a short distance, and he hit the side of the cave wall again. Liam regained his stability by staying down on one knee, but he now had to use every last bit of his upper body strength to pull Galen up to his position. Me'ira knew he had to be straining to his limits. The distance was at least one and a half times what Caleb had to travel.

Galen finally stabilized himself halfway up the ascent. Although he couldn't help Liam pull himself up, he kept himself away from the cave wall with his other hand to prevent himself from swaying. After that move, things seemed to go more smoothly. Once Galen's arm became even with Liam's, Galen held onto Liam's arms with both hands. Liam pulled him over the large boulder. Me'ira lost sight of them for a few minutes. She then saw them stand and embrace. Her heightened adrenaline, now draining, made her legs wobbly as she breathed a sigh of relief.

Now it was just a matter of all of them getting back to where she and Liam had started.

"Come on, Lois, let's go meet them." She led Lois back the way she and Liam had come. Although anxious to get back quickly, she kept her steps slow and methodical; she wanted Lois to follow her confidently. They had come too far to make a crucial mistake now.

Once they got back, Noah and Caleb were already there. Lois went over and gave Caleb a hug. Tears came, and she let them flow. Noah wrapped his arms around them both. Tears of happiness and released anxiety flowed.

They were still in their group hug when Liam and Galen arrived. Me'ira ran over and wrapped Galen in a big hug.

"*Umph*," Galen said, squeezing out some air.

Me'ira immediately let go. "Galen, are you OK?"

He smiled weakly. "I will be. My wrist and shoulder are very sore at the moment. I guess we have something in common."

She chuckled, then looked in his eyes. He leaned in and she didn't move. His lips touched hers and she felt a tingling sensation rush through her. He wrapped his arms around her; she returned the warm hug.

After a minute, Liam tapped them on their shoulders. "That was my gift. Back to decorum, please."

Galen released Me'ira. His cheeks turned red.

Me'ira smiled. "Thanks, Liam."

He gave her a wink.

Lois and Noah came over and hugged Galen. This latest group hug lasted several minutes.

Caleb turned to face Galen. He held out his hand and Galen shook it.

Liam came over and put a hand on each of their shoulders. "There's a lot of catching up to do for everyone," he said. "First, let's get out of here and back to the house."

Everyone nodded.

"Come on, everyone. I'll lead the way," Caleb said as he picked up a lantern. Noah and Lois followed Caleb. Liam followed them. Me'ira grabbed Galen's hand and followed Liam. She almost lost Galen and was now going to hang on to him. She didn't care about protocol right now.

She remained worried about the vetting process that would still have to take place, but she was determined not to lose him again.

CHAPTER 21

"Dear, your pacing isn't going to bring them home any faster." Jeremiah walked up to Kyla and held both of her shoulders. "Besides, your pacing is going to require this section of the floor to need repolishing."

Kyla slapped his arm lightly. "Don't you get smart with me," she said. "I can't believe you let her go all the way to Australia alone in the first place."

"Darling, she's not alone. Liam is with her."

"Oh." She waved a hand at him. "You know what I mean." She sat down in one of the chairs. "You didn't send anyone else with them?"

"Sending too many people can sometimes be a hindrance."

She shot a stare at him with pursed lips.

Jeremiah walked over and took a seat beside his wife. "Kyla, sweetie, we know they're fine. Liam sent me a text saying they made it all right and that they had found Caleb, the Shafirs' son."

Kyla nodded. "I know. But we haven't heard anything else from them."

He patted her hand gently. "Just be patient. I'm sure we'll get an update sometime today."

Kyla sighed and put her hand to his chest. "I just don't like not knowing."

Jeremiah nodded. He felt the same way, but he wasn't about to add more worry to Kyla by admitting it.

Kyla's T-band beeped.

"Oh, it's a call. Uh, what do I do again?"

Jeremiah smiled. She had never been very technological. "Just touch the T-band and then press answer."

She did this and Nyssa's holographic image appeared.

"Nyssa. It's good to hear from you. Everything all right?"

"Uh, Mom, either please hold your wrist still or put the T-band on a stable surface. You're making me seasick the way you're moving your arm."

"Oh, sorry." She gave a confused look to Jeremiah.

He smiled. "Hold a minute, Nyssa."

He turned the holographic image off but kept the communication open. He took the T-band off Kyla's wrist and stood it up on the low table in front of Kyla, facing her, and then reengaged the holographic display. Nyssa's image returned to view.

"Is that better, Nyssa?" asked Kyla.

"Oh, much better. Thank you."

Kyla gave a sheepish smile. "Sorry. I'm still getting used to this thing."

Nyssa smiled. "That's good. I'm sure you'll have it mastered in no time."

"Why did you call? Everything all right?" Kyla asked.

"Oh, yes. Everything's fine. Just busy. Too busy, actually. I wondered if you could come help with Sarit's wedding planning. The date is approaching fast and there is still so much to prepare and so many decisions to make. You're so good at these things and make quick decisions that turn out perfect. Would you please come help me?"

"I would have thought Liam would have stayed to help," she said.

Nyssa's expression changed to one of mock terror. She held up her hand. "No, no, no. I wouldn't trust his decisions at all. I can't imagine what the wedding would look like if he helped plan it. My instruction to him was to just show up.'"

Kyla smiled. "Well, you have a point. Detail was never his strong suit."

"So, you'll come?"

"Certainly, my dear."

"Wonderful. You know, if you get here by noon, you can help me with my meeting with the caterer."

Kyla laughed. "OK. I'll see you shortly." They ended the communication.

Kyla sat there and looked at her T-band. Picking it up, she seemed unsure what to do.

Jeremiah chuckled lightly to himself. "Just flick it back on your wrist. It'll snap back into place."

She straightened it. "What, just slap my wrist with it?"

Jeremiah nodded; she did just that. It wrapped around her wrist. Kyla looked up and smiled.

Jeremiah raised his eyebrows. "So, it sounds like you'll be visiting Nyssa and Sarit for a while."

Kyla nodded. "Yes, they need—"

She stopped in midsentence, shaking her finger at him. "You! You put her up to this, didn't you? So I'd take my mind off Me'ira."

Jeremiah smiled. He reached over and gave her a kiss. "Darling, you both can help each other. You're worried about Me'ira. She's worried about Liam, although she would never admit it. And she's getting Sarit's wedding together. I just thought this would be a good time for you three girls to support each other."

Kyla smiled. "I guess that's why the King chose you."

He tilted his head, unsure what Kyla was trying to convey.

"You care about everyone and have such good ideas for solving problems," she said.

He gave her another kiss. "Especially when it comes to you."

She smiled, then jerked her head. "Oh, what time is it?" She glanced at her T-band. "Oh my, if I'm going to get there by noon, I need to get ready." She jumped from her seat and headed to their bedroom.

Jeremiah looked at his T-band. "But it's not even 10 o'clock."

He heard her call back. "Yes, I know. I barely have time to get ready."

Jeremiah shook his head and laughed. He started to give a retort but then remembered the incident with his cufflinks. No. Experience and wisdom taught him that, sometimes, it's just best to say nothing. This was one of those times.

He sat back in his chair and thought of Me'ira and Liam. He was glad Liam went with her. His oldest and youngest together. This would likely create a stronger bond between them.

Still, Jeremiah couldn't help but worry. He had told Kyla he was sure everything was fine, but he wasn't that sure. He thought about calling Liam but didn't want to interrupt if his oldest son was doing something important—or dangerous.

He hoped Liam would call soon with an update. Jeremiah headed for his office.

CHAPTER 22

"I hope this one will fit. We're not exactly the same size." Caleb handed Liam a shirt. It was obviously a little snug, but Liam seemed satisfied with it.

"I can't believe Me'ira didn't retrieve my shirt but just left it there to fall into the pit."

Me'ira gave Liam a stare. "Well, that wasn't high on my to-do list at the time."

Liam laughed. "I guess that's understandable." He sat down at the table with the others.

Lois brought tea and shortbread cookies to the table. She poured tea for everyone.

Me'ira took her tea. "Thanks, Lois. But I think I need to hear how all of this came about."

Lois looked at Noah and sighed. She handed Liam his cup and sat down. "Even before I became pregnant with Caleb, Noah and I became involved with The Order."

Caleb choked on his tea. "Mom, Dad, really? Why?"

"Isabelle contacted us. I guess she knew we were excavating for all sorts of artifacts. She said they had been searching for a specific one and wanted us to help them and would even fund our digs if we did. We didn't have to do anything out of the ordinary, she said, but only needed to dig at certain sites they might select. Everything else we found we could keep—except, of course, the item they were searching for."

Me'ira turned up her brow. "*Who* is Isabelle?"

Noah shook his head. "Not entirely sure. Both she and the Leader are pretty secretive, as you probably discovered this afternoon. We think she's his wife, but there was always some question about that. Anyway, they were a very tight team." He turned to Liam. "You're probably the only one who has gotten close enough to see the Leader."

"Liam, did you see his face?" Me'ira turned to Liam with anticipation. If they could identify him, it might shed more light on Galen's heritage.

Liam shook his head. "He had on a hood and a cap. I didn't get a good look at his face. He looked about my height. That's the only detail I can tell you."

Me'ira sighed.

Lois passed the cookies. She cleared her throat and look embarrassed. "Being around them so much, we got caught up in their diatribe against the King."

"They kept talking about how the Overtaker would make things so much better," Noah said, shaking his head. "We . . . came to a place where we believed it."

Liam waved his hand. "That's what I'm having a hard time understanding. What did you expect to get better?"

Lois shrugged. "Well, it was touted that the Overtaker would bring total freedom—no reprisal for any thoughts or actions one may decide to think or do."

"But Lois." Me'ira reached for her arm. "The King's ways are best, and he only wants the best for everyone. What made you so dissatisfied with the King?"

Lois's eyes watered. "In hindsight, it seems pretty petty. It angered me we had no children. I guess I let that sway my thinking."

Me'ira scrunched her brow and took a sip of tea. "So, how did you two agree to live a double life?"

Lois shook her head. "Before I knew I was pregnant with Caleb, Isabelle asked me to be the mother of her child." Her eyes moistened. "I had become so desperate for a child I didn't even try to rationalize the reason for making that decision."

"What reason did she give for asking you?" Galen said.

Lois turned her head and gave Galen a sympathetic look. "Oh, sweetie. She said their lives were so hectic they wouldn't be able to take care of you properly, and they wanted a more stable home."

Galen squinted. "But, Mom . . . Lois . . . "

Me'ira saw the pain that this change in words caused on Lois's face.

Galen went on. "Your life was anything *but* stable. I stayed with the nanny a lot more than with you."

Lois held up her hand. "I know, I know. Like I said, sweetie, I wasn't thinking rationally. I was just thinking I would be having a child, which I wanted desperately." She gave another sympathetic look. "Galen, we really did enjoy you and thought of you as our own—especially as time went on."

Galen's eyes now began to water. "What do you mean?"

Noah jumped in. "Galen, this couple never took you or visited you. They would periodically ask about you, but they never wanted to see you. Over time, we stopped asking if they wanted to visit. You just felt like ours and, after a while, we didn't think any differently."

"And when you found out about *me*?" Now it was Caleb's turn to ask a tough question.

Noah put his hand on Caleb's shoulder. "Caleb, that became one of the happiest days of our lives."

Lois nodded. "We were willing to raise both of you together, but Isabelle was adamant we not do that. I guess she felt that would raise questions, and she didn't want their decision to come back and haunt them."

"We had started the dig here in Mulka's Cave, so she suggested we raise you, Caleb, here," Noah said. "We would spend a lot of time here anyway, so it seemed reasonable." He held up his hands. "I know you don't think it sounds reasonable, but at the time, it did to us. We were willing to help them out. They provided nannies and we went back and forth. We spent as much time as possible with each of you."

Liam drummed his fingers on the table. "OK, so you go from here to Israel. And you were here to look for what? The stone plaque?"

Noah nodded. "They felt it could potentially be here. Everything else we put into our shop and museum in Israel." He shrugged. "One day, I found it. I asked Caleb to hide it. As you heard earlier, I— we -intended to use it as leverage to become higher within The Order."

Lois held up her hands. "I know that sounds petty, but these people are so secretive. We felt used and wanted more." She put her head in her hands and shook her head. "I feel so ashamed now." She looked up, tears rolling down her cheeks. "They never cared about us. She only wanted to position their cause for the Overtaker." Lois looked at Caleb and then Galen. "I'm so . . . so sorry. Will you ever forgive us?"

Me'ira looked at Liam; it was as though a light bulb went off. "Maybe that should have been our translation. Maybe 'he will overtake' should be translated 'Overtaker.'"

"Wait. Wait." Noah's eyes widened. "You translated it?"

"You *didn't*?" Me'ira looked from Noah to Lois and back. "But you found it."

"I didn't have time before we were called back by the Leader." Noah's eyes darted from Me'ira to Liam. "Can you tell us what it means?"

Caleb got up from the table and walked to the kitchen. He opened a drawer and pulled out a piece of paper. He set it in front of his father. Noah read it silently.

He will overtake, the morning star.
Wished by many. Driven by two.
One near the prince. One through afar.
His power they ignite, renew.

"This is what they wanted?" Noah looked confused. "This doesn't clear up anything."

Noah handed it to Lois. She looked it over. "It confirms their suspicions," she said. "But if this supplies details, I don't understand them."

"Suspicions?" Me'ira now took the paper and looked at it again. "What suspicions?"

Lois pushed her teacup to the side. "There are two people who are supposed to help prepare the way for the Overtaker."

Me'ira looked confused. "I thought you said that's what this Leader was doing."

Noah shook his head. "No. The Order is preparing people to be ready for his coming, but there are supposedly two special people to prepare the way." His hands flew in the air. "Or that's what they believed anyway." He sighed. "I'm not sure this ... this ... " He did air quotes with his fingers. " ... 'Prophecy Plaque' is much of a prophecy at all."

Lois nodded. "To me, these words are way too general to be

anything specific enough to identify anyone."

Me'ira wasn't so sure. She looked again at the phrase "one near the prince." Could that mean *her*—or *Galen*? Was that why this Leader wanted Galen in Israel, so he could get near her father?

Suddenly, she gasped softly and brought her hand to her mouth. She looked up, but no one looked her way. The word in Hebrew, she knew, was the *feminine* form. It wasn't talking about a man, but a woman.

Perhaps she was involved in this prophecy after all.

CHAPTER 23

Me'ira rose before anyone else, made tea, and went to sit on the back patio. She stopped, stunned. In the distance were large rocks looming out of the ground, but between where the yard ended and the rocks began swayed a sea of yellow. Buttercups by the thousands were growing. She sat down on one of the chairs, sipped her tea, and looked at the beautiful spectacle. The light breeze sent ripples through the sea of yellow. *Breathtaking.*

How could such a perfect world have people against the King? It seemed unfathomable. Yet she had met them yesterday. If she hadn't experienced it for herself, she was unsure she would have believed it. And what of this Prophecy Plaque? Was it really a prophecy? Was *she* really part of it? Was *Galen*? If the prophecy was true, would marrying him or not marrying him cause it to happen? It all seemed very puzzling.

She turned when she heard the door open. She smiled as Galen approached.

"Well, aren't you the early bird?"

Me'ira chuckled. "I suppose. I couldn't sleep any longer. Did you sleep well?"

He sat next to her in a nearby chair. He shrugged. "Well enough, I guess. It's been an interesting last few weeks." He gave a half chuckle. "I don't even know who I am."

She put her hand on his knee. "Galen, it doesn't matter to me. I love you for who you are, not for who you may be."

He put his hand on hers and spoke softly. "Yes, I know." He smiled. "And I'm thankful for that. Truly, I am." He shook his head. "But I need to know more."

Me'ira took his hand in hers. "Galen, maybe to understand your past you need to understand your future."

Galen squinted. "Mind explaining that?"

"You remember our last conversation about the King?"

He nodded.

"Have you thought any more about it?"

"Some." He displayed a thin smile. "But I've been a little preoccupied."

Me'ira laughed. "Yes. Yes, I guess you have." She turned somber. "Galen, it is really a very important decision. I do want you to consider it."

"I want to. Really, I do. But . . . I have these doubts."

She put her hand on his arm. "What kind of doubts?"

"Is he good if he allowed me to . . . have no parents?"

"Oh, Galen." She put her hand to his cheek. "You're looking at it all wrong."

He scrunched his brow. "What makes you say that?"

"Would you want him to make you love him?"

He shook his head. "No, of course not. That wouldn't be love at all."

"So, if your parents chose not to love him, or maybe not even love you, how could the King show his love to you?"

"Uh, well, I've never considered that." He thought for a few seconds. "I suppose to find me a family that would love me."

"Is that not what the King did?"

155

Galen's head jerked back just a bit. "Well, uh, yes. I guess he did."

She took his hand again. "And because of that, we met." She smiled. "Can that be bad?"

He grinned and shook his head. "No, of course not."

Me'ira heard the door open and saw Caleb step through. "Will three be a crowd?"

Me'ira smiled. "Hi, Caleb. We were just talking about how the King loves us."

Caleb's eyebrows went up. "Really? Well, I had wanted to talk to Galen about that as well."

"Why don't the two of you talk, and I'll start some breakfast?" Me'ira said.

Caleb waved his hands. "No. No, please stay, Me'ira."

Me'ira resettled in her seat as Caleb pulled another chair closer.

"Galen, I have to say I was not a big fan when I first heard about you," Caleb began.

Galen gave a sheepish smile. "I'm sure you weren't. But I had no idea you existed. I didn't even know your parents weren't mine." Galen shook his head. "I don't even know what to call them anymore. I've called them Mom and Dad for so long."

"And you still should," Caleb said.

Galen looked at Caleb, his eyes darting over his face as if trying to assure himself Caleb was being truthful. "You really mean that?"

Caleb nodded. "I've had some time to think about it. And as you just said, you were an innocent party in all of this." He gave a weak smile. "I did some praying last night and the Messiah helped me sort some of this out in my head. If we had been put together as kids, we would be treating each other as brothers. Why not now? It's like two brothers being separated at birth. We've now been reunited."

Galen squinted. "You really feel that way?"

Caleb nodded. "I do now. I really want to get to know you, Galen."

Galen smiled. "I do too."

"And since you're my brother, I want you to experience the joy of my Messiah and King as I do."

"Me'ira was just talking to me about him." Galen looked from Caleb to Me'ira. "Hey, are the two of you working together on this?"

Both chuckled and shook their heads.

"But maybe it's another way the Messiah is showing his love toward you," Me'ira said.

Galen laughed. "You're really pushing this topic, aren't you, Me'ira?"

"Well, think about it, Galen. There are a lot of scenarios as to how all of this could have played out."

"Such as?"

"Such as, you never met either of us and The Order dominated your life. Or, Caleb could have not known the Messiah and thereby resented you for the rest of your life for stealing part of his parents' time. Or, any other number of scenarios." She put her hand on his knee and looked into his eyes. "But that's not how the Messiah worked this out for you. You now know the truth of The Order. I would think that has turned you off to them."

Galen nodded.

"Your parents are sorry for what they put you through, so there's a good opportunity for mending and having a better, open, and honest relationship with them," Me'ira went on. "And you now have a chance to get to know your brother. You see, the Master had good things in store for you even though they initially looked bad. We're both here with you and love you."

Galen smiled. "You make it sound as if it was all part of a grand plan from the beginning."

"And you think it wasn't?" Caleb asked.

Galen's gaze shot to Caleb. "You think it was good for you as well?" He shook his head. "How could you?"

Caleb smiled. "That's what I struggled with last night. I didn't see what was good about any of this for me. Yet, Ruach HaKodesh helped me work through all that. If I wasn't living here, I may not have met someone like Shepherd Malcolm, who has helped me put a lot of things into perspective and accept my King as the hope for my future. I probably wouldn't have gotten the job I have now. I could go on, but you get the point. My life could have been very different, but I'm not sure that would have been a good thing. So, yes, I can see the King's love through all of this."

"So, knowing who my parents are doesn't bother you?"

"No offense, Galen, but I don't like your parents."

Galen leaned back and put his hand to his chest. "Even *I* don't like my parents."

Caleb laughed. "See, we already have something in common."

Galen smiled.

"Look, Galen," Caleb went on. "I can't hold who your parents are against you. After all, my parents haven't been squeaky clean either." He paused and then turned serious. "I may not like your parents, but I think if I get to know you better, I will you."

Me'ira rubbed his arm. "So, Galen, if you don't want to follow The Order, and you feel you can't solve your future yourself, who are you going to turn to to understand your future?"

Galen shrugged. He began to look uncomfortable and kept rubbing his palms on his pants legs. Me'ira knew he was having lots of inner conflict. He likely wanted to trust the King but was having trouble getting over the threshold of faith.

"Galen, we both have put our faith in the King," Me'ira said. "We both would really like for you to also."

Caleb nodded. "Well, I hear what you're saying, and it does make sense," he said. "But my parents . . . "

Me'ira shook her head. "This is about *you*, not your parents. This is a personal decision. It's between just you and the King."

Me'ira saw beads of sweat forming along Galen's brow. He was close to the right decision. "Just talk to him, Galen. Pretend he's in another chair sitting with us right here. Just talk to him."

Caleb got up and pulled another chair over. He patted the seat. "Galen, here. Look at this chair and place the King right here in your mind. Just talk to him."

"What do I say?" Sweat formed under Galen's lip and he kept licking his lips like his mouth had gone dry.

"Whatever is on your mind," Caleb said. "Just talk to him."

Galen nodded. He turned to the empty chair. "My King, I . . . I know I haven't really been following your teachings. I would avoid many of Shepherd Franklin's lessons. I think I've really been messed up in my thinking. I understand what Caleb and Me'ira have been telling me, and I think that is what I want. They tell me you love me, and I can see now how you have been looking out for me in spite of my circumstances. I want to know you like they know you. I put the hope of my future in your hands. I trust you with it."

Galen turned back to Me'ira. "Is that what—"

Galen gasped. Me'ira and Caleb smiled.

"I can hear someone talking to me."

Caleb patted him on his shoulder. "It's Ruach HaKodesh connecting you to the Messiah. Welcome to the family, buddy. We're definitely brothers now."

Me'ira gave him a hug. "Galen, I'm so happy for you."

Lois called from the door. "Galen. Me'ira. Caleb. Breakfast is ready."

"There in a sec," Galen yelled, his voice now light. He turned to Me'ira, smiled, stood, and held out his hand.

Me'ira took his hand, stood, and walked with him back toward the house. Caleb wrapped his arm around Galen's shoulder. The three walked in together.

"Now, Galen, you can help me work on Mom and Dad," Caleb said softly.

Galen laughed. "Four against two. How can they resist?"

Caleb opened the door and held it for Galen and Me'ira to enter. He slapped Galen on the back as he entered. "That's the spirit."

Me'ira felt elated. One of her concerns had come true. Galen had accepted the King. Her father should be very happy about that.

It would surely help with the vetting process as well.

CHAPTER 24

Caleb gave a simple but elegant blessing before breakfast. Lois served eggs, cheese, and fruit. Me'ira sat next to Liam and across from Galen. Unable to stop herself, she kept smiling at Galen.

After a short while, Liam leaned over. "Me'ira, what's going on with you?" he asked quietly.

She turned his way. "What? What are you meaning?"

He gave her a smirk. "I haven't seen you smile this much—ever."

She gave a broad smile and whispered in her brother's ear. "Liam, Galen has accepted the King for his future."

He raised his eyebrows. "Congratulations." He looked at Galen, nodded, and smiled.

Liam leaned over to Me'ira again. "So why are you being secretive about it?"

She whispered back. "I don't know. I think he and Caleb are waiting for the right time to tell their parents."

Liam nodded. "OK. I'll keep my mouth shut."

She smiled back. "Is that possible?"

He opened his mouth and sucked in a short breath. "You wound me, My Lady."

Me'ira giggled. "I'm so glad you came with me on this trip, Liam."

Liam smiled. "In spite of my wounds, so am I." She laughed again.

Caleb stood. All eyes turned to him as he lifted his glass. "I wish to propose a toast."

After a few seconds, when he didn't continue, Lois asked, "To whom do you propose the toast, dear?"

Caleb smiled. "Good question, mother. I wish to propose a toast to our King."

"Oh, uh, OK. Why so?"

"It's the King who has turned a search of mystery to a find of family." He looked at Galen. "I have found a long-lost brother—in more ways than one." He looked at Me'ira and Liam. "I have met part of our Royal Family and count them as friends." He turned to his parents. "And I have regained my parents, leaving all deception aside." He raised his glass. "My King, I thank you."

Everyone clinked their glasses of water or juice. There were sounds of "Hear, hear."

Noah turned to Caleb. "Son, I never would have considered that perspective. That does make one think."

Caleb looked at Galen and gave him a wink.

Lois chimed in. "I'm happy to hear you and Galen are getting along so well. I was worried about that. But what did you mean by 'in more ways than one' when you talked about Galen being your brother?"

Caleb looked at Galen and smiled. "Brother, do you wish to explain?"

Galen turned to Lois. "Mom . . . are you OK if I still continue to call you that?"

Lois's eyes watered. "Galen, that would make me very happy."

Galen smiled back. "Mom, both Caleb and Me'ira . . . " He gave her a smile. "Both helped me understand that while I felt somewhat of a pawn in all this deception in the beginning, the King was still looking out for me by providing me with a loving family, even if . . . " He looked Caleb's way. "It was not yet complete."

Caleb nodded.

"I realized this morning that if the King did love me like this even when I didn't know it, I could do nothing less than return my love to him once I discovered it," Galen said. "I placed the hope of my future in the King this morning." He smiled. "I am now connected to him by Ruach HaKodesh." He looked from Lois to Noah. "Mom, Dad, the only thing that both Caleb and I feel is missing is that both of you would come to the same realization."

Lois and Noah looked at each other but said nothing.

Caleb sat next to Noah and put his hand on Noah's arm. "Dad, what is your opinion of the Leader and The Order now?" He turned to Lois. "Mom?"

The two of them looked at each other again. Noah shook his head. "Son . . . " He looked at Galen, then over to Caleb. "Sons . . . it's like you said, Galen. We were all pawns in the beginning. I see now that neither the Leader nor Isabelle really cared about us. It was all about them."

Lois nodded. "I don't want to follow someone who is so caught up in themselves they can't see the needs of others." She looked at Caleb. "I liked your toast, Caleb, and can see the logic in it. Though we were duped in the beginning, I wouldn't trade where we are now for anything. I have both of you now with us. I can see the truth in you saying the King was at work."

Noah took her hand and nodded. "Yes, it's hard to refute that."

Caleb put his hand on Noah's shoulder. "Dad, would you like to tell the King that? I'm sure he would like to hear that from you."

Galen put his hand on Lois's shoulder. "You, too, Mom?"

The two of them looked at each other and nodded. Noah swallowed, then began. "My King, thank you for giving us such wonderful sons. They have helped us see not only our deception by The Order, but your love for us as well. You have united Galen and Caleb and brought them both back to us. They have shared your love with us. We accept it and trust you for our future."

Lois breathed in and said, "Thank you, my King. I too put my trust in you for my future. I can't thank you enough for bringing both of our sons together to be with us going forward. I am sorry for my earlier decisions and poor choices. I see your wisdom resides in our sons. I look forward to our family bringing you glory."

With their eyes wet, but a smile on their faces, Noah reached over and gave Lois a hug. They both suddenly looked shocked—at the same time. Smiles spread across the faces of both Galen and Caleb.

Noah pulled back from Lois. "I feel such freedom. This is how I always wanted to feel." He began to openly weep. "If only I had known earlier."

Lois nodded.

Me'ira and Liam went around the table to where they were.

Me'ira hugged Noah. "The King's timing is perfect. You now have a complete family."

Noah nodded, and they hugged again.

Me'ira walked over to hug Galen. "I'm so happy for you.

You now have a complete family and one blessed by the King."

Galen pulled back from her hug. "You forgot one thing."

"What's that?"

"The King has also put you in my life. I am the most blessed man in his kingdom."

She kissed his cheek. "You're sweet. I feel the same way." She smiled. "I mean, most blessed woman."

He quickly kissed her on her lips. She felt tingly all over once again.

When she looked at Liam, his eyebrows were raised. Me'ira smiled, but he didn't return the sentiment this time. Maybe he was thinking that the full vetting had not yet taken place. There was still one hurdle to overcome: Galen's heritage.

Lois wiped away her tears. "I feel so light—like a burdened is removed. I think we should sing a song."

"That's a great idea." Me'ira tried to think of an appropriate song. "What about, 'All Creatures of Our God and King'?"

Caleb smiled. "Perfect. We sing that one sometimes at Shepherd Malcom's meetings." He started in with a beautiful baritone voice.

Everyone joined in. Galen, Noah, and Lois had a difficult time with the words, but once they understood the tune, they sang with all their hearts.

> *All creatures of our God and King*
> *Lift up your voice and with us sing,*
> *Alleluia! Alleluia!*
> *Thou burning sun with golden beam,*
> *Thou silver moon with softer gleam!*
> *O praise Him! O praise Him!*
> *Alleluia! Alleluia! Alleluia!*

They sang the stanza three times. By the end, all were singing strongly. Lois had a beautiful soprano voice and Noah a deep bass. Me'ira couldn't help but feel their Messiah smiling at the beautiful fragrance of sounds lifting up to him.

CHAPTER 25

Caleb answered a knock at the door. A smile spread across his face. "Shepherd Malcolm, please come in."

An evenly tanned man with extremely blond hair entered. His glorified skin made his tanned appearance glow nearly like that of an angel. "Hello, Caleb. It's great to see you again."

Caleb smiled. "Likewise, Shepherd. You remember my parents?" He turned their way.

"Of course." He shook their hands. "Lois. Noah. It's great to see you again."

Both smiled but didn't say anything.

"And this is my brother, Galen."

Galen smiled. "It's my pleasure to meet you."

Malcolm shook his hand but then turned and squinted at Caleb. He mouthed, "Brother?"

Caleb chuckled. "I'll explain shortly." He took Malcolm's shoulder and gently turned him around. "And I believe you know . . . "

"Your Grace! Your Highness!" Malcolm bowed. "Always a pleasure." He smiled. "Welcome to my neighborhood. I don't think I've ever had the pleasure of such a visit."

"Well," Me'ira said, "I'm glad we could change that."

Malcolm chuckled. "As I, Your Grace."

"Please, call me Me'ira."

"And me, Liam." Liam bowed ever so slightly.

Me'ira smiled. Her brother showed such great tact giving respect to this Shepherd of the King.

"Thank you for the honor," Malcolm said giving a genuine smile back.

Caleb gestured toward the living room. "Hey, let's all have a seat."

After everyone had settled on the sofa, chairs, or ottoman, Caleb stood. "Shepherd Malcolm, I have wonderful news to share with you."

Malcolm looked at everyone. "Well, I can't wait to hear it. To be honest, I'm a little surprised I don't already know about it. The Master usually keeps me in the loop, so I guess he's allowing me to hear something special."

Caleb laughed. "Well, not that the Master couldn't explain it, but it is rather complicated."

Malcolm's eyebrows went up. "Now I'm really intrigued, Caleb."

Caleb went through the entire backstory of Galen and himself, The Order, the Prophecy Plaque, the Mulka's Cave ordeal, and what happened the previous day with Galen and his parents.

Once finished, Caleb looked at Malcolm. "Well, that's the story. What do you think?"

"Wow. Quite the story, Caleb. First of all, I'm thrilled all of you have put your future in the Master's hands. Our King wants the best for everyone. I'm glad you've discovered that."

Galen looked at Caleb and nodded toward Malcolm.

Caleb cleared his throat. "Shepherd Malcolm, we want to set our sacrificing ceremony. Do you think you can present us?"

Noah interjected. "While, technically, my wife and I are

from Naphtali, we don't really know Shepherd Franklin that well. Caleb knows you and wants you to present him, and we want to be presented with him."

Malcolm held up his hand and chuckled. "Don't worry, Noah. We're not territorial. I'll talk to Franklin. Believe me, he will be thrilled. It's not about who presents, but that you have accepted. It will be such a thrill to present an entire family."

Me'ira squeezed Galen's hand. She could tell he was thrilled that Malcolm called him a part of Noah and Lois's family after hearing the entire story.

Galen fidgeted. "Uh, Shepherd Malcolm, how long does it take to set up the ceremony?"

"Oh, not long." Malcolm thought for a few seconds. "Actually, there's an honoring ceremony in two weeks. Sacrificing ceremonies are usually right before those. I can probably get you slotted in if you feel that's not too soon."

"Sounds good to me," Caleb said, looking at the others. They nodded. He looked back at Malcolm. "Set it up, Shepherd Malcolm."

Malcolm smiled. "OK. I'll contact Administrator Eldridge and get it on the official agenda."

Lois stood. "OK, everyone. I've made some hors d'oeuvres." She paused. "Just stay put and I'll bring them out. Just keep talking."

Me'ira followed Lois into the kitchen. "I thought I'd help," she said.

"Oh, you don't have to do that."

Lois turned and Me'ira gave her a hug. "Lois, I'm truly happy for you and your family."

"Thanks, Me'ira."

Lois took several trays out of the oven. Me'ira helped her put them on serving trays and took them to the living room.

Lois followed with some sweets.

The group spent the next few hours eating and talking. Seeing everyone treat Galen as if he belonged thrilled Me'ira. She couldn't have been happier for him. Despite his beginnings, he was now part of a family and feeling the love not only of a physical family but a spiritual one as well.

Me'ira decided to slowly wander outside as everyone else talked. She sat in one of the patio chairs and sipped her tea. A short time later, Liam came out and joined her.

"Can I join you? I don't want to intrude on their family joy."

Me'ira smiled. "Sure. Take a seat."

Liam cocked his head. "But why are you out here? I'm sure Galen thinks of you as more than just a third wheel."

Me'ira laughed. "I just wanted to give them space and let them work out their relationships. Plus, I wanted some time to think."

"Do you want to be alone?"

She smiled and shook her head. "No, I actually think I could use someone to bounce my thoughts off."

Liam leaned back. "So what's on your mind?"

"I was thinking about the last time Galen kissed me. You weren't smiling."

Liam sat up and cleared his throat. "Me'ira, it's just that we can never be like everybody else. Not only is there protocol, people *expect* us to be different. Our standards have to be higher to inspire others to be all the King wants them to be."

Me'ira nodded. "Yes, I can understand that." She looked deep in thought. "Liam, how was Nyssa vetted for your marriage? I mean, did you know her heritage before you met her?"

Liam took a deep breath and tilted his head with eyebrows raised. "Me'ira, it was very different for me. I didn't even get to date anyone before they were vetted. Mom and Dad knew everything about Nyssa and even her great-grandparents."

"So, you're politely saying I did everything backwards."

"Look, sis. I like Galen. I really do. But I don't want you to get hurt either."

"He just accepted the Messiah as the hope for his future," she countered. "That has to be a positive for the vetting process."

Liam sighed and took Me'ira's hand. "Me'ira, don't get defensive. I'm on your side. I really am."

Me'ira sighed. "I know. I'm sorry."

"Please understand. Accepting the King as the hope for one's future wasn't a requirement of the vetting process. It was a requirement to *start* the vetting process."

Me'ira stared at Liam. "What? Say that again."

"Me'ira, I don't want to be the bearer of bad news. But if you had done things by protocol, it is only now that Galen would even be considered for vetting. You wouldn't have even dated him yet."

The realization of what Liam said hit—hard. Me'ira suddenly felt weepy, like tears could flow any minute if she allowed them. She had made an emotional investment before she knew if she could possibly marry Galen. Well, he hadn't asked, but still, what if he did? Would she have to break his heart—and hers?

Tears trickled down her cheeks. "Liam, what if he doesn't pass the vetting process? Is there no hope?"

Liam leaned forward and took her hand. "Me'ira, I'm sorry. But I don't see how you can maintain your status as princess and marry someone who doesn't pass the vetting process." He shook his head. "I . . . I don't know of any way around it."

Me'ira let go of Liam's hand and put her hand over her mouth. She had always thought of her mom as doting and somewhat of a busybody. But that wasn't the case at all. Mom had been truly looking out for her. More tears came. "There's no way around it?"

"There's only one way I know of." Liam shook his head. "But I wouldn't want you to consider it."

Me'ira perked up. "What is it?"

Liam swallowed—hard. "You would have to disown your heritage."

Me'ira gasped. "What?" More tears fell. "That . . . that would break Mom and Dad's hearts."

"Me'ira, don't count him out before you know the answer. Isn't that what you told me?"

Me'ira smiled as she wiped her tears. "Yeah. Yeah, I did say that, didn't I?"

Liam stood and kissed her on her forehead and headed back inside.

She watched him as he walked away. Why couldn't she be more like her big brother? He always did things by the book and yet had fun at the same time. She had always acted the rebel and bucked the system. *Why do I do that? Mom always said that would come back to bite me.*

She wiped away another tear. It looked like her mother might be right.

CHAPTER 26

Me'ira stepped off the teleporter and took a deep breath. The familiar aromas and sounds sent a relaxing feeling through her. There was nowhere like Jerusalem. She stepped aside as the others came through. They would all stay here until the sacrificing ceremony next week.

Liam and Me'ira gave Noah, Lois, Caleb, and Galen hugs.

"Shepherd Malcolm got you rooms at the Guest House just down from the palace," Liam told them.

Noah nodded. "Thanks. We can never thank you enough."

Liam patted Noah on his shoulder and nodded. "Me'ira, are you ready?"

Me'ira held up a finger to indicate she needed another minute. She turned to Galen. "I'll see you at the sacrificing ceremony, OK?"

He gave her another hug. "Me'ira, I love you."

Me'ira's eyes were watery. "I know. Let's take it one step at a time, OK?" She loved him also, but didn't want to give him false hope.

Galen nodded. "I understand." He smiled. "I'll see you next week."

The Shafir family turned and walked toward the Guest House. Me'ira and Liam headed to the palace. They went to the dedicated teleporter between the King's palace and their palace in the city proper. In a matter of seconds after entering the teleporter, they were home.

Me'ira turned after her vision was no longer blurred and saw her parents and Nyssa waiting for them. Her father gave her a hug, followed by a huge one from her mother.

"Me'ira, I am so happy to have you home," Kyla said.

"Thanks, Mom. It's really great to be back."

"Let's all go in and you can catch us up."

"Sure, Mom."

She walked with everyone back inside the house. Liam and Nyssa, after their own huge hug and kiss, were arm in arm. She smiled, delighted that Liam had a happy life with a family who truly loved him. *Will I ever have that?*

All found seats in the living area. Me'ira allowed Liam to do most of the talking and explaining; she didn't want to say anything inappropriate. She had already done way too much of that already. Liam supplied all the necessary details they would want to know but chose to leave out some of the details that would make his wife and their mother upset. Me'ira smiled to herself. He had such great tact. Maybe that was why he chose to go with her: so some of what he had would rub off on her. She wondered, though: was it too late for that?

After some time, Liam and Nyssa said their goodbyes. Kyla went to see them off leaving Me'ira alone with her father. He smiled. It seemed as if he wanted some time with her alone. That was not necessarily a good thing.

"Me'ira, I wanted to talk to you in private," Jeremiah said.

"Yes, Father." She gave a wary smile. "I assumed you would."

"Anything else you want to fill in that Liam didn't?"

"Well, there is one thing." She stopped, nearly in midsentence.

Jeremiah cocked his head and raised his eyebrows. "Which is?"

"Liam helped me understand that by not following protocol I've put everyone in a tough spot. I put my feelings before my responsibility."

Jeremiah leaned back. "Well, I should have put you on a trip with Liam a lot earlier."

Me'ira chuckled. "Maybe. At any rate, I want to . . . officially apologize."

Jeremiah nodded. "Well, I'm glad to hear it." He smirked, just a bit. "Although I'm expecting to hear a 'but.'"

Me'ira sighed. "Just because I've learned what I did wrong doesn't change the emotional investment I've already made. I can't just turn it off."

Jeremiah put his fingertips to his temples and rubbed them. He looked back at Me'ira. "Me'ira, I realize that. But I'm not sure if I can make things work out the way you want."

"I know, Dad." Her tone became very low. "Liam explained it to me."

"I thought after the sacrificing ceremony we would have the Shafirs and Elsbeth over to hear what she's found out," Jeremiah said.

Me'ira nodded. "Any previews?"

Jeremiah shook his head. "I haven't spoken with Elsbeth about her findings. We'll all hear it at the same time."

She wondered if that was a good thing or not. And yet, would it matter? She had a lot of thinking to do to prepare for each outcome.

After a few moments of silence, Me'ira looked up. "Dad?"

"Yes, dear."

"If Galen passes the heritage test, is he free and clear?"

Jeremiah raised his eyebrows.

"I mean, would there be further vetting?"

Jeremiah rubbed his chin. "Well, that depends on what else Elsbeth has found. If she is able to find out his true parents, then we would need to search further and ensure there are no dangers. Otherwise . . . "

This time Me'ira's eyebrows went up.

"Well, let's just say, we have to decide how much of a threat everyone feels the Leader would be for us." He shrugged. "I'm sorry, Me'ira. I can't say for sure further investigation will not be needed." He gave her a sympathetic look. "I'm sorry."

She nodded. Her eyes moistened but she was determined not to cry—at least not in her father's presence. "Anything else, Dad?"

Jeremiah shook his head. "No, dear. That's all for now."

As she stood, Jeremiah grabbed her hand. He kissed the back of it and smiled. She gave a weak smile back and headed for her bedroom.

Once there, Me'ira let the tears flow. She had no idea what she would do. Yes, she had done everything backward, but she couldn't undo it either. Her heart ached for Galen. A life without him in it seemed unimaginable. She thought about her conversation with Liam. That made her cry even more. It seemed no matter the outcome and no matter what decision she would make, someone would get hurt. One of Shepherd Franklin's teachings came back to her: *There are consequences to all our decisions.*

If only she had taken that to heart much earlier.

But then, the more she thought about it, if she had stuck to protocol, would she have met Galen? The odds seemed remote. Would that have been better, to never have known him at all? Yet every time she thought of him, the anticipation of seeing him made her heart race. Would it do that for any other? She didn't want to have to find out.

She fell to her knees beside her bed and cried out to the only One she knew who understood everything. "My Messiah, you know my heart. You already know the outcome. Please let me make the right decision. Is there a path where all can be happy?"

She felt a calmness wash over her and a still small voice respond in her mind. "My child, no matter the outcome, I am always with you."

Her eyes became watery again. It was comforting to know her Messiah's love was not dependent on her choices. "Thank you, Master. Your love means so much to me. Galen has accepted you. Will that be sufficient for us to be together?"

No answer came. "Master?"

"Your path is chosen, Me'ira. Yet it cannot be revealed before it unfolds. It is your decision, your free will, based upon all you have been taught and on what you have learned."

She felt confused. "But if it is known, then you know what I should choose. I would appreciate your guidance."

"My child, your guidance is already in my Scripture. Your choices cannot change my plan for you, but the choice is yours to make, and so are the consequences. All choices come with consequences. Some bring joy, some bring regret, and some even bring both. Yet my love is constant."

Me'ira rose and lay on her bed. She knew Scripture was truth, but it would certainly be helpful to know the correct decision she should make.

CHAPTER 27

Me'ira sat in the Royal Family's reserved section to observe the sacrificing ceremony before the honoring ceremony. She looked at the crowd in the courtyard between the temple and palace. The area filled quickly. The light of the large menorahs cast dancing shadows on the temple and palace walls. The excitement building through the crowd was almost palpable.

An angel chorus began. Everyone settled and became quiet listening to the ethereal, yet haunting, music. Many swayed to the music with their eyes closed. Me'ira never tired of hearing such awe-inspiring beauty.

Ya'akov came to the front of the South Gate of the temple. Everyone in the crowd was standing. Me'ira and her family now stood as well. "Citizens of our King's earth, we come this evening to hear from several who have placed their faith and their future in the hands of our King, now their Messiah."

Applause went through the crowd.

The King sat in the balcony overlooking the courtyard and facing the South Gate of the temple. Ya'akov genuflected before addressing him. "My King, there are several here this evening who now pledge their lives to you. There are some individuals and one entire family." He smiled. "For that, I turn the presentation over to Shepherd Malcolm from the Western Territory of Australia."

Ya'akov stepped back and Shepherd Malcolm stepped forward. He genuflected to the King. "My Lord, presenting individuals to you is one of the highlights for every Shepherd you have assigned in your kingdom. This evening I bring as a burnt offering to you the entire Shafir family. Before you are Noah and Lois Shafir and their two sons, Caleb and Galen. They each have a testimony to share."

Malcolm stepped back and Noah stepped forward. He genuflected before his King. Me'ira could tell he was extremely nervous; she noticed his hands shaking. Yet once he started talking, his voice became stronger. "My King, I am pleased to be before you this evening. I offer myself as a burnt offering before you by pledging my life to you and to the betterment of your kingdom. I am ashamed it has taken me this long to recognize the truth of who you are. Yet it thrills me to stand here, and I look forward to becoming a positive part of your kingdom going forward."

The King stood. Everyone bowed. "Noah Shafir, you may stand."

Noah slowly rose and looked toward his Master.

Me'ira couldn't help but notice the admiration Noah now had for the King.

"Noah, your sacrifice is pleasing to me and I accept it wholeheartedly. Please take your animal for sacrifice and present it to the priest, who will offer it as a memorial to what you have committed to me this day. Enter the South Gate, exit the North Gate, and wait there."

"Yes, my Lord."

Noah took his lamb from Shepherd Malcolm and carried it through the South Gate of the temple. The King sat down once again, and the people again stood and faced the temple for the next presentation.

All eyes focused on Lois, who stepped forward . . .

She, Caleb, and Galen each made statements similar to Noah's, and the King responded in a similar manner to each. Lois knew that when they stepped through the North Gate, Administrator Eldridge would take them to the King so he could speak to each of them individually.

There were a few more individuals who pledged themselves to their King as well. Two were from Japan, one from China, and one from India.

Me'ira also looked forward to the honoring ceremony. Japan was the territory to pay homage to the King on this night through song, poetry, and skits. Later there would be presentations in the civic center of various types of paintings, sculptures, and artistic influences, as well as scientific discoveries. Those from this area of the world were so meticulous in their designs; Me'ira always found their inspirations mesmerizing.

The honoring ceremony would not start until the King came back to his balcony overlooking the temple after talking to each person who had just offered themselves. The angels sang again to the enjoyment of the crowd. They would sing until the honoring ceremony began.

Me'ira excused herself and headed to the palace steps. Lydia rose and went with her. Me'ira couldn't wait to hear what the King said to Galen. As she sat at the bottom of the stairs waiting for him to exit, she thought back to her time with the King after she had pledged herself to him. Being with him was mesmerizing. He was so kind and gentle yet commanding and awe-inspiring at the same time. There was a conflict of emotions. While wanting to run to him and hug him, she also felt so awed by him that she only wanted to bow before him. The memory made her smile. The King, of course, had come to her and wrapped his arms around her. The memory, even now, caused her to feel the warmth of his touch that had enveloped her and went through her. At the time, she didn't want that moment to end. She knew the experience would be the same for Galen and each member of his family.

Me'ira heard footsteps above her. She stood and turned. The entire Shafir family was coming down the palace steps together. Each wore a smile or grin. They were talking and laughing. When they saw Me'ira, they stopped.

Lois reached out to Galen. "We'll meet you at the honoring ceremony."

He nodded. Noah, Lois, and Caleb walked toward the festivities while Me'ira and Galen stayed on the palace steps. Lydia stood a distance away to give them some privacy but remained very much in sight.

Galen held out his hand. Me'ira took it.

"Galen, I am so proud for you. And for your family, also."

Galen smiled. "Thanks. It felt very special to be treated as one of the family as I pledged myself to the King."

Me'ira sat on one of the steps and pulled Galen down next to her. "So, how did your talk with the King go?"

A huge smile swept across his face. "It was so awesome, Me'ira. I really can't put the experience into words."

Me'ira nodded. "I completely understand that. But . . . what did he say?"

Galen's eyes got misty. "He told me I was very special to him." He looked down and shook his head. He gave a slight chuckle as he looked back into her eyes. "No one had ever told me that. Except for you, of course."

She smiled.

"I asked him about my past and my parents and what that all meant."

Me'ira looked at him in anticipation; she had also wanted to know about that. "Well, what did he say?"

Galen paused. "He answered—and didn't—at the same time." Galen tapped his fingertips together as he talked. "He first said he looked at people on an individual basis and not their heritage. I was special because of me and not because of what family I came from." Galen glanced up at her and smiled.

"Well, that sounds very positive."

Galen nodded. "He then said that the choice of my parents was their choice and they would have to bear the consequences of their decisions just as everyone has to."

"He didn't say anything more specific?"

Galen shook his head. "But that's OK. At least he answered the most nagging question I had. I'm someone important to him." He smiled. "I can live with that."

She reached over and squeezed his hand. "That's wonderful, Galen. What else did you talk about?"

"Well, I told him I didn't know what to do with my life. He asked me what I truly wanted to do." Galen shrugged. "I told him I had been managing antiques and I really liked doing that. He said every job in his kingdom is important as long as it is done for his glory. He saw no reason I couldn't keep doing that."

Me'ira smiled. "Galen, that's great. That means you'll stay in Israel then?"

Galen's smile dissipated. "Well, I don't know. He then said something strange. I've been trying to understand it, but I'm unsure what he really meant."

Me'ira turned up her brow. "What did he say?"

"He said heritage does not define importance, but it does

define responsibility. Then he said to not forget the whole earth belongs to him, and that distance does not define his loving and caring."

"He didn't explain further?"

Galen shook his head. "He just hugged me and reminded me I will always be important to him."

Me'ira smiled. "And you'll always be important to me as well." She gave him a hug.

"Shall we go and see the honoring ceremony?" Galen asked. "I hear the angels just finished."

She nodded and stood. They walked together, but not hand in hand. She knew protocol was important and, being in public, she didn't want to start rumors that would put her father in an unfavorable light. Lydia came up and walked beside them.

Galen found his parents and sat with them while Me'ira went to sit with her parents. Although she had looked forward to this particular honoring ceremony, she couldn't help but think about herself and Galen and whether they had a future together.

After the performances, many went to the civic center to view all the displays being hosted. Me'ira went with her family. All the beauty and scientific findings amazed her. She was impressed with the presentations many people had brought to share and devote to the Messiah, their King.

That night she prayed again. She knew the next few days were going to be very hard. Important decisions for her were coming; she prayed she would make the right ones.

CHAPTER 28

Jeremiah sat at his desk. His heart felt heavy knowing the possibility Elsbeth would present on this day that might not be what everyone wanted to hear. At least not what Me'ira wanted to hear. On one hand, frustration filled him as Me'ira had not followed protocol, and this had caused her to become infatuated with a young man who might not even be capable of passing the vetting process. On the other hand, he wanted her happiness more than anything, so being able to see her wishes fulfilled would be satisfying.

A knock at the door caused him to look up. His administrative assistant, Azariah, peeked in. "Sorry, Your Highness. Galen Shafir is here and wishes to speak to you. He said he knows he's not on your agenda at this hour but would like an audience with you."

Jeremiah nodded. "Send him in, Azariah."

"Very good, sir."

The door opened wider and Galen entered and bowed. "Thank you, Your Highness, for agreeing to see me."

Jeremiah smiled and gestured to a chair. "Please, Galen, have a seat."

Galen sat facing his desk. Jeremiah stayed seated.

"Sir, I know my family and I are to meet with you and

Administrator Isakson this afternoon, but I wanted to speak to you before that meeting."

Jeremiah nodded. "What's on your mind?"

Galen fidgeted in his chair. "Well, sir. I have a request that may seem premature, but I must at least ask it."

Jeremiah's eyebrows went up. He believed he knew what Galen would ask but wanted to see how he would make his request.

"Uh, when I first met Me'ira, I didn't know anything about there being protocols to follow." He licked his lips as if his mouth had gone dry. "Sir, I really regret that. But, I don't regret knowing her. She is one of the most wonderful people I have ever known. I have really grown to love her." He held up his hands. "I know what I'm saying is really premature with the vetting process still going on. Still, I wanted you to know my true feelings for her. If you could see it within your grace to give your blessing for me to ask for her hand in marriage, I would be most grateful."

Jeremiah opened his mouth to respond, but Galen interrupted.

"Not now, sir. I know you have a lot of things to take into consideration. I just wanted you to know my true feelings. I will do whatever is necessary to prove myself to you. Just let me know what that would entail."

Jeremiah set back and interlaced his fingers. "Galen, I admire your courage for coming here and stating your true feelings. I can't really tell you anything at this point. We need to get a full picture before I can make any kind of ruling on this matter."

Galen nodded. "Yes, sir. I understand. Thank you for listening." He stood, bowed, and left the room.

Jeremiah tried to turn his attention and concentration to

the documents before him, but he found himself unable to focus. Frustrated, he went out onto his balcony. He let the sun shine on his face and took a deep breath. Decisions seemed to come easily when he had to make them for others, but now, well, this involved his own family, and he found himself conflicted. Would he be able to make an objective decision?

Jeremiah looked out toward the city. The Messiah had chosen him to be the Prince to these people. While King David ruled over them as a nation, he led them in the proper way to worship their Lord and King. Yet his job went beyond Israel to the entire world. Every citizen of every nation needed to worship the Messiah, the King of kings, and he led them in that endeavor. He couldn't, or shouldn't, let personal issues compromise his responsibilities.

For quite some time he remained seated on the edge of one of the oversized planters. When he heard the French doors open, he assumed Azariah had come to get him for his meeting with Elsbeth and the Shafir family.

When he turned, however, he was looking at King David.

Jeremiah's eyes went wide. He instinctively genuflected. "Your Majesty, may I assist you?"

David smiled. "That was going to be my question for you."

"Sir?"

David sat on the edge of the oversized planter and gestured for Jeremiah to sit next to him.

"I can only imagine you are conflicted about something to sit out here for so long." He smiled. "I saw you out here when I left for a meeting and then saw you still here when I returned. Care to get anything off your chest?"

Jeremiah gave a weak smile. "It's my daughter, my lord."

David nodded. "Yes, children can sometimes prove difficult."

"Yes, my lord." He sighed. "She didn't follow protocol and met a young man to whom she has grown very fond. Actually, he just came to me and asked for her hand in marriage."

"I see. And you're unsure if he will pass the vetting process."

Jeremiah nodded. "I'm unsure if I will be able to follow what is prescribed by law and still be able to make my daughter's desires come true."

David raised his eyebrows. "Well, I'm not sure I'm one to give family advice. Unfortunately, most of my failures are recorded in Scripture for the entire world to know and understand."

Jeremiah smiled. "So, I do have something to be thankful for?"

David chuckled. "Indeed. Yet, in spite of all my blunders, I found God to be faithful. He will be that for you as well. He looked at my heart and knew I loved him. He sees your heart as well. I know it's true. So does he."

Jeremiah smiled. "Thank you, Your Majesty."

David patted his shoulder and stood. Jeremiah also rose.

The balcony doors opened and Azariah stepped through. He stopped and genuflected immediately. "Your Majesty, forgive me." He looked at Jeremiah. "Your Highness, Administrator Isakson is here."

David smiled. "I see you have some business to attend. Goodbye for now." He turned and headed to the French doors on his side of the balcony. Azariah hurried to the door and opened it for him, bowing as David entered.

Azariah then hurried to the other side of the balcony, opened the door, and bowed to Jeremiah as he returned to his office.

"Are the others here as well?"

"Yes, my lord."

"Send them all in."

Azariah opened the door and motioned for everyone to enter. He had already put extra chairs in the office so everyone could have a seat.

All four members of the Shafir family entered along with Me'ira, Liam, and Elsbeth. Everyone found a seat.

Jeremiah turned to Elsbeth. "OK, Elsbeth. Please tell us all you've discovered."

She nodded. "Yes, Your Highness." She turned to the Shafir family. "As the biggest question is whether either of you are Israeli, that is what I will focus on here. Also, to explain, when I say Israeli, I mean both Israeli and Jewish. The other information about your DNA heritage is informative. I can supply that to you, but it's not critical for today's discussion."

All four members of the Shafir family nodded.

"I know we have some relatives who go back a way in the Northwestern Territory of America," Noah said. "But both my and Lois's ancestors have lived in Israel for the past couple of centuries."

Elsbeth nodded. "That's a good point, Noah. A person can be from a place but not be one hundred percent ethnically from that place. One's ethnicity is a combination not only of one's parents but several generations back as well. So what I'm presenting here is how much each of your individual DNA contains Israeli ethnicity. We have made strides in determining from which tribe a person is from, but today I'm just presenting all that in totality to answer the most pressing question: do you qualify to live in Israel?"

Lois grabbed Noah's hand. "What do you mean by 'qualify to live in Israel'?"

Liam leaned forward. "Lois, when the Messiah established his kingdom, he gave the land here to the twelve tribes of

Israel. They have precedence. Others do live in Israel, but they are here for specific purposes or have been invited to live here."

Lois nodded but still looked concerned.

Elsbeth smiled. "Well, Lois, let me put your mind at ease. The average percent of Israeli DNA in your total DNA is 37 percent. Noah, yours is 42 percent. Therefore, you certainly qualify to be classified as Israeli."

Noah and Lois looked at each other and hugged.

"Caleb, since you are their biological son—"

"Oh, it doesn't matter." Caleb shrugged. "I plan to stay in Australia."

Elsbeth smiled. "That is certainly your prerogative. But just so you know, your DNA is 40 percent Israeli."

He gave a satisfied look as he nodded with lips pressed together.

"Now, every test has a percentage of error. Today, it is 2 percent. This becomes very important when we start talking about low percentages." Elsbeth sighed. "That is true in your case, Galen."

Galen nodded but didn't say anything.

"Galen, the percentage of Israeli DNA as a part of your entire DNA is 4.8 percent. With the error rate of 2 percent, it means the highest value with this level of accuracy is . . . 4.9 percent."

She glanced at Jeremiah and Liam. "Now, I don't make the rules here. Yet, customarily, 5 percent has been the cutoff for determining one to be legally classified as an Israeli."

Galen nodded, but his expression remained stoic.

Jeremiah saw Me'ira's eyes growing watery. His heart went out to her, but the facts were the facts. He grimaced, but mostly to himself, while thinking: Why couldn't Galen have been at least an even 5 percent?

"Thank you, Elsbeth. We really appreciate your help in this."

"Dad," Liam said. "While she's here, can we hear what she's discovered about Galen's parents?"

"Good idea, Liam." He looked back at Elsbeth. "Do you have anything to share on that?"

Elsbeth shook her head. "While it was, theoretically, a good idea to use DNA information to produce a teleporter signature, it didn't prove very trustworthy."

Liam tilted his head slightly. "Why is that?"

"Well, there were just too many false positives. It could still be done but would probably take a couple of years to be at a place we would feel confident." She shrugged. "We never considered the need to do something like this, so we would be starting almost from scratch to develop the science to do it."

Liam nodded. "Well . . . " He shrugged. "It was worth a shot anyway."

Elsbeth nodded and then turned to Galen. "I'm sorry, Galen. I know none of this is what you really wanted to hear."

Caleb quickly stepped in. "If I don't live in Israel, would that mean Galen could take my place here?"

Liam smiled. "Caleb, that is very generous of you, but that's not how it works. We don't have a quota of who lives here, just the qualifications for those who can."

Me'ira had sat for some time with her hand over her mouth. Jeremiah was unsure what she was thinking, but she looked nearly in shock. He hoped she was going to be OK. She looked up and her gaze met his. He gave a sympathetic look. Her eyes watered and she blinked faster to keep the tears at bay.

"Your Highness?" Noah quietly asked.

Jeremiah looked at Noah.

"What does all of this mean for Galen? He's lived with us

since a he was baby. Surely that means something."

Jeremiah sighed. "Noah, it would if he had been adopted by you and Lois. Yet, he was never adopted. He is now a man and cannot be adopted." He sat up and put his elbows on his desk with his fingers interlaced. He sighed, pausing again.

"Now that I have all the information, I have to make some decisions. I'll give you my decision in a couple of days as I check the various laws, protocols, and options."

They all rose and stepped from the office. Me'ira turned to look back at her dad.

"I love you, Me'ira."

She nodded and wiped a tear from each cheek as she left.

CHAPTER 29

As Me'ira left her dad's office, she stepped off to one side of the hallway. She knew she had to get her emotions in check before she could talk to anyone. She felt as if she would fall apart at any moment. This was certainly not the news she had wanted. She really thought that since Galen had put his faith in the King for his future, all would work out.

The key question was this: would her dad be able to find any way to pass Galen through the vetting process?

Liam came over, stood next to her, and rubbed her back. "Are you OK, sis?"

She shook her head and breathed in and out through her mouth; she was determined to not cry. The breathing technique partially helped with that goal.

"I'm really sorry, sis."

She nodded. "This was not the news I expected."

"I know."

After getting her emotions under control, she looked at Liam. "I need to talk with Galen. Can you chaperone if we go to the garden?"

He nodded.

"At a distance."

He chuckled. "Sure. Just stay in sight."

She reached up and kissed him on his cheek.

Turning, she saw Galen still talking with his parents and Caleb near Azariah's desk. She could only imagine what was going through their minds. Their emotions were probably as frazzled as hers.

As she approached, Caleb tapped Galen on his shoulder. As Galen turned, his gaze locked with hers. A sheepish smile came across his face.

"Can we talk for a while?" Me'ira asked.

Galen nodded. He turned to the others. "I'll meet you back at the Guest House, OK?"

Each nodded. Caleb patted him on his back, turned, and left with his parents.

Me'ira took Galen's hand and they walked together down the hallway and into the gardens. She glanced back and saw Liam following, but at a distance, which gave them some privacy—at least in conversation.

They walked around some of the planters, through the wisteria arch, and over to the corner, which had the bench next to the fountain. She made sure to keep within Liam's sight.

The noise of the fountain helped drown out any conversation. Although she wasn't necessarily afraid for Liam to hear their conversation, she felt better knowing her words would be heard by Galen only.

Galen rubbed her index finger with his thumb as he held her hand. "So, what do you think all this means for the two of us? Will there even be an 'us'?"

"Well, it doesn't sound too good," she said. "But I'm not sure Dad has all of the facts to make a completely informed decision." She put her other hand on top of theirs. "He knows I care about you, but he may not know your intentions are . . . more." She lowered her voice. "Are they more?"

Galen smiled. "I met with him earlier today and told him I wanted to have his permission to ask for your hand in marriage."

"Really?" She was so impressed he had the courage to do that not knowing what would come later. "What did he say?"

"I didn't let him say anything. I didn't think that fair. I told him I just wanted him to know my intentions so he could take that into account after he heard the news this afternoon."

Me'ira nodded.

"Since he agreed to say nothing, I took that as a good sign since he didn't refuse immediately."

She giggled. "Galen, he really likes you. So does Liam."

He sighed. "I like your family too, Me'ira. But what are the odds I'll pass laws, protocols, and . . . options?"

She patted his hand. "Don't lose faith, Galen. It can still happen. If anyone can find a way, he can."

Galen gave a weak smile. "I hope so."

"Besides, I have a couple of options of my own."

Galen looked confused. "What options?"

"Oh, don't worry about it. No sense going there if we don't have to."

"Me'ira . . . "

She frowned. "Don't say my name like that. You sound like my mother."

He laughed. "Sorry. I just don't want you to do something you may regret."

"Let's just see what Dad comes up with."

He nodded, turned, and exhaled a sigh.

Me'ira stood, went to the wall, and looked down at the street below; she wasn't looking at anything specific. Should she ask him the other questions she had? *Well, it can't hurt, can it?*

"You OK?" He stood and walked next to her, leaned his back against the wall, and crossed his arms. "Something's on your mind."

"Yeah. I was just thinking . . . " She put her forearms on the top of the wall and looked at the city before her. "Did your mom or dad talk any more about the Prophecy Plaque?"

Galen turned so that he was facing the same direction as Me'ira. "Some. I'm not sure they know what it's supposed to mean."

She looked his way. "I think I do."

"Wh— I mean . . . how?"

She turned to him and leaned her shoulder against the wall. "It said 'one near the Prince and one from afar.' I think . . . it's talking about me."

He faced her. "Me'ira, how could you possibly think that? It could mean anyone."

"These phrases are using feminine Hebrew words. It's talking about two women, Galen."

"But . . . "

"I'm a woman who is near the Prince."

He put his hand on her shoulder. "Yes, but not the only one."

"Maybe."

She took a few steps toward the fountain, reached down, and flicked the water. Me'ira wondered if she should continue, and if Galen would think she was losing it if she did. Well, she'd come this far. She turned. "Galen, you remember the first time we met?"

He chuckled. "How could I forget? You were the most beautiful person on the ship."

"Why were you on the ship? Not just anyone could get on that cruise."

195

Galen's smile faded. "What? You think I planned the meeting with you?"

"No, Galen. No." She put her hand on his chest. "But I'm wondering if someone else planned it."

He looked confused. "What are you talking about?"

"So, how were you able to get on the ship?" Me'ira repeated.

Galen thought for a moment. "A customer came into the store, wanted a vase dated to pre-Refreshing times, and offered the cruise ticket as partial payment. She was so persistent; I finally caved and took it." He laughed lightly. "After I had it, I decided it was foolish not to go on the cruise."

"Who was your customer?"

He shrugged. "I don't know. Does it matter?"

She put her hand on his arm. "Galen, I believe it was your mother."

It looked like he had turned to stone. He didn't move for several seconds.

"Galen, are you OK?"

He sat down on the edge of the nearest planter. "You know, a few days ago, I would have thought you crazy for that statement. But after what went down in Australia, you might be right." He shook his head. "But to what purpose?"

"It has to be something to do with the prophecy."

He looked up at her. "Do you believe in the prophecy?"

"I . . . I don't know. But she certainly does."

"But again, to what end?"

"I think . . . she somehow feels we're part of the prophecy."

"How?"

Me'ira shrugged. "I'm not completely sure."

Galen stood. He squeezed his forehead between his index finger and thumb. He paced between the planter and wall.

196

"This . . . this is crazy." He gave a half laugh. "What are we? Puppets?"

"Priest Ya'akov did say they were masters of manipulation."

He stopped pacing and faced her. "OK, let's say you're right. If you're the one close to the Prince, how do *I* fit in? You're already close to the Prince. Whether you met me or not, that doesn't change."

Me'ira shook her index finger as she thought. "I think . . . I think they wanted us to get together to keep me close to my father."

Galen shook his head. "I'm not following you."

"They know, or at least feel, they can manipulate us and thereby get to my dad through us."

"What?"

"And I think they had this planned for over twenty years."

CHAPTER 30

Jeremiah sat at his desk and thought about whether Galen could be classified as Israeli. On the one hand, it could potentially be justified that 4.8 percent could be rounded to 5 percent. Yet he also knew that in the beginning of the kingdom many were not allowed to live in Israel who had similar levels of Israeli DNA unless they already had family living in the land.

He thought about that. He had a hard time classifying Galen in this way. Galen was never officially a Shafir because he had never been adopted. Actually, Noah and Lois had been deceptive about things. That was the bad part. It was all an act of deception. How could he reward that?

On the other hand, he wanted Me'ira's happiness. She would be heartbroken if he ruled against Galen. Yet, once again, she hadn't followed protocol. Should she now be rewarded for that?

He made a growling sound and began to pace. The pros and cons kept going through his head. He felt so conflicted. Should he behave as a ruler or as a father? Should he stick to the letter of the law or be more lenient?

Jeremiah dropped to his knees and then fell totally prostrate on the floor. He knew he had to turn to the only One who could be completely objective. He began his prayer. "My Lord and King, I come to you as I am so conflicted with the decision I have to make. As Prince, I'm not convinced Galen should be classified as an Israeli. Yet, as Me'ira's father, I wonder if it would be wrong to do so. Please help me make the right and wise decision."

Jeremiah knew Ruach HaKodesh would relay his concerns and deliver a response back to him. He also knew he would likely not get a direct answer as the King usually gave words of wisdom but did not directly answer questions because he wanted people to assume the responsibility of their decisions.

"Jeremiah, I appreciate you have come to me with your heartache. Your question is an important one, but not necessarily one Scripture can answer directly."

"Yes, my Lord. I do realize that, but I need the ability to be objective in this issue that involves one I love."

"Although difficult, a less emotional decision is best. Think back on what you know of the principles of Scripture and talk to those you trust for their advisement. Please know I am always with you, even if heartache comes."

"Thank you, my Lord."

Jeremiah rose from the floor and went back to his desk. He called both Ya'akov and Franklin and asked if they could come by. The Master was right. He had not sought counsel from wise friends. Although this was not entirely a spiritual issue, these two also dealt with legal issues as well. He would not expect them to make a decision for him, but their insight could prove extremely helpful.

In less than an hour, Azariah announced both men had arrived. Jeremiah invited them into his office. Franklin was the epitome of someone who did not look Israeli but was so:

he was rather tall with sandy brown hair and blue eyes. Still, Jeremiah could think of him as nothing but Israeli since he had done so much for the nation through the centuries and had carried out many assignments for the King.

Ya'akov had the looks of someone most would think of as Israeli. His skin and hair appeared darker than that of Franklin, and he had a pin-striped beard. But his father was Edvin, who, although he had Levitical DNA, had come from Europe while his mother Elsbeth was Jewish and a descendant of Zadok, also from the family of Levi. This heritage allowed Ya'akov to perform temple sacrifices as a priest.

Both men had both become trusted friends. Jeremiah had sought their advice many times before. He was unsure why he didn't consider it this time. It must be because he was too close to the situation.

Both men took a seat and Jeremiah sat next to them; he didn't sit behind his desk this time. These two men were respected friends, and he wanted them to know he was seeking their advice as friends.

"Before we get started, I want you to know I have invited you here as friends and not in an official capacity," Jeremiah said. "So, please, feel free to address me as Jeremiah. I would appreciate that."

Both nodded.

Franklin scooted his chair a little closer. "So, what's on your mind, Jeremiah?"

He went through the entire story with Galen and Me'ira: Galen's background, their meeting outside protocol, how they were now in love with each other, how The Order was likely involved, and Elsbeth's findings.

Jeremiah then asked his nagging question. "So, my biggest quandary is about Galen's heritage. How close is close enough to declare him Israeli?"

Franklin gave him a sympathetic look. "Jeremiah, I understand why you are so conflicted about this. But for five centuries, this has never been a question. We have always used 5 percent as the cutoff."

Ya'akov quietly spoke up. "I'm not sure that's entirely true, Franklin."

Jeremiah turned to Ya'akov. "Why is that?"

"Well, it was certainly that way when the kingdom was first established, but to my knowledge this question has never come up again." He shrugged. "So I think Jeremiah's dilemma is not unfounded. I think the question is, do we still use what was used five centuries ago, or do we redefine it?"

Franklin nodded. "Good point. But I think we need to remember that everyone who had to abide by that initial guideline is still around today. I know in pre-Refreshing times a new decision could be made five centuries later and no one would have been alive to make a rebuttal. Today, however, I think we have to remain consistent."

Jeremiah looked at Ya'akov. "What do you think of what Franklin has just said?"

Ya'akov tilted his head slightly side to side. "It's a very compelling argument." He paused and then grimaced. "I want to be supportive, Jeremiah. But I think Franklin's argument is stronger than mine."

"There is another point, Jeremiah," Franklin said.

Jeremiah turned his way. "Yes? And that is?"

"Well, you may think this unfounded, but knowing what I've heard of this Leader and his organization, and if it's true Galen is their son, then having their son part of the Royal Family may not be a good idea."

Jeremiah squinted. "Why is that?"

Ya'akov interjected. "I've had some firsthand experience with him, and this man is quite crafty. Although Galen is now united with our King, his parents may still be able to manipulate him to some degree. For what purpose, I can't really say. It's just . . . I feel it does put you at a higher risk."

Jeremiah sighed. "I can see the wisdom in your words."

After a couple of seconds of silence, he tapped his legs. There was really nothing further to say. "Well, I really do appreciate your insights. Thank you both for coming." He stood, and they did also. Each man shook his hand, bowed, and exited.

Jeremiah returned to his desk, sat, and put his head in his hands. His heart was heavy. He now knew the decision he had to make.

He couldn't think of anyone who would be happy with it.

CHAPTER 31

Me'ira walked through the garden grounds. It had been a day and a half without hearing from her father. She wondered: *Is that a good sign or a bad one?* As she looked over the edge of the wall to the courtyard, she saw Liam step off the teleporter. She ran downstairs to meet him.

She met him as he entered the living area. "Liam!"

He turned. "Me'ira, hi."

"What brings you back?"

"I think Dad's made a decision."

Me'ira turned her head. "Really? Why didn't he tell me?"

At that moment, Azariah appeared. He bowed. "My Lady, your father requests your presence in his office."

Liam produced a thin smile. "I think he just did."

"Me'ira." It was a familiar voice, from behind her.

She turned and there was Galen.

"Galen." She smiled. "The moment of truth, I suppose."

He gave a nervous smile. "I guess so."

They walked together behind Liam. She resisted the urge to hold Galen's hand.

Azariah opened the door for them to enter her father's office. Me'ira realized it was just the three of them and her father who would be present. Jeremiah motioned for them to take a seat.

"I have all three of you here because you each have been involved with understanding Galen's past," Jeremiah began. He cleared his throat. "Let me first begin by saying, Galen, I think you are a remarkable young man. Through no fault of your own, you have been plunged into some type of conspiracy. Still, you were able to see through that to the Master's goodness and accept him as the hope for your future. No matter the outcome here today, you will be eternally blessed for that decision."

Galen smiled and nodded. "Thank you, Your Highness. I do feel blessed in that regard."

"Now for the matter at hand." Jeremiah interlaced his fingers and laid them on his desk in front of him. He sighed. "There are things that occurred which should not have occurred." He gave a slight nod. "I think we all bear some responsibility for the way events have come about." He looked at Me'ira and then at Galen. "First, protocol was ignored when you two first met and then when you met several times unchaperoned. This caused the two of you to grow very fond of each other before a vetting process could be held. It is likely that, had that not occurred, neither of you would have even known each other." He paused.

"And, as we found out the other day, Galen, the amount of Israeli DNA is not sufficient to classify you as an Israeli."

Galen nodded. He looked dejected.

"Unfortunately, I must now institute protocol, which dictates that any member of the Royal Family must marry someone classified as an Israeli and living in Israel. You meet the second part of that statement but not the first. Both have to be true."

Me'ira's eyes were getting teary. She knew what was coming: her worst nightmare.

Jeremiah looked at each of them, his eyes sad and a bit wet as well. "It is with the utmost regret that I cannot allow the two of you to continue to see each other." He looked at Galen. "And, son, I cannot give my approval for you to ask for Me'ira's hand in marriage."

Galen nodded. His bottom lip quivered and his eyes welled with tears. A couple of them ran down his cheeks. "Yes, Your . . . Your Highness. I appreciate all the care you have granted me." He looked at Me'ira and gave a shaky smile. "I can't regret meeting you. Only through you did I find the truth of the Messiah, my King." He stood and bowed, ready to fully accept this decision. "I bid you all a very fond farewell."

Softly, Jeremiah asked a question. "Where will you go from here?"

Galen turned to face the Prince again. "Likely to the Northwestern Territory of America. My parents have some relatives in a city there. Vancouver, I believe. And they will help me open an antique shop there. My parents will still be one of my major suppliers."

"Well, I wish you all the best, Galen."

He bowed again. "Thank you, Your Highness." He turned and left the room.

Me'ira thought her heart would break. She looked at her father. He gave her the most sympathetic look he could. She shook her head.

"Me'ira, I am truly sorry. In time—"

Suddenly, she ran from the room to find Galen. She couldn't let him leave like this—not when a way out still existed. He had to know that. She caught up with him as he stepped out to the courtyard that held the teleporter.

"Galen, wait! Galen!"

He turned revealing his tear-stained face. "Me'ira." He shook his head. "We shouldn't prolong our goodbye. It . . . it hurts too much."

She grabbed his hands. "But Galen. We don't have to. If you really want to marry me, I have a way."

Galen scrunched his brow. "What?" He shook his head. "How? Your father just said—"

"Just answer one question. Do you want to marry me?"

"Yes, of course. But . . . "

She smiled. "No buts. I can fix this. I really can. Just . . . just don't leave Jerusalem until you hear from me. OK?"

Galen held his confused look, but said, "OK."

"Good." She kissed his hand. "I'll see you soon."

She ran back while wiping tears from her cheeks. She had to find Liam.

As she walked into the living area, Liam entered from the other side.

"Liam, can I talk to you?"

"Sis, I'm so sorry. Are you OK?"

"That's what I want to talk with you about. I have a decision to make, and I want you to understand why I'm doing it."

Each took a seat on the settee opposite the sofa.

"So, what's on your mind?" Liam asked.

Me'ira took a deep breath. "This is going to sound weird. So let me finish before you say anything, OK?"

Liam turned up his brow. "I'm already not liking this."

"Remember the Prophecy Plaque?"

Liam gave her a hard stare. "Of course," he said slowly, the words slightly drawn out. "What about it?"

"I think Galen and I are part of it."

Liam's eyes widened, followed by a sigh. "Me'ira—"

She held up her hands. "I said, let me finish."

He gestured a hand toward her to invite her to continue.

"The prophecy said, 'one close to the Prince, one from afar.'"

Liam shook his head.

Me'ira gave him a stare and sighed. "What? What is it?"

"It said, 'one close to the Prince, one *through* afar.'"

Me'ira shook her head. "Does that make a difference?"

Liam shrugged. "I don't know. But just be sure you think about the right words."

Me'ira's eyes widened briefly and she gave a small shrug. "OK. Anyway, the plaque used the feminine form of 'one.' That means these are *women*. I met Galen on a Sea of Galilee cruise that, as you know, required a special invitation. A woman offered him the ticket for the cruise as payment for a vase in his shop. I'm pretty sure that woman was his real mother. I think his actual parents planned for us to meet and get together so they can, somehow, influence us to help achieve whatever they feel the prophecy is supposed to fulfill. I think the one close to the Prince is . . . *me*."

Liam waited a few seconds. "Anything else?"

Me'ira shook her head.

"Me'ira." He sighed and looked up at the ceiling as if thinking. He then locked his gaze with hers. "What you're saying is a real stretch in my opinion. The words of that prophecy are just like Noah and Lois said. They're very vague. There's probably other scenarios one could take out of them as well."

"Really? And what about all that happened in Australia? Why would they have otherwise involved Galen?"

Liam shrugged. "I . . . I don't know."

"I know how to foil their plan."

"How?" Liam seemed stunned at his sister's statement.

"I can abdicate my inheritance."

"Wh—" He put his hands on his head. "Me'ira, do you hear what you're saying?"

"I can thwart their plans and we can still be together."

"Me'ira . . . Me'ira. You're not thinking straight."

She grabbed his arm. "Liam, you're the one ignoring the facts here."

"You have always been headstrong, and I've sort of admired you for that," Liam said. "But this . . . " He shook his head. "This is taking it too far."

She sat back. "Liam, you agree Galen is the son of Isabelle and this Leader, right?"

He nodded.

"And you agree they are extremely manipulative, right?"

He nodded again. "I know they've ignored him his entire life and were willing to sacrifice his life to get the Prophecy Plaque."

"That's my point. Liam, they're willing to do anything. I think they want to get to the King through our father. Getting Galen close to me was all part of their plan. They then plan to somehow use their manipulation through him—us—to achieve . . . something. I just don't know what."

"But that's all moot now," Liam said. "If you can't be together, then he can't get to Dad or the King. Dad has actually solved your dilemma."

Tears welled within Me'ira's eyes. "I can't . . . I can't lose him."

"Oh, Me'ira." Liam embraced his sister in a tight hug. "I'm truly sorry. But the heartache will ease over time."

She let go of his embrace and shook her head. "He's my soulmate. I value him too much."

Liam shook his head in puzzlement. "So, you're going to throw away your inheritance for him? That will break Dad's heart. Not to mention what it will do to Mom."

"I know. I know." Me'ira's voice sounded barely audible. Tears spilled onto her cheeks. "But I have to, Liam. I just have to." She wiped the tears from her cheeks. "I know if I had followed protocol, I wouldn't be making this decision. But I also know if he and I had not met, he and his parents likely would not have accepted the King. I think . . . I think it was all for a purpose. This decision is an extension of that purpose."

Liam's eyebrows raised. "You think you giving up your inheritance is the will of the King?"

Me'ira nodded.

Liam put his hands to his head. "I . . . I . . . " He cupped his temples with his palms. "Wow." He took a deep breath and lowered his hands. "Have you asked him that? The King *told* you to take this course of action?"

"I have prayed about it," Me'ira said. "You know the King doesn't tell his followers exactly *what* to do."

"Well, he doesn't leave you totally clueless either."

Me'ira gave him a hard stare. "And what is *that* supposed to mean?"

Liam sighed. "Me'ira, he wants the best for you, so he would guide you in a certain direction."

Me'ira bit her lower lip while trying to prevent herself from saying something she might later regret. "Liam, I *have* prayed, and I *have* asked for direction." She shook her head. "You'll probably say I'm letting my bias prevent me from hearing him, but he really hasn't given me a specific direction. He's kind of left it up to me."

Liam put his thumb and forefinger to his forehead again, shaking his head slightly. He looked back at her. He started to say something, but chose not to. He sighed. "You also know he doesn't usually ask people to shirk their responsibility."

209

"I'm *not*." Me'ira knew she had to help Liam see things from her perspective. "I'm accepting a greater responsibility. I'm sure Galen's parents will try to use him in the future if I'm not a part of his life. I can help prevent that from happening. He's been through so much. I don't want him to go through more. I can help him, and I can serve my King."

"Me'ira, I'm not sure what to say."

"Surely you can see the logic in this," she said quietly.

"Can I?" He sighed and looked into her eyes. "Your reasoning is not devoid of logic. Yes, I can see that. But if you were not a princess, it would make more sense to me."

"But Liam," she said. "My being a princess is why all of this happened in the first place. I want to do my part to thwart the plans of this so-called Leader. Will you support me in this?" She paused. "But you can't tell Dad all I've told you."

Liam's eyes widened. "But then, Me'ira, he'll think you only did it for selfish reasons. That will break his heart even more."

"OK. But you can only tell him once Galen and I have left. I don't want him trying to talk me out of it."

Liam's eyebrows rose. "Oh, have no fear. He will do that anyway."

CHAPTER 32

Me'ira took a deep breath and knocked on the door. She smiled at the tall sandy brown-haired man with a glorified body. "Hello, Shepherd Franklin. Thanks for setting this up."

He smiled and motioned for her to come in. "My Lady, this is Shepherd Hayden from Vancouver."

Hayden bowed and kissed her hand. "My pleasure to meet you, My Lady."

Me'ira smiled. It was uncanny how much alike he and Shepherd Franklin looked. "Thank you, Shepherd Hayden. After today, that title will not apply anymore."

Hayden nodded and smiled. "Until then."

"Me'ira, please have a seat," Franklin said.

"Thank you, Shepherd Franklin." She sat in one of the umber and tan plush chairs. "Where are the others?"

"Oh, they'll be here shortly," he said. "I first wanted a chance to talk with you privately to be sure you still want to go through with this. I mean, after all, this is a most highly irregular decision."

Me'ira gave a short sigh and slight smile. "Shepherd Franklin, I assure you I do not do this lightly. I have thought long and hard about this and, yes, I am confident I want to go through with it."

Franklin's shoulders drooped. "Very well, My Lady. You understand, I have to be sure, because once it is done, it can never be revoked."

Me'ira nodded. "Yes. I am aware."

Shepherd Franklin answered a knock at his door.

"Shepherd Franklin, you asked to see me."

"Come on in, Galen." Franklin turned to direct Galen toward Hayden. "This is Shepherd Hayden."

Galen entered and shook Hayden's hand. When he turned, he saw Me'ira. His eyes widened. "Me'ira!" He looked from Hayden back to her. "What . . . what are you doing here?"

Franklin motioned for Galen to have a seat. He sat next to Me'ira.

She grabbed his hand. "Galen, I told you a way existed for us to be together. This is it."

"Really?" She saw his eyes develop that twinkle again. "Me'ira, do you really mean it?"

She nodded. He kissed her hand. "How . . . how did you convince your father?"

"Well—"

Another knock at the door once again interrupted things. Jeremiah and Liam entered.

Jeremiah looked from Hayden to Me'ira and Galen. He perfunctorily shook Hayden's hand and nodded. "What's going on?" He turned back to Franklin.

"Please, shall we all sit?" Franklin gestured to the empty seats. "There is a matter which Princess Me'ira has brought to my attention and wishes to have addressed."

Jeremiah looked at Me'ira with a slightly contorted face. He turned a questioning look to Liam. "And why is Shepherd Hayden present?"

Franklin held up a palm. "Please, Your Highness. All in good time."

Me'ira looked at Liam and hoped for a smile. Instead, he returned an expressionless gaze and gave a slight shake of his head.

Franklin looked at Me'ira. "My Lady, shall I continue?"

Me'ira swallowed hard but nodded. Franklin then turned to Jeremiah.

"Your Highness, as you well know, you decreed Me'ira and Galen could not marry because he did not meet the qualification as an Israelite. That is, per decree, a requirement for one of royal birth. There is only one way Me'ira can still legally marry Galen."

Jeremiah's face went pale. He looked from Me'ira to Franklin. He shook his head. Slightly at first, but then more forcefully. "No. No, I forbid it!" He looked at Me'ira. "You . . . can't. Me'ira, please tell me this isn't true."

Galen looked dumbfounded. "Wait. What's going on here?" He looked at Me'ira. "Me'ira, I thought you convinced your father." He looked at Franklin. "I don't understand."

"Me'ira has decided to renounce her heritage," Franklin said.

Galen stared at Franklin. "What?" He looked at Me'ira. "No. No, you can't. Me'ira, I can't let you do this. Not on my account. I'm . . . I'm not worth it."

Me'ira's eyes watered. "Yes. Yes you are, Galen."

He shook his head, looked at Jeremiah, and responded. "Your Highness. I'm sorry. I . . . I had no idea." He turned to Me'ira and fell at her feet. "Please, Me'ira. Don't do this." Tears began to roll down his cheeks. "Please, don't."

Me'ira wiped his tear-stained cheeks. "Galen, don't you want to be with me?"

"Oh, Me'ira. Of course. More than anything. But . . . " He shook his head. "Not like this." He put his head in his hands, muffling his voice. "Not like this." He looked back up. "Is there no other way?"

Me'ira shook her head. "No, Galen. This is the only way."

"But your family," Galen said, shock still on his face. "Your family is more important."

"I love my family." She looked at her father, tears now rolling down his face. "I really do." She looked back at Galen. "But I want you and me to be family. I . . . I choose you, Galen."

"Oh, Me'ira. No one has ever made me feel this special." He shook his head. "But the cost is so high."

She smiled and wiped tears from her cheeks and then from his. "You're worth it, Galen."

Liam rubbed his chin. "Shepherd Franklin, have you explained everything to her?"

Franklin nodded. "I think so. Is there anything you want to add?"

"Me'ira, you know you also will not be considered an Israelite," Liam said. "You won't be able to visit. Mom and Dad won't be able to attend your wedding. You will be as any other non-Israelite."

Me'ira nodded. "Liam, I know all that and I have considered all that. This is not a decision I have taken lightly. Believe me, if another way existed, I would take it."

"Me'ira." Jeremiah's voice sounded hoarse. "Your decision breaks my heart. Yet, I can to some extent understand it." He shook his head. "I feel partly to blame. I think I became more lax with you than with the others, you being born so many years after my other children." His eyes got wet again. "Yet I never dreamed of anything like this."

Me'ira came over. She knelt next to him. "Dad, it's not your fault. This doesn't mean I don't love you. But my heart can't turn away from Galen. Please understand that."

Jeremiah nodded. "My main concern is that this will most assuredly break your mother's heart."

Me'ira's eyes filled with tears again. "Yes, I know it will. I will talk to her later."

Franklin stood. "I have made some edits to the document to help in this decision so it cannot appear rash. Once everyone signs it, the decision can be revoked within one month. If not rescinded by that time, it will be irrevocable." Franklin bowed. "My Lady, I know Princess Sarit will be married in less than a month, so that gives you time to attend."

"Thank you, Shepherd Franklin. That is most considerate."

Franklin held the stylus to Me'ira. She came forward, signed, and then had it scan her fingerprint. Jeremiah slowly walked forward. His hand shook as he signed. Franklin then signed as the officiating member. Liam signed as a family witness, and Hayden signed as a witness and as the Shepherd under whom Me'ira and Galen would now reside.

Franklin pressed a button on the tablet and laid it back on his desk. He turned to Me'ira. "My Lady, you have one month from today to revoke this decision. In one month and a day, this document will be officially entered into the system, and it will never be able to be revoked. Are you completely aware of this condition?"

Me'ira nodded. "I am, Shepherd Franklin."

"We will all leave now so Me'ira and Galen can get to know Shepherd Hayden, under whose direction they will soon reside."

Liam came over and gave Me'ira a hug. "I will miss you, Me'ira. Perhaps we can at least see you at festivals or honoring ceremonies."

She nodded and whispered in his ear, "Don't forget our agreement."

He nodded. "I promise."

Me'ira walked over and hugged her father. "Dad, I still love you so much. Please know that."

"And I you, Me'ira." He wiped tears from his cheeks once more.

"I'll walk you to the teleporter, Your Highness," Franklin said.

"Thank you, Franklin."

Jeremiah and Liam stepped from the room with Franklin.

Me'ira took a deep yet staccato breath. This had been even harder than she had envisioned. Still, she knew she had made the right decision. She looked forward to getting to know Shepherd Hayden. This would be a new experience for both her and Galen. Having a friend to help guide them and to introduce them to other members of the community would be welcome.

She reached for Galen's hand and interlocked her fingers in his. She was no longer bound by protocol.

She looked at Shepherd Hayden. "So, Shepherd Hayden. Fill us in on Vancouver."

CHAPTER 33

Me'ira woke and slowly stretched. The memory of the night before flooded into her mind. She was glad the ordeal was over. While she knew telling her mom would be hard, her mother took the news much harder than she had imagined. While there would likely still be tears, things should now go better. At least she hoped.

An idea came to her. She called Liam. His holographic image appeared over her T-band on the nightstand.

"Hi, sis. What's up?"

"Well, I told Mom last night."

"And you're still alive. Congratulations."

"Ha ha." Her tone turned somber. "It was rough, though. I never thought it would be that hard."

"I'm sure it was."

"It's only a couple of weeks until Sarit's wedding. You think maybe she and Nyssa could use some help? I want to give Mom some time to process things, and I can't see Galen until we leave, so I need something to keep my mind busy."

"I'm sure they can use all the help they can get. Let me ask them."

"Liam?"

He turned back.

"Have you told anyone?" Me'ira asked.

He shook his head. "No, sis. I'm good to my word. I won't tell anyone else until after you leave." He paused. "I can tell you, though, the others will not be happy you kept them in the dark."

"I know, but I just can't go through what I went through with Dad and Mom all over again. I just can't."

"Understood. Let me go get Nyssa." She saw Liam step away.

In a few seconds, Nyssa's beautiful face, with her dimples showing around her bright smile, appeared onscreen. Me'ira smiled to herself. She had, of course, seen Nyssa a thousand times before, but this time Nyssa's dimples stood out to her, and they reminded her of Galen and how much she missed him. Evidently, a weakness for dimples was something she and Liam shared. "Hi, Me'ira. Liam tells me you want in on the chaos."

"Absolutely," Me'ira said. "OK to stay and help out, or should I come back and forth?"

"Oh, feel free to stay. Sarit will love it."

"OK. I'll see you this afternoon."

"OK. See you then." She blew Me'ira a kiss and the connection ended.

* * * * *

The next couple of weeks went by quickly and kept Me'ira's mind occupied, just as she had hoped. She helped with place settings, analyzing and discussing with Sarit who should sit next to whom, coordinating flower arrangements with table placements, selecting hors d'oeuvres based on taste and color, and picking out the music for the string quartet. And she did any other odds and ends either Nyssa or Sarit asked of her.

When Me'ira woke up the morning of the big day, everyone was already scurrying at a frantic pace handling last-minute details. She went outside to help Liam with arrangements at the gazebo where the ceremony would take place.

She always loved Liam's place. The house overlooked the Mediterranean Sea. The clear blue water with its occasional whitecaps captivated her as she stood on their back patio. The grounds gradually sloped down from the patio to the seashore, and the gazebo sat next to the edge of their property atop rocks overlooking the sea and surrounded by beautiful yellow rosebushes. These made the overall ambience look gorgeous but also gave off a wonderful floral fragrance. Me'ira sat there for a few minutes taking everything in.

She felt happy and sad at the same time. While happy for Sarit, as she knew the wedding would be beautiful, she also knew her own wedding would be so different from this one. She did a small, sad half chuckle. Who would even be at her wedding other than Galen's family? Maybe a few of Galen's parents' distant relatives they didn't even know. But then she reminded herself the wedding was only the brief part. Spending her life with the person she loved was the thing to focus on. And she couldn't wait for *that* part.

Liam came by and sat next to her. "Resting already?"

Me'ira laughed. "Getting married is hard work." She looked over the backyard; everything was decorated in yellow and white with yellow gladioli and white orchids scattered throughout. "Liam, you must be so proud."

He nodded. "My son-in-law will be working with me. He's going to be taking over many of my current duties, and I'll branch out to look at the needs of citizens outside Israel."

Me'ira smiled. "Congratulations. Sounds like a promotion."

Liam chuckled. "Sounds like more work to me."

Me'ira laughed. "It suits you, though."

Liam nodded. "Oh, I'm really excited about it." He looked at his T-band. "Speaking of excited. You'd better go get ready for the excitement about to begin."

She looked at her T-band and her eyes widened. "Oh my. Yes, I should." She stood. "See you in a few."

Me'ira's dress, composed of a pastel yellow chiffon that flowed from the waist to her ankles, was adorned with a thin clear gemstone waistband and sleeves coated with the same gemstone but crushed and fused onto the fabric.

She looked at herself before heading out to the ceremony. This was one final chance to look like a princess.

Sarit had a very traditional Jewish wedding with all the trimmings. The all-white chuppah had its poles decorated with white orchids. Liam wore an all-white tuxedo with a boutonnière of a yellow gladiolus. There were *oohs* and *ahhs* all around when people saw Sarit's dress. It too looked all white, but both its bodice and sleeves had the clear crushed gemstone look. The bottom of the dress had a satin sheen with strategically placed sequins that sparkled in the sunlight. Her bouquet of white orchids and yellow gladiolus flowers tied the theme together. Me'ira was so impressed with Sarit's choices.

Me'ira felt as if the wedding went by in a blur, yet it was a beautiful blur. Once the ceremony ended, the celebration began. Everyone drank, ate, and danced. Liam came by and took her hand.

"Dance with me, Me'ira."

Me'ira laughed. "One for the road?"

Liam frowned. "Oh, don't say it like that."

"Sorry. I guess I'm being melancholy."

They took the floor, and she twirled as he let go of her hand and brought her back again.

As they were dancing, Liam broke in with a statement she hadn't expected.

"I know few will understand why you're doing what you're doing, but the more I've thought about it, the more impressed I am," he said.

"Really?"

"You're giving up your station in life for someone else to have a better life. It somewhat reminds me of what Shepherd Franklin talked about the other week of how the Messiah gave up so much for us."

Me'ira smiled. "Don't put me too high. I have too far to fall."

Liam laughed. "Oh, not to worry. I can make a list of your faults very quickly."

She playfully slapped his arm. "Hey now."

He chuckled. "I just mean, not everyone would sacrifice so much. Don't get me wrong. I know you're getting happiness out of the deal as well, but you're giving up a lot also."

Me'ira's eyes began to tear up. "Thank you, Liam. That means a lot."

"So only a week left, huh?" he said.

She nodded. "I'm excited, sad, and happy all at the same time."

Liam's next statement came out flatly, and it hadn't been unexpected.

"There's still time to back out," he said.

She shook her head. "No. I'm committed. Galen is the one for me."

The song ended. Liam walked Me'ira back to the table. He took Nyssa by the hand. "I believe the next song is calling our names," he said to his wife.

Nyssa smiled and went to the dance floor with him.

Me'ira sat and watched the two of them. They seemed so perfect. She knew they had their issues, but they truly loved each other. She hoped she and Galen would be that happy together.

Yes, there would be challenges. With The Order so close to Galen's background, she knew challenges would arise. Yet they had both committed themselves to their King. Even though she would no longer be part of the Royal Family after next week, she knew she and Galen would not be abandoned by their King. They were secure in him. That fact alone provided a great deal of comfort.

Me'ira dreaded the goodbyes that were coming, but she really did look forward to being with Galen and starting a life together. After next week, she would be helping Galen sell antiques. *What will that be like? Will I need to find out about each piece and what makes each one so special?*

She smiled. She always did like a good mystery.

CHAPTER 34

Me'ira walked through the palace gardens where she always spent so much time. She would definitely miss this place. Being here always helped her think. Tomorrow would end it all. This chapter of her life would end, and a new chapter would begin. The thing that troubled her the most was, after tomorrow, her parents would be as out of reach to her as they were to the rest of the world. Her dad would be her Prince and model of how to worship the Messiah. Perhaps periodically she would be able to see them from afar, but she would never be in their presence informally again. That was going to be hard. Very hard.

Me'ira scolded herself. *No. You can't get back into a melancholy mood. You must focus on your new adventure.*

When Me'ira looked up, there stood her mother, father, and Liam in the doorway to the garden. She smiled and walked over. "OK, I know something's up for all three of you to be standing there like that. What's up?"

Jeremiah wrapped his arm around her shoulders. "I thought we would go serve a fellowship offering to our Messiah. This will be the last time we can do that as a family. Since Liam is the only one of your siblings who knows about your new life at this moment, I've asked him to join."

Liam came over and gave Me'ira a big hug. "Oldest and youngest together again," he said.

She smiled. Yes, their last time together. She was really going to miss Liam. They had become closer these last couple of months than ever before.

As they walked to the teleporter, Kyla wrapped her arm around Me'ira's shoulders. "We thought it appropriate to spend part of our last day with you in family worship."

"Thanks, Mom," she said. "I appreciate this. I couldn't think of anything more special to do before Galen and I start a new life."

They each took the teleporter to the King's palace and then walked to the South Gate of the temple. Azariah met them with a bull from Jeremiah's herds for them to offer as a sacrifice. Ya'akov met them at the Inner Eastern Gate and held the bull as Jeremiah placed his hands on its head while Ya'akov said a prayer for the family.

As Jeremiah stood at the gate, Ya'akov took the bull to the Northern Inner Gate to prepare it for sacrifice, the place where all the tables for sacrifice preparation were located. Jeremiah entered the gate, going through the vestibule, past the chambers in the gate, and stood at the doorjamb but did not enter the inner court where the priests were preparing the sacrifice. Me'ira waited with Kyla and Liam in the outer court at the vestibule of the gate.

As the sacrifice took place, Ya'akov approached the family and said a prayer. "Our King and Messiah," he began, "I ask you to bless this family and bring them your peace. Because they bring a fellowship offering, part is offered to you, part is given to your priests, and part is shared with each family member in your presence. Many changes will occur with this family very shortly. Therefore, my King, I ask you to continue to give your peace to each family member as the relationship with them and with Me'ira changes. Yet, we know you are still in control of all. Help them to know and feel your favor upon them."

Ya'akov directed them to the northern corner of the outer court where their portion of the sacrifice would be cooked and served to them.

Jeremiah exited the Inner Eastern Gate and the others followed him into the northwestern corner of the temple where one of four kitchens was located. By the time they arrived, the meat had been boiled and was ready for consumption. Liam carried it, along with additional trimmings, into one of the nearby chambers located on the outer temple wall.

They divided the meal among them. Jeremiah prayed.

"Our King and Messiah, we partake of this meal knowing you are in our midst. By eating this part of the sacrifice, we symbolize we continue to incorporate you and all you represent into our lives. Please fill us with your peace as we know our future is secure in you. Although our family dynamic will change, we know you never change, and we can rest in the surety of that. Help our lives to continually give you glory."

Me'ira was delighted to have this time with her father, mother, and oldest brother. As they ate, they told stories of past experiences, laughed at many of them, and shared of future desires. Me'ira knew she would treasure this time with her family for the rest of her life.

When the meal ended, Me'ira hugged and kissed each of them. Her eyes began to get watery. "Thank you all so much for this. I couldn't imagine a better memory to have as I begin a new life." She smiled. "I know the relationship with each other will change, but my love for you never will."

Kyla hugged her again. "We feel the same way, Me'ira."

They exited the North Gate, walked back to the King's Palace, and took the teleporter back to their own palace.

The next several hours were spent in the living area again telling stories—sometimes they cried, but mostly there was laughter as they reminisced. Me'ira felt thankful for this time to remind her of all the experiences she had with her family.

After a time, Liam said he had to leave but would come back in the morning to see Me'ira off. She walked with Liam back to the teleporter.

"Liam, I've really enjoyed our time together over the last couple of months. I will always cherish it."

He gave her another big hug. "Me too, sis. I'll see you tomorrow, OK?"

She smiled and nodded.

He entered the teleporter and soon disappeared. Me'ira wiped tears from her cheeks and went back inside the palace.

She didn't sleep well that night. She couldn't help but feel a small amount of regret. Still, a great deal of excitement overlaid that regret, and this left her in a series of mood swings as she lay there waiting for morning. It had been a couple of weeks since she had seen Galen in person, even though they had talked by hologram.

Knowing she would see him in the morning heightened her anxiety.

In the morning, Me'ira was surprised to see Liam waiting for her at the dining table.

"Hello, sleepyhead."

Me'ira smiled. "You're just early."

Liam laughed. "So, are you ready for your new adventure?"

Me'ira took a deep breath. "I think I am. I have a tinge of regret, but I'm really excited at the same time."

After a few bites, Me'ira pushed her plate away.

"Done?"

She nodded. "I think I'm too anxious to eat."

"OK. All set?"

She could feel her heart racing. She took another deep breath and followed Liam into the living area.

There, seated with her parents, were Galen and Shepherds Franklin and Hayden.

Galen's gaze locked with hers as she entered. He gave a broad smile, which she returned. Just seeing him helped her pulse calm. He stood and gave her a hug. His touch was what she missed most these last few weeks. All her anxiety immediately quelled. She knew she was doing the right thing.

She shook the hands of both Shepherds. "So, what's the next step?"

Shepherd Hayden motioned for everyone to sit. "Let's go over a few things before we embark on your new life."

Me'ira sat next to Galen. They held hands; neither of them had to worry about protocol any longer. She looked at Shepherd Hayden with anticipation.

He first turned to Galen. "Galen, your parents have found a place for an antique shop you can run. There are living quarters above the shop, so that should be very convenient for you. It isn't large, but it is a great place for a couple starting out."

He then looked at Me'ira. "We first need to talk about your name. Unfortunately, you will need to change it."

She nodded. "Actually, Mom and I talked about this yesterday. What about May Irena?"

Hayden smiled. "I think that is perfect." He looked at Galen. "What do you think? You're the one who will be saying it the most."

Galen chuckled and focused on Me'ira. "I like it. I think May is a beautiful name."

Me'ira smiled and squeezed his hand.

Hayden shifted in his seat. "Now. About the wedding."

Me'ira saw her mom get up and leave the room. She glanced at her father. "Is she OK?"

He nodded and smiled. "She'll be back."

Me'ira turned and focused again on Shepherd Hayden.

"Your wedding will be a week from today," Hayden said.

Me'ira's eyes popped wide. "Wow. So soon?"

Hayden nodded. "We want you to integrate as fast as possible. Me'ira, you will stay in a hotel room until the wedding. The Shafir family will stay in another room at the hotel and help you get the business and living quarters set up."

"You will be doing the ceremony, right?" Me'ira asked.

Hayden smiled at Me'ira and nodded. "I will. There is a lovely park that overlooks the ocean. Liam felt you would like that, so we have secured that for your wedding."

Me'ira looked at Liam, her eyes moistening, and mouthed, "Thank you."

Liam smiled back.

Kyla returned holding a large box. "And since I can't be there for you," she said, "this is my donation."

Me'ira gave her an inquisitive look. Tear stains on her mother's cheeks revealed she had been crying again while she had been alone. Me'ira's heart went out to her mom, but she decided not to address it or they would both be crying uncontrollably. Instead, she smiled. "Do I get to open it now?"

Kyla nodded. "Open it, but best to keep it in the box for now."

After Me'ira opened the box, she put her hand over her mouth, her eyes got even more wet, and she couldn't hold back the tears. "Mom, it's beautiful." She ran her hand over the fabric of a gorgeous wedding dress. Although simple in design, it had sequins and beading placed in strategic places. She knew it was going to look stunning.

She gave the box to Galen, who sealed it up as she stood and gave her mother a hug.

"Mom, that is the sweetest thing. It's so beautiful. Thank you."

"You're welcome, Me'ira . . . May Irena."

Me'ira smiled and kissed her mom on her cheek.

Shepherd Hayden stood. "OK, everyone. The time has come."

As they stood, Me'ira saw Lydia in the doorway. She looked at Shepherd Hayden. "Could I have just one more minute?"

He nodded.

Me'ira walked over to Lydia. As she got closer, she could see Lydia's cheeks too were tear-stained, her eyes red from crying, and they were now watering again.

Me'ira gave her a hug and Lydia began openly weeping.

"Oh, Me'ira. What on earth will I ever do without you?" Lydia asked. "You have always been in my life. Can't . . . can't I go with you?"

Me'ira rubbed Lydia's upper arm lovingly. "Lydia, you have always been like a sister to me. Thank you for your friendship. But, as I have to say goodbye to Mom and Dad, I have to say the same to you."

"I'm going to miss you so much, Me'ira."

Me'ira's eyes were tearful again. "Same here." She smiled,

or tried to, but her emotions were beginning to overwhelm her. "I know Mom will have good things for you to help her with. You won't have to follow me around and make me follow protocol anymore."

Lydia nodded and released a small chuckle between sniffles. "I didn't mind." She shook her head slightly, her voice now catching in her throat. "Not really."

Me'ira opened her arms. Lydia fell into them for a final hug. No additional words were spoken. Me'ira locked gazes with Lydia and smiled. Lydia gave a quick nod.

Me'ira turned, wiped tears from her eyes, and went back to the others. They all walked to the teleporter.

Shepherd Franklin took out an electronic tablet and held it up. "Me'ira, I think I know the answer, but I have to ask one more time. Once you teleport from here, you will not be able to teleport back again. You will no longer be Me'ira, but you will be May Irena. You no longer will have a royal birthright. Is that your wish?"

Me'ira nodded. "Yes, Shepherd Franklin. That is what I choose."

He handed her a stylus. "OK. Please sign your new name on this line."

She wrote *May Irena* on the line and handed the stylus and tablet back to Franklin.

He nodded and pressed a confirm button with the stylus. "It is done. It is now public record. As soon as you teleport from here, this teleporter will be locked out from your access."

Me'ira gave a slight nod with a half smile. "I guess that's it then."

Shepherd Franklin leaned in and gave her a kiss on her cheek. "I wish you much happiness, May Irena."

"Thank you, Shepherd Franklin, for . . . everything."

Liam came up and gave her one final large hug. There were handshakes, hugs, and kisses all around.

When she came to her mother, more tears came. "Oh, Me'ira, I don't want to let you go." She drew a sharp, staccato breath. "I . . . I don't know if I can." She pulled Me'ira to her again.

Me'ira hugged back. This was even harder than she anticipated. She pulled away from the hug and looked at her mom. "I know you would do the same for Dad if the situation was reversed."

Kyla nodded as her tears continued. "I would. I just never thought you would have to."

"I love you, Mom."

"You have my love forever."

Me'ira gave a slight smile and nodded. "I know." She turned to her father.

Jeremiah wrapped his arms around her. "I will always love you. Your position changes, our interaction changes, but not my love. Always remember that."

Me'ira nodded and tried to smile, but tears ran down her cheeks and she kept wiping them away. He wiped away a tear and kissed her cheek.

Kyla wrapped her arms around both Me'ira and Jeremiah. "I know you will be radiant in your dress. I can't be there, but Shepherd Hayden can get pictures to me. OK?"

Me'ira nodded. She choked up and had a hard time speaking. She managed to squeeze out, "I will, Mom . . . Your Highness."

Kyla smiled as she once again wiped tears from her own eyes.

Me'ira turned, and Liam's strong arms embraced her again. "Bye, sis. I will always love and respect you. I wish you and

Galen much happiness." He kissed her on her forehead.

"Thank you, Liam. Tell everyone . . . tell everyone . . . " She couldn't seem to formulate the words she wanted, so she just gave a weak smile. "You know what to tell them."

"I will. I'll be sure they all understand."

She nodded. More tears fell. As she turned, Galen took her hand and gave a slight squeeze. She smiled at him and took a deep breath as she wiped away still more tears.

Galen stepped onto the teleporter still holding her hand and holding the box with her dress in his other arm. He pressed the Engage button. Her vision of her family blurred . . .

The thought hit her hard. They were no longer her family . . .

Once at the King's palace, they stepped aside and waited for Shepherd Hayden. Galen turned to her and kissed her on her cheek. "Me'ira, I will never let you regret this sacrifice you made for me."

She smiled and put her hand to his cheek. "It's never a sacrifice when done out of love."

He took her hand and kissed it.

A few minutes later, Shepherd Hayden appeared next to the teleporter. He smiled. "Ready to head home?"

Me'ira took another short breath and nodded. It was done. There was no going back. Her life with Galen would now begin.

As they headed for the long-range teleporter, Me'ira thought about Shepherd Hayden's last remark. *Home.* Me'ira realized her definition of home would now be different for the rest of her life.

CHAPTER 35

When Me'ira's sight came back into focus, she stepped off the teleporter pad in Vancouver. Her surroundings had changed drastically. A breeze blew in from the bay. It seemed the temperature here would be a few degrees cooler than in Jerusalem. Me'ira recalled pre-Refreshing stories her grandfather told of how temperatures across the earth varied widely, but with the King's return came uniform temperatures so crops could grow year-round on all continents. It was hard to imagine life during pre-Refreshing times. As she panned the scenery, she saw fishing boats anchored in the harbor as well as several sailboats with colorful sails gliding across the water. She took a deep breath. This was her new home.

Shepherd Hayden walked with them across town and down a street with several shops. He stopped in front of one with a large glass storefront.

"This is it," Hayden said.

Galen's eyes widened. "Oh, this will be great. We'll be able to display items for customers to browse even before they come in."

Me'ira peered in. "Galen, I see your mom and Caleb inside."

"You two go in," Hayden said. "I'll leave you now and check in later."

Both shook Shepherd Hayden's hand. Me'ira turned her handshake into a hug. Hayden smiled. As Hayden turned to leave, Galen and Me'ira entered the store.

Lois saw them first. "Galen! May! You're here." She came over and gave them a hug.

Caleb also hurried over.

"Where's Dad?" Galen asked.

Caleb released his hug. "Oh, he's upstairs with Miriam getting things ready there."

Galen's eyes widened. "Miriam? She's here?"

May looked from Galen to Caleb. "Who's Miriam?"

Galen smiled. "She was my nanny for many years."

"Why is she here?"

Lois came over. "May, you have the final answer, but I asked her, and she has agreed to be your housekeeper. She can also be your nanny . . . " She gave May a couple of eyebrow raises. "When the time is right."

May blushed slightly. "Oh, well, that's nice of you. Uh, but where would she stay?" May had not seen the living quarters upstairs yet, but she knew they weren't large. She wanted time alone with Galen and not have another person underfoot.

Lois rubbed May's upper arm. "Don't worry, honey. There's a building out back. Noah has prepared it for Miriam to stay there. Feel free to set up your own schedule with her."

Caleb came over and gave May a dust cloth. "Ready to get your hands dirty?"

May smiled. She had never really done manual work but was determined to do her part. After all, this would now be her and Galen's business, and she wanted the shop to look excellent as much as he did.

She spent the rest of her day dusting, cleaning windows,

sweeping, and even doing a little painting.

Galen came over, looked at her, and giggled.

"What are you laughing at?" she asked.

He took a cloth and wiped a spot of paint off her nose. "You only need to paint the shop. You don't have to match."

"Hey." She gave him a nudge with her hip since her hands were full.

He laughed and blew her a kiss. "I'll check back with you soon. Dad needs my help upstairs."

"OK." She pointed her paintbrush at him. "Then it's my turn to critique *your* work."

He chuckled. "I guess turnabout is only fair."

As May went back to painting, she had a sense of pride in herself. Never, prior to the last few weeks, would she have dreamed of doing anything like this. Yet she felt content in this work. When finished, she washed up and walked around to the back of the building. There, stairs led to living quarters upstairs. After she climbed to the top of the stairs, she stopped and thought: *Is this a landing or is it considered a porch?* Either way, the view from this height nearly took her breath away. She could see the bay through the trees from where she stood. The green went all the way to the water's edge and then solid blue stretched out from there. Sailboats were visible and added color to the scene before her. She hoped a window inside would allow her to have this same view.

She also noticed Miriam's place behind theirs. It looked quaint with its walls painted pastel green and outlined in tan trim with the windows displaying laced curtains. The building looked to have a dark green tin-style roof.

She opened the door to her place and stepped into a living room combined with an open kitchen area. While not large, it appeared to have plenty of room for the two of them. Off the living room ran a small hallway that led to the master bedroom. It looked to be almost as large as the living area. Another door off the hallway opened to a smaller bedroom.

On the kitchen counter were many samples of paint and wallpaper swatches. She looked at them for a few minutes, then wondered where everyone had gone. Noticing a door in the corner of the living room, she walked through onto a large-sized deck. It had the same spectacular view she had seen earlier, but an even better, unobstructed one.

Galen came around the corner. He smiled. "Just in time."

"In time for what?"

"Come see."

He led her around the corner. May gasped. This part of the deck attached to the master bedroom and had been transformed into a garden reminiscent of the one she loved at the palace, just much smaller. Her eyes moistened and her hand went to her mouth.

"Oh, Galen, it's beautiful." She gave him a hug. "This is what you've been doing all this time?"

He nodded. "I wanted a place for you to relax, so I thought it important to start here."

"I love it." She turned to the others who were there. "Thank you all so much."

Galen waved someone over. The woman had long flowing black hair and dark eyes. She was definitely much older than she and Galen, but May thought her lovely.

"May, this is Miriam," Galen said.

Miriam smiled. "I am so pleased to meet you, May. Galen told me you were lovely, but he didn't do you justice."

May felt heat rush to her cheeks. "Thank you. I can say the same for you."

"Well, I look forward to getting to know you. I'm here for

whatever you need me to do."

May smiled. "Thanks. It looks like you've done a lot already."

Miriam laughed. "Oh, we're just getting started." She gestured toward the main house. "Did you see all the swatches on the counter?"

May nodded. "I did. Some are quite lovely."

"Why don't you tell me what you like so we can get started on the inside tomorrow?"

May followed Miriam back into the house and viewed the samples with her. Miriam took careful notes on what colors and patterns May chose for each room. When Noah came through the room, Miriam handed the plan to him.

He looked at the list and then back to the two of them. "Well, it looks like you have the rest of my afternoon planned for me."

Miriam laughed. "Yes, and the rest of the week as well."

Noah smiled. "Well, I guess I'd better get started then." As he left to get the materials, he called back, "No one will have an excuse for not being here bright and early tomorrow."

Miriam laughed and turned to May. "I know you were going to sleep at the hotel, but why don't you sleep at my place instead? That will give us a chance to get to know each other better. What do you say?"

May smiled. "Sure. I think that's a great idea." It seemed as though Miriam would be around a long time, so the earlier they could bond and understand each other, the better.

Once Noah returned and unloaded the supplies, they all headed to dinner together. Shepherd Hayden met them at a local restaurant. This time allowed May to get to know each member of Galen's family better. By the end of the evening, she felt more relaxed around them. They ended up back on her garden deck for tea.

After a long day of chores, May knew she would be sore tomorrow since she had never done so much manual work in her life. Yet she knew she chose this life, and she had no regrets. Everyone called it an early night as they each needed an early start to the next day, and they had a lot to accomplish.

Everyone went back to the hotel except for Miriam and May; they stayed up for another hour talking and getting to know each other. Miriam gave her a history on Galen, telling stories of his early life and what he was like as a child and teenager.

She was going to like Miriam after all, she was sure. Miriam seemed warm, witty, and knowledgeable about so many things. Not having grown up with domestic knowledge, May realized Miriam would be a lifesaver.

May smiled to herself. That was likely what Lois knew but had been too gracious to make her feel bad about. The more she learned of this family, the more she was growing to love them. She hoped they felt the same about her—and would visit often.

CHAPTER 36

The week went by quickly. With a day to spare, the upstairs living area was completed. May looked around. While not palatial, it had a homey feel, and this was quite all right with her. The paint, wallpaper, and furnishings all matched and contrasted well. She couldn't have been happier with how everything turned out. It now had a light and airy feel, and a large part of that was contributed by the wraparound deck that gave a feeling of so much extra room. She couldn't wait for her and Galen to begin their life together.

The downstairs shop was also clean, but empty. They would have plenty of time to work on that after the wedding. More importantly, they now had a place to live while they worked on their business. May felt fortunate. It definitely wasn't regal, but everything was new and fresh—a great way to start out.

She had concentrated these last few days on getting the house prepared but hadn't focused on their actual wedding. Now the realization that her wedding would occur the next afternoon hit her like a tsunami. She felt so behind—and overwhelmed.

Sleep did not come easy that night. The next morning brought panic; May felt she didn't have enough time to prepare and get herself and everything else ready for the wedding. Although the day was still early, she found Miriam up and breakfast prepared.

"Miriam, I can't believe how much energy you have," May said as she entered the kitchen. "There is no way I can keep up with you."

Miriam laughed. "Don't even try, May. Lois used to tell me the same thing. I guess that's just my makeup. I have to be doing something at all times."

May ate her eggs and toast quickly.

"Whoa! Slow down, young lady. What's the rush?"

"Oh, there is so much to get done today. The wedding's this afternoon!"

Miriam waved her hand. "Don't worry. It's all under control. All the food is catered. Caleb has scheduled a string quartet. Shepherd Hayden has the locale planned out. So you can actually concentrate on you."

"Really?"

"I'm going to give you as much of a stress-free day as possible."

Miriam took May for a facial, a body scrub, and had her nails and hair done. She then took her back to her place and helped her get into her dress.

"Oh, May, you look absolutely gorgeous. Galen will literally faint."

May laughed. "Well, I hope not. That would complicate things."

Miriam giggled. "Yes, I guess it would."

May fluffed her ringlets and turned in front of the mirror. Seeing herself in the dress made her eyes get teary. If only her mother could see her. She quickly reminded herself her mom would get to see pictures.

Miriam snapped her fingers. "Step out of that melancholy moment, May. You need to look fresh and vibrant for Galen."

May laughed. "You're right, Miriam. This is our day. I need to stay in the moment."

"Absolutely."

Miriam looked out the window and then turned back to May. "Now, Galen has done something old school here, so just go with it. There is a back trail that goes down to the bay where the wedding will be held."

May scrunched her brow. "OK. But I'm not following."

"You will. Go on outside."

When she stepped outside, she stopped, stunned. There, in front of her, stood an all-white open carriage pulled by two white horses. The color inside the carriage and where the driver sat looked a dark maroon.

She looked back at Miriam, who had followed her outside. "It's . . . it's beautiful," May gasped.

She looked up and noticed Caleb was the driver! He was dressed in a white tuxedo and even wore the traditional coach-man hat, white in this case to match his tuxedo. She noticed several sprigs of wildflowers had been placed in the hatband adding a shot of brilliant color. He grinned and hopped down. "Your carriage awaits, My Lady."

"Caleb, this is beautiful—and overwhelming."

He took her hand and helped her into the carriage. Miriam helped reposition her dress.

"Are you coming, Miriam?"

"I'll be there, but this is your moment," Miriam answered.

The horses led the carriage down the trail. May sat back and took a deep breath, trying to relax and take it all in. As they got near the bay, the number of people who had gathered for her wedding surprised her. Caleb pulled up under a large tree, tied off the horses, and then came around to help her down. Somehow Miriam, already present, was repositioning her dress again.

May gave her a curious look. Miriam smiled. "Horses are elegant, but an AGA is faster."

May laughed. "Knowing you, you outran the horses yourself."

Miriam touched her index finger to her lips and winked. "Shh. Don't give away my secret."

May laughed even more. As this would not be a Jewish-style wedding, she wasn't exactly sure of the next step. When she turned to ask Caleb what she should do next, she gasped.

There stood *Liam* with his hand out to her.

"Need someone to escort you down the aisle?"

"Liam, what . . . what are you doing here? How are you allowed to be here?" Her eyes instantly got teary. She fanned them to try and calm herself.

"Oh now, don't shed any tears," he said. "You have to look beautiful for Galen."

She slapped his arm playfully. "Well, you shouldn't surprise me like that."

Liam laughed. "It's good to see you, sis. My new job allows me to visit other places, so I chose to visit here first."

She smiled. "I'm so glad you did." She gave him a hug but was careful not to crush her dress.

"And I'm glad you chose white tuxedos. I got a chance to recycle."

She laughed. "Oh, anything for you."

He smiled back and held out his arm. "Are you ready?"

She took a deep breath and nodded.

Miriam handed her a bouquet of colorful wildflowers

pulled together with white lace. "This will give you something to do with your hands," she said.

May kissed Miriam on her cheek. "Thanks, Miriam. Thank you for everything."

Miriam smiled and directed her forward.

The quartet began to play more loudly. Everyone stood. Liam walked her slowly down the aisle between rows of chairs. Everyone smiled at May as she glanced from one side of the aisle to the other, smiling back—and yet having no idea who these people were.

Looking forward, there stood Galen at the end of the aisle, looking so handsome in his white tuxedo—and those dimples. She could never resist those dimples. She was glad she would finally not have to.

Liam escorted her next to Galen. There was no chuppah, but there was a variety of colorful wildflowers on both sides of Shepherd Hayden arranged in what looked like large strawberry pots that had been painted white. She had never seen anything like it, but thought they looked stunning and matched her bouquet perfectly.

The ceremony was held on a large overlook. Behind Hayden was blue water. There were some whitecaps and several colorful sailboats traveling behind him at the time. They looked like extensions of the wildflowers in the foreground. She thought it all so beautiful. This area next to the bay was naturally beautiful and picturesque. It was a wonderful spot for her wedding.

May couldn't remember everything that took place. It all seemed so surreal. Yet she knew she had repeated the words to Galen asked of her by Shepherd Hayden. Galen slipped a wedding band on her finger and they kissed. Then she remembered Shepherd Hayden saying, "I present to you Mr. and Mrs. Galen Shafir."

Everyone cheered. As they walked back down the aisle, people showered them with bubbles. May had never experienced this, but found it to give an ethereal feel to the ceremony. Galen walked her to the other side of the string quartet where a large paved area connected with another overlook.

Galen took her hand and placed his other behind her lower back. They danced as the others watched. The enjoyment of just being in his arms made her content.

"Galen, you have outdone yourself. Thank you for all of this."

He smiled and displayed those dimples again. "You deserve it, May Irena. No matter what, you are my princess, and I wanted you to feel like one."

She smiled and put her head on his chest. "I do, Galen. I do."

Once the song ended, others joined them on the dance floor. Liam came over and Galen turned her over to him. "I'm going to mingle," Galen told his bride.

"I'll bring her to you when I'm done," Liam said.

Galen smiled and stepped off the dance floor.

"Does anyone know you came?" May asked as they began a graceful waltz.

Liam's eyebrows raised. "You think I'm here to see you?" He shook his head. "Oh, no. I'm here on official business. I came to meet with Shepherd Hayden. I heard he was officiating a wedding, so I came to see what a non-Jewish wedding is like." He looked into her eyes, winked, and smiled. "This, My Lady, is just research."

She chuckled. "Well, I'm glad I could help you out. How are you enjoying your experience of a local wedding?"

"Very much, actually. Surprising, really."

"Oh. How so?"

Through a mischievous smile Liam replied, "To find how someone so plain could capture someone so handsome."

She gave a mock look of shock. "I've never heard of anyone needing glasses, but I guess there is a first time for everything."

He laughed. "Sis, I'm going to miss your banter."

"As am I."

"In all honesty, you look absolutely beautiful. As beautiful as any princess."

Her eyes started to tear up again. "Thank you, Liam. That means a lot to me." She gave a smirk. "Especially from someone needing glasses."

Liam threw his head back in laughter. "Oh, sis. You are precious." He kissed her forehead and had her twirl one final time.

Once the song was over, Liam gave her a kiss on her cheek. "Well, sis. I do have to go. I am so glad I got a chance to see you so radiant and beautiful as you begin your life with Galen." He held out his arm and she took it. "I'll deliver you to your husband and I'll be off."

Galen was talking to several people near the food table. Liam took her over, gave her one last kiss, and left her with Galen. He gave Galen a brief hug and then left.

Galen took May's hand and introduced her to several people. She kept looking back, watching Liam weave through the crowd. He glanced back once. Their eyes met. He winked once more, turned, and disappeared; her view of him became blocked by a group of people in the distance. Would she see him again? That tinge of regret came back. But when she looked back at Galen, it vanished in an instant.

She couldn't believe how many people he introduced her to.

No way she could ever remember that many names. She found Galen amazing and his actions drew her to him even more. He didn't know most of these people either! But he looked at ease with them, and he even took the opportunities to talk up his business. Awe of her husband filled May as Galen did all this without coming across as self-serving but actually making people feel he was doing them a service by mentioning the business.

For the next several hours they dined, talked, and danced until after the sun set. By the time they left, everyone treated them like they had known them for years. Most of the crowd gathered around and saw them off as Galen helped May into the carriage. He climbed in the other side and Caleb hoisted himself into the coachman seat.

Everyone waved until they were well down the trail; Caleb had the horses take them back to their house. Galen wrapped his arm around her, and she put her head on his chest. She thought back to the morning, when she had felt so stressed. Now, feeling so relaxed, she couldn't imagine how she could be more content.

Caleb had the horses stop next to the house. Galen helped her down and Caleb drove on. Galen helped her up the stairs and then carried her across the threshold into their new home. He set her down and leaned in. They kissed, and she had the same tingling sensation she did the first time they kissed. This time, however, he prolonged the kiss and she went a little weak. She found he had stronger arms than she realized.

Once he released the kiss, she turned and saw something on the kitchen counter.

"Oh, look, more goodies."

She unwrapped a beautifully decorated basket containing

sparkling cider, nuts, and chocolate. She got some glasses while Galen opened the bottle and brought the treats to the sofa.

They spent time talking and snuggling. He would feed her a bite and she would do the same for him.

"You're quite the schmoozer," May said.

Galen laughed. "What do you mean by that?"

"I mean, I was very impressed how comfortable you were with people you didn't even know. That's quite a skill."

He shrugged. "I guess I've been able to do that ever since I can remember. I never knew it to be a skill. It's just something I do." He smiled. "It always came in handy with customers as I tried to make them feel comfortable and willing to open up to me as to what they were really looking for."

She gave him a wry smile. "So, is that how you captured me in your web? You schmoozed me with your charms?"

He wrapped his arms around her. "Well, it seems it worked, didn't it?"

"Yes, I guess it did. Now what are you going to do about it?"

His eyes darted between hers. He leaned in. "How's this for a start?"

His lips touched hers, and he leaned farther in, turning it into an extremely passionate kiss.

"Well, that was nice for starters," she said.

He smiled. "Well, let's see what else I can come up with."

He stood, scooped her up in his arms, and carried her toward the bedroom.

"I have all night to help you know you made the right decision," he said.

"Well, I'm hard to convince, you know."

"Oh well. I'm a good schmoozer. Or so I'm told."

She laughed as he closed the bedroom door with his foot.

CHAPTER 37

Over the next several months, May helped Galen get the shop in order. She knew she would enjoy being Galen's wife, but never knew it would be this special. He really did live up to his promise of making her feel like a princess. He didn't necessarily dote on her but did small things that showed his love and devotion. She would never have the lifestyle of Liam and Nyssa, but that didn't matter to her. She felt content. Happy. Special. She did her best to make Galen feel the same. Plus, her interest in antiques grew stronger each day, which she knew made Galen excited and happy. They were becoming united in interests and what made the other tick, so to speak. Plus, with Galen's ease of communication with anyone he met, they both became acquainted with many of their neighbors in short order. Everyone treated her as one of them. She liked that.

Me'ira manned the store while Galen did a good deal of traveling between Israel, Australia, and home to get unique artifacts that others would find attractive. In very little time they developed quite a diverse clientele. They also did a lot of business with various museums by utilizing the universal nebula drive for electronic ordering.

One particular morning, May came in the back entrance

bearing two cups of tea. Galen looked up from unpacking a crate and smiled.

"You read my mind."

May smiled and nodded toward the crate. "Is that from your folks?"

Galen nodded. "Yeah, and some of these are fascinating." He handed her some papers. "Here is some information about them. They're sending more information through the nebula drive."

She scanned the list of items as she sipped her tea. Her eyebrows went up. "It says there's a helmet here. They think Egyptian."

Galen looked up with furrowed brow. "Egyptian? I don't think Egyptians wore helmets." He cocked his head. "Maybe from a mercenary army?"

"Maybe the Cairo museum would authenticate it."

Galen stood. "Maybe. Good thinking. I'll take it there this morning. You think you'll be OK to run the store until I get back this afternoon?"

May nodded. "I think so."

He found the item. "I'll go change and head out. The faster I leave, the faster I can get back."

She gave him a prolonged kiss. "Just remember that. And hurry back."

Galen smiled and gave an enthusiastic "Yes, ma'am."

May finished her tea as she removed the remainder of the items from the crate and placed them on the counter. She found a cloth and started to clean them to be ready for presentation.

She heard the door open and looked up to see a woman enter.

"Good morning. May I help you with anything?"

The woman looked her way and smiled. "I thought I would just look around if that's OK?"

"Certainly. Just let me know if you need any help."

The woman scanned the aisles and occasionally picked up an item, looked at it, and returned it to its place. She seemed to take her time as she browsed.

May thought it a little odd that the woman never took off her sunglasses even though she was inside and didn't need them. She also wore a colorful scarf over her head which she didn't remove. The only identifying aspect of her face was a small tuft of auburn-colored hair in the front of the scarf.

When the woman came near her at the back counter, May said, "I love your scarf."

The woman smiled. "Thank you. It's so silky soft I just love wearing it."

May smiled. Still, it seemed a little rude to take off neither the glasses nor the scarf when talking to someone inside. "The floral print is quite beautiful. I can tell you like beautiful things."

The woman nodded. "That's why I stopped by. You have your shop so elegantly displayed, and the pieces you have . . . they are lovely."

"Thank you. Did you find anything you like?"

"Oh, quite the opposite."

May's eyes widened. "Oh, how so?"

The woman laughed lightly. "Sorry. I didn't mean it to sound that way." She glanced around. "Actually, I love everything you have in your shop." She turned back and sat a large purse on the counter. "I was looking around to see how knowledgeable you would be about dating objects." She smiled. "I can see by the pieces here you know what you're doing."

May chuckled. "Well, we think we do. Actually, my husband, Galen, is much more qualified than I."

"Well, I have something I think is pre-Refreshing, but I'm not sure how old. I was wondering if you could date it for me."

May gave a slight shrug. "Maybe. What do you have?"

The woman pulled a vase from her purse. It had a beautiful blue-green iridescent hue to it with a design that looked to be peacock feathers. The vase was larger at the top than at the bottom. The iridescent hue turned more of a deep cobalt blue color as it approached the bottom of the vase.

"Your vase is very beautiful." May turned the vase over to look at the bottom to see if it had an identifying mark. She ran her finger over the scarred bottom. "I do see a monogram, but it's hard to see clearly."

"Yes, I've noticed that as well. It looks to be a 'T.'"

May nodded. "And it seems to be superimposed with an ampersand." She brought it closer to her eyes. "There are letters on either side, but they're very hard to make out. Maybe a C or an O?"

The woman nodded. "Is that significant?"

"Could be." May looked back at the woman. "My husband may know more."

"Is he here?"

May shook her head. "Unfortunately, no. But he will be back later today."

"I see." The woman drummed her fingers on the counter. For some reason her tone sounded like she was happy about that simple fact—even though her mannerisms seemed irritated.

"Would you be able to bring the vase back later today or tomorrow?" May asked.

For some reason the woman looked at her T-band and then

shook her head. "I have to leave this afternoon." She perked up. "I know. I'll just leave it with you. Your husband can assess it. I'll stop by the next time I'm in the area and pick it back up with the results of his assessment. Would that be OK?"

May shrugged. "Well, I suppose." She picked the vase up again. "It's so beautiful, though. Don't you want to keep it and bring it back with you later?"

The woman held up her hands. "No, no. I really want your husband to see it. So, I don't mind waiting a while to get the results."

"Should I call you when he has it evaluated? If you leave your number—"

The woman held up her hand and smiled. "No. No need. I'm sure I'll see you around."

May chuckled and gave a small shrug. "OK. If that's what you want." She pointed at the window. "I may put it on display to be sure it doesn't get sold accidently."

The woman smiled. "That's a wonderful idea. That way others will get to enjoy it as well."

"You have a great attitude about such a beautiful piece." May tapped the counter. "So, what else can I do for you today?"

"Oh, you've been most helpful, believe me. Just show it to your husband, and I'll see you soon." She stuck out her hand. "I'm Isabelle, by the way."

May nodded and shook her hand. "Very nice to meet you. I'll be sure Galen sees it when he gets back."

The woman turned and left the shop.

May had never seen anyone act so strangely. The woman seemed so fixated on Galen seeing and evaluating the vase, yet she acted unconcerned about getting the results quickly. Then there was the way her face was covered. May shook her head and shrugged as she set the vase on the counter close to the wall so Galen would be sure to see it.

As the day went on, May forgot about her strange morning. She completed the unpacking and cleaning she had started before the unusual woman entered her shop. Several other customers came in. Most browsed and asked a few questions, but two made selections. In between customers, May packed up and shipped items other customers had ordered over the nebula drive. All in all, she felt this had been a good day.

As she packed up the last order of the day, she heard what she thought was another customer entering the shop just before the store's closing.

"One moment, and I'll be right with you."

"Well, I sure hope so."

May stood quickly and turned around at the familiar voice. She gave Galen a huge smile. He came over and gave her a hug and a lingering kiss. He hugged her again.

"I missed—"

May giggled. "Yes? Your next word should be 'you.'"

"Where . . . where did you get that?"

"What?" May turned and saw what had captured Galen's attention: the vase the woman had brought in.

"Oh, that. Well, that is your project to find out. If it's pre-Refreshing, and who made it."

Galen's face went pale. "Oh, it's definitely pre-Refreshing. And it was made by Tiffany and Company."

May looked from Galen to the vase. "How do you know that without even looking at it?" She saw him licking his lips as if his mouth had gone dry. She didn't like how pale he looked. "Galen, is something wrong?"

He sat on a nearby stool and ran his fingers through his

hair. He glanced at May. "You remember when you asked me how I met you, and I told you a woman gave me a ship cruise ticket to pay for a vase?"

May nodded.

Galen pointed at the vase. "*That's* the vase."

May's mouth dropped open. "What did the woman look like?"

Galen shrugged. "Hard to say. She wore sunglasses and a scarf over her head. I didn't get a good look at her."

May put her hand on his arm. "Galen, the woman today was dressed the same way." She ran her hand over her mouth. "I thought it odd she would wear those glasses while inside. Now I know why." She paused. "She said her name was Isabelle. I . . . I don't know why I didn't make the connection earlier."

Galen took her hand. "What else did she say? Did she give a last name?"

May shook her head. "No. She just wanted you to see the vase and said she would come back at a later date to hear what you discovered about it." May ran her fingers through Galen's hair. "But she already knew you knew everything about the vase. What do you think she wanted?"

Galen looked at May. "I think she just wanted to leave us a message."

May scrunched her brow. "What kind of message?"

Galen swallowed. "She wants us to know they're watching us."

CHAPTER 38

For many weeks May looked over her shoulder whenever she was out and about to see if she could spot the woman who came to their shop. Over time she became more relaxed and stopped thinking about her. Every so often, she would see the vase in the display window and think about how she and Galen might be under surveillance. Yet the woman never returned—at least as far as she knew.

One evening as she and Galen walked home from a night out, May was the first to notice someone sitting at the door to their shop. She put her arm out to stop Galen.

He glanced at her. "What's wrong?"

She nodded forward. "Someone's at the shop."

Galen turned to look. "Really? At this hour?"

"You . . . you don't think it's that woman again, do you?"

Galen gave her a shocked look. "I sure hope not. But there's only one way to find out."

May reached for his hand and he took hers and squeezed lightly.

As they got closer, the woman stood and walked toward them. That silhouette. That walk. *I know that walk.* May gave a sigh of relief.

It wasn't the mysterious woman after all.

May quickened her step. "Lydia?"

As the distance between them decreased, May saw a huge grin spread across Lydia's face. They embraced.

Lydia hugged her as tightly as she could. "I have missed you so much, Me'ira."

"Same here."

"Hi, Lydia. Welcome to Vancouver."

Lydia smiled. "Hi, Galen." She gave him a hug. "It's good to see you too."

"What brings you here?" May asked, still stunned.

"Oh, I was given the day off and just wanted to visit." She looked between the two of them. "I hope that's OK."

Galen smiled. "Absolutely. May, I'll go upstairs and prepare some tea for you two." He gave May a kiss and headed around the side of the building.

"Thanks, hon."

May turned to Lydia. "Did you want to go upstairs or see the shop first?"

"Oh, I'd love to see the shop." She looked at May. "Me'ira . . . " She shook her head. "I mean, May." She smiled weakly. "It's hard to picture you running a shop."

May laughed. "I know. Who would have ever thought?"

May walked Lydia to the shop door. As she opened the door, the lights came on. As they stepped inside, Lydia looked around, turning several times to take it all in. "Wow, May. This is very classy."

May laughed. "And you expected?"

Lydia shook her head. "Sorry. I went into some of the other shops waiting for you to come home. They were not nearly as nice as this."

"Thanks."

Lydia walked down one of the aisles looking at the items.

She paused by a couple of artifacts and looked at the small monitor next to each one. Looking from a monitor to May, she said, "May, this is really awesome." Glancing back at the monitor, she pointed at it. "You have a map of where the artifact was found and a lot of information about it. That makes me want to know more about it."

"That's the plan." May smiled. "Galen knows everything about everything, but he's not always here. I suggested we do this so the customer can explore and have a better understanding of the artifact. Then I can follow on my tablet and see what interests them. Asking additional questions often results in them buying more than one item because I'm able to make a connection between artifacts for them."

Lydia laughed.

May furrowed her brow. "What's funny about that?"

Lydia shook her head. "Nothing. It's absolutely brilliant. It's just . . . "

"What?"

"I never would have placed you to have a mind for business. You . . . this . . . " She looked around again. "All of this is very impressive."

A pause lingered between them. Lydia walked up to May. "I just have one question. Are you happy?"

May took Lydia's shoulder and gave a slight squeeze. "Yes, Lydia. I'm happy. I'm very happy."

Lydia nodded. "I'm so glad, May." Her eyes got teary. "That's what I've always wanted for you."

"Thanks, Lydia. You were always more than a friend." She gave her a hug and then released the embrace. "Now, let's go get that tea."

Lydia smiled and nodded. May led her out the back and up the stairs.

Galen was in the kitchen putting something on a tray.

Lydia looked around. "May, Galen, I love your place. It's quaint but colorful."

Galen chuckled. "Wait until you see the outside." He picked up the tray with their tea and some shortbread cookies and headed to the back side of the deck. Lydia and May followed. He put the tray on a table between two lounge chairs. He turned, smiled, and said, "Enjoy." Galen stepped inside to leave them alone.

Lydia took a seat. "May, this mini garden reminds me of the palace garden. Just in miniature."

May sat back and nodded. "This is what Galen and his family did for me before anything else. I was so grateful, and I enjoy it immensely."

They each sipped tea a few moments in silence. After having a cookie, May asked, "So, Lydia, what about you? How are things at the palace?"

Lydia swallowed a bite. "Everyone misses you terribly. That was one reason I came to see you. I just had to know you were doing well."

May chuckled. "I think you can stop worrying about that part."

Lydia nodded.

May scrunched her brow and squinted. "And how's Mom and Dad?"

"They miss you, May. But they're dealing with it. Don't worry about them. They'll pull through." Lydia gave a half laugh. "Your mom has turned me into one of her projects."

May grimaced. "Sorry."

Lydia waved her hands. "No, no. It's fine." She paused. "I've met someone."

May's mouth fell open. "What? When? How?"

Lydia giggled. "About two months ago."

May waved her hand in a rolling motion. "Come on, give me details."

"Well . . . I sort of owe it to you and Galen."

May looked puzzled. "How's that?"

Lydia turned to face May straight on. "As you know, Liam's office keeps track of everyone on the planet to know who is related to whom."

May nodded. "Yes, I think it was first started to know who should be allowed to live in Israel. Over time, the role expanded."

"Avner, Azariah's nephew's great-grandson, works for Liam. They have been trying to track down this Leader."

May raised her eyebrows. "Wait, am I starting to hear about the love interest? Avner?"

Lydia's face developed a reddish hue and she giggled just a bit. "I think he may be the one. He hasn't really made that clear yet, but . . . " She shrugged.

May smiled. "Well, if I know Mom, she'll make sure."

Lydia chuckled. "She's already helped me so much. She's already talking plans." Lydia's voice trailed off and she developed a sheepish look.

May reached over and patted Lydia's arm. "It's OK, Lydia. I'm happy for you. And I'm happy Mom is helping you."

Lydia suddenly got a bit of a sad look. "It's only because you're not there."

May shook her head. "Don't feel bad about it, Lydia. I'm happy. You're happy. You allowing Mom to help you makes her happy. Just go with it." She smiled and patted Lydia's arm again.

Lydia smiled. "I'm glad you feel that way. I don't want you to feel I'm trying to take your place."

"I told you, Lydia. I'm quite fine with it. Really."

Lydia had another cookie. It looked as if all the tension had melted from her body. *Poor girl,* May thought. *That was likely the main reason she had come.* Lydia wanted to feel OK with May's mother doting on her. May could only feel happy for Lydia.

"So, what did Avner find out?"

Lydia sat up in her chair. "Oh, yes. The most important part. He found nothing."

May furrowed her brow. "Nothing? How is that possible?"

Lydia shrugged. "I'm not sure. Avner said he and Liam could find no trace of this Leader. It seems he's been off the grid from the very beginning of the kingdom. Maybe because it was at least a decade before non-Israelis were tracked as carefully as they are now."

May sat back and shook her head. "Wow, this guy is an enigma. He seems to always be one step ahead." She turned to Lydia. "Did Liam or Avner say what they plan to do next?"

Lydia gave a slight shrug. "Avner said Liam was going to keep investigating, but he doesn't feel it's promising." She gave a grimace. "Sorry."

May shook her head. "No need to apologize." She reached over and took Lydia's hand. "Lydia, I'm so glad you came. I hope you plan to stay the night."

"Unfortunately, no. I have to get back." She smiled. "Morning starts earlier there."

May nodded. They stood and gave each other a tight hug. This time tears freely came to both women. Lydia kissed May on her cheek.

May walked Lydia to the door and down the stairs, gave her one last hug, and Lydia was gone.

CHAPTER 39

May and Galen's life went along uneventfully for another month. One morning, as usual, Miriam came in to prepare breakfast for May.

May, groggy, stepped from the bedroom and scrunched her nose. "Miriam, what on earth are you cooking?"

"Nothing unusual. Do you not want eggs and cheese?"

May held her nose. "Did you use rotten eggs or something?" She went and opened a couple of windows.

Miriam turned. "My eggs smell wonderful, thank you. I'm not sure why you have an issue with them."

May held her stomach. "Oh, my, I feel—"

She raced to the bathroom and retched a couple of times. She came back into the living area. "Miriam, what's wrong with me? I've never been sick. How could I be sick?"

Miriam smiled at her. "Congratulations."

May turned up her brow. "What on earth for?"

"You only get sick like that for one reason."

"What? I've only heard of people getting sick when . . . " Her eyes widened and her hand covered her mouth. "Miriam. I'm . . . I'm pregnant?"

Miriam laughed. "Seems you are."

"Oh my. Oh my." Her hands went aflutter. "Galen is going to be so happy."

Miriam gave her a hug. "I finally get to take care of a little Galen."

May laughed. "That's a 'we,' Miriam. *We* get to take care of the baby."

Miriam laughed with her. "Oh, of course. Of course."

Both of them were giddy for the rest of the day.

When Galen came home that night, May had placed small stuffed animals in various places throughout the house.

"What are all of these stuffed animals for?" Galen, looking tired, asked with a slight tone of annoyance.

May shrugged. "I don't know. You tell me."

"I didn't put them here. So how can I tell you?"

"Well, what are stuffed animals used for?"

"Used for? They're not used for anything. Usually people with—"

His eyes widened, light suddenly dawning. "Really?" He rushed to her and gingerly put his hand on her stomach. "We're having a baby?"

She smiled and nodded.

He grabbed May and gave her a kiss.

"So, you're happy about it?"

"Are you kidding me? I'm ecstatic." He twirled her around.

Whether they walked down the street or entered a store or restaurant, Galen would tell people he was going to be a father. May felt as though, by the time they got back home, everyone in Vancouver would know she was pregnant.

As they were walking back from the restaurant, they came across Shepherd Hayden.

Galen needed very little time to speak. "Shepherd Hayden! Guess what? I'm going to be a father."

Hayden shook Galen's hand and gave May a kiss. "Congratulations. I'm assuming May will be a mother as much as you're going to be a father."

Galen's cheeks turned red. He turned to May. "Sorry, honey." He turned back to Hayden and nodded. "Yes, Shepherd Hayden, you are correct."

"Actually, I'm glad I ran into the two of you," Hayden said. "In a couple of months is our scheduled honoring ceremony. This time, selected individuals will get an audience with the Prince and King David."

May's eyes widened. "Really?"

Hayden held up his hand. "Now, I can't promise you will get chosen. But I will certainly put your names into the drawing."

May nodded. "Yes, of course. Thank you, Shepherd Hayden." She shook her head. "I'm not asking for special treatment, but just the thought . . . " She smiled. "It's . . . it's wonderful."

After a few more minutes of small talk, they said their goodbyes and started for home.

Galen squeezed May's hand. "I will pray we're chosen."

"Thanks, Galen. It would really be great for Mom . . . I mean . . . Her Highness to know we're soon to be parents."

Galen and May went about a regular schedule for the next several weeks. May tried not to be anxious, but she was having a hard time waiting.

One evening, about a week and a half before the scheduled honoring ceremony, there was a knock at their door.

May answered. She gasped as she saw Shepherd Hayden in their doorway.

"Who is it, honey?" Galen called from across the house.

"It's Shepherd Hayden."

"Well, invite him in," Galen said as he entered from another room, motioning for Hayden to enter.

"Is this a social call? Or do you have news for us?"

Hayden smiled. "I do indeed." He smiled and looked at them both. "Your names were drawn." He turned to May. "You will get to see the Prince, his wife, and King David."

May turned and gave Galen a hug. Tears ran down her cheeks. She turned and hugged Hayden. "Thank you, Shepherd Hayden."

He laughed. "Really not my doing. But you're welcome."

Later, when asked, Miriam agreed to keep the store open for them while they would be in Jerusalem.

In a week, May found herself back in her former home city. This time, though, she stayed with Galen in the Guest House he had stayed in the first time he visited her, just down the street from her dad's and King David's palace. The visitation with the Royal Family was to take place the day before the honoring ceremony.

May and Galen walked several blocks to the Prince's palace from the Guest House. They were just one of one hundred families who were scheduled to visit the Royal Family that day. No one else knew of her background, and she knew she could not show any public display of affection when she saw her parents.

She greatly looked forward to meeting her parents once again—no matter how short it might be—but still felt nervous at the same time.

There was no special order for those visiting the Royal Family. One simply had to have the special invitation. She and

Galen drew number sixty-three. They waited a little more than three hours before they reached the throne room. As they got closer and closer, May's heart began to race, and her hands became sweaty. Galen rubbed her back.

"Don't be nervous. It will be fine," he assured her.

She nodded and gave a small smile. Still, she couldn't keep herself calm.

As the couple in front of them finished talking to the Prince, Kyla's eyes met May's. Kyla gasped but caught herself quickly. May genuflected. Galen did the same.

"Your Grace. Your Highness," May said as she rose. "It's my pleasure to see you."

Kyla's eyes moistened, but she seemed able to keep her emotions in check.

May put her hand on her stomach.

Kyla's eyes widened and a smile crept across her face. "I see you are pregnant." Kyla glanced between the two of them. "Congratulations to you both."

"Thank you, Your Grace. It's a boy."

"You both must be very happy," Prince Jeremiah said.

May looked to the Prince. "Indeed, Your Highness, we are."

"I'm very happy for you both."

May and Galen genuflected again. "Thank you, Your Highness," Galen said to Jeremiah. He nodded to Kyla. "Your Grace."

Kyla caught May's eye. "Some motherly advice?"

May's eyes widened slightly. "Yes, Your Grace?"

Kyla's smile softened. "A mother's love is forever."

May's eyes moistened and her hand went to her chest as she caught her breath. She was fully aware Kyla was telling her of the love her mother still held for her.

"That's true for a father's as well," the Prince said. Jeremiah's eyes didn't water, but they did glisten.

May and Galen genuflected again. "Thank you, Your Highness. Your Grace. May you always be blessed."

Both Jeremiah and Kyla smiled. "And you, my child," Jeremiah said.

Both he and Kyla turned their attention to the couple behind them, but May saw Kyla glance her way a few times as they talked with King David.

Galen genuflected before King David. "Your Majesty. It's our honor to see you."

May genuflected. "May you be ever blessed."

King David nodded. As he looked up, his gaze locked with hers and he gave her a wink. She smiled.

Galen and May turned and left the throne room. As they did, May glanced back at her mother as they passed the door most people were using to enter. Their gazes locked for a final time. Kyla gave a brief smile. May nodded and kept walking. Galen put his arm around her shoulders and gave a light, supportive squeeze, and they exited the palace.

May knew she might never get another opportunity like that again. But she had seen her parents, they had seen her, and they knew she was happy and starting a family. That would have to suffice.

CHAPTER 40

As they walked hand in hand from the palace, May looked up at Galen. "Let's go to the Overlook."

Galen looked at her and smiled. "Really?" He chuckled. "I was just thinking about that very same thing but wasn't sure how you would feel about it."

May leaned into his shoulder. "My life is with you." She shook her head. "I have no regrets. It may be a long time before we get a chance to come back. We should make the most of this trip."

Galen smiled. "OK. Let's head to the local teleporter and step off near the temple complex."

Once they arrived there, they walked slowly through the temple complex on the way to the Overlook. This brought back so many memories: her sitting on the dais looking at Galen sitting with Adelina; her waiting on the palace steps for Galen to finish talking with the King; her last fellowship offering with her mom, dad, and Liam; and the many festivals she had attended with her family. All were happy memories. She couldn't deny there was still a tinge of regret she would not experience those times again. Yet, as she looked at Galen, she was more excited about their future together.

When they came to the Overlook, they stood at the railing

admiring the view. Each year the view became more and more spectacular. She wondered what the landscapers thought about it now. Was this the vision they had from the beginning? She tried to imagine what this area would look like without all the flowers and vegetation. She smiled. They had to be true artists at heart to have such a vision of beauty starting from a blank and rugged landscape.

Galen pulled her to a seat on the nearest bench. "I lived in Israel all my life, and it wasn't until I met you I even knew this beautiful place existed." He turned and looked into her eyes. "You've opened my eyes to so many things. I will always do my best to make sure you never regret choosing me over all you had."

May put her hand on his cheek. "Galen, I don't regret my choice." She smiled. "I never will." As she put her head on his chest, Galen wrapped his arm around her. There was no way she could be more content. When she was with him, nothing else seemed to matter.

They must have sat there for a couple of hours. Time seemed to stand still.

Galen kissed her on her forehead to wake her from her daze, trance, or whatever altered state she was in. "Ready to go?"

She looked up at him and nodded. They slowly walked back to the teleporter. One more night here and then back to Vancouver. She was actually looking forward to getting back to their own home.

A line awaited them at the teleporter. She didn't mind. Being in a hurry wasn't on today's agenda. Today, she was determined to live in the moment.

The line dwindled quickly, however, and soon was down to

only one couple in front of them. She wondered if they were as happy as she was.

Only at that moment did it dawn on May that the woman in front of them wore a scarf over her head. It brought an uneasy feeling and reminded her of the time Galen's mom came into the shop. She shook her head slightly. There was no sense getting paranoid.

Galen rubbed her back. "You OK, May?"

She smiled and nodded. "Yeah, just had a déjà vu moment."

He turned up his brow. "Why? What happened?"

She patted his chest. "Oh, the woman in front of us wearing that scarf just reminded me of—"

May's eyes widened. Her gaze locked with that of the woman in front of them, who had turned. . . . *No, it can't be!*

"May, what's . . . what's wrong?"

"Hello, Galen."

May put her hand to her mouth. Galen quickly whirled around. In a blur, the woman forcefully grabbed Galen, pulled him into herself, and the man pressed the Engage button. Before May could even blurt out a word or a shout, all three were gone.

May sucked in a breath and then screamed, "Galen!" She turned. No one was around. She looked back at the teleporter. *How . . . why?* Her mind whirled in total confusion. *Why would Galen's parents take him now?* Her eyes began to water. A couple of tears spilled over her eyelids and ran down her cheeks. She stumbled to the nearest bench and sat. Numbness filled her. A need to do something rose from within.

Where did they go? What can I do?

Elsbeth. She had helped her and Liam track Caleb. Maybe she could do the same here. May looked at her T-band. It wasn't that late. Maybe she'd still be at her office.

May walked as fast as she could, without literally running, to the Science Center. When she reached Elsbeth's department she was out of breath. She headed around the outside counter for Elsbeth's office as she had done so many times before. Yet this time a man stepped in front of her causing her to stop in her tracks so she wouldn't run into him.

"Oh, excuse me," May said. "I need to see Els— . . . I mean, Administrator Isakson."

The man remained in her way, refusing to budge. "Do you have an appointment?"

May stiffened and stood straighter. *Appointment?* She hadn't even considered one needed such a thing. She shook her head.

"No, but I'm Me— . . . I mean, I'm May Shafir, and I have an urgent matter to bring to Administrator Isakson's attention."

"Impossible," the man flatly said. "Administrator Isakson is extremely busy." He gestured toward the counter. "If you come over here and tell me your issue, I'll schedule an appointment for you."

She sighed heavily but walked to the counter with the man. Evidently Elsbeth had a new assistant. She didn't remember seeing this man before. Although a nuisance, she realized she now had to behave as a non-Israelite. Her eyes began watering again.

"What's the issue?" He poised himself in front of a screen to enter her complaint.

"My husband was just kidnapped."

The man's eyes went wide. "What?" His eyes narrowed as though he was trying to see if she was telling the truth. "That's . . . that's impossible."

May's patience was wearing thin. She wasn't used to being totally ignored—or challenged. Did this happen to others?

"Don't tell me what's impossible. I was there! I need to talk to Administrator Isakson!"

"Calm down, Miss."

"Don't tell *me* to calm down!" May said, now erupting. "Did you hear what I said? My husband was kidnapped."

"I'm sorry. It's just . . . "

"Unusual? Yes, I know. That's why this is so urgent!"

The man looked unsure of himself. "I'm sorry. I've never heard of such . . . "

May grew even more impatient and her voice escalated even further in tone and volume. "Does that matter? Just because *you've* never encountered it doesn't mean it didn't happen." She suddenly became very loud. "I demand to see Administrator Isakson!"

The man held up his palms and patted the air. "Shh, shh. Please, Miss."

May's eyes widened. "Did you just *shush* me?" Her aristocratic air instinctively came back to her. She didn't try to suppress it. "The audacity!"

The man's eyes widened. "I'm sorry. It's just—"

"Go tell Administrator Isakson the former Me'ira Ranz is here to see her!"

The man froze—his eyes wide as saucers. She pointed. "Go. *Now!*"

He dashed to the back. In about a minute, Elsbeth came out.

"Me'ira?"

May ran into her arms. "Oh, Aunt Elsbeth. It's Galen. He's been kidnapped."

Elsbeth pulled May off her shoulder. "What? Here, come into my office and tell me what happened."

The man looked at Elsbeth. "Administrator, I'm very sorry.

271

I had no idea."

Elsbeth patted his shoulder as she passed. "It's OK, John." She gave a weak smile. "It's OK."

He nodded but still looked shaken.

Elsbeth led May to a chair in her office, had her sit, and brought her a glass of water.

May looked up and gave a sheepish smile. "Thanks. I'm . . . I'm sorry for the commotion. But I didn't know where else to turn."

Elsbeth pulled up a chair next to hers. "OK, tell me all that happened."

CHAPTER 41

May felt like she had been sitting in Elsbeth's office too long. The longer they waited, the more time there was for Galen's parents to get away. May looked at her T-band. Nearly an hour had passed since Elsbeth had left the room to check on Galen and his parents' teleporter signal and, hopefully, determine where they went.

As she sat drumming her fingers on the chair's armrest, she heard movement in the doorway. She turned to see what Elsbeth had found out, but it wasn't her.

"Liam!" She jumped to her feet and dashed to his arms. This was something she never thought would happen again. She couldn't help it as her tears returned.

Liam brought her back to her chair and sat next to her. "Aunt Elsbeth just filled me in. Are you OK?"

May nodded and let out a small, sharp breath. "I'm . . . I'm OK, but I'm very worried for Galen."

"Any idea why they would take him now?"

She took another staccato breath. "I've been thinking about that. The only thing I can think of is that we foiled their plan."

Liam cocked his head. "Come again? Why do you say that?"

May was surprised Liam didn't think it obvious. "Liam, for all these years, Galen's parents have not had any direct contact with him except by subterfuge. Now all of a sudden they come out of their hiding to have direct contact with him." She shrugged. "Why else would they do that?"

Liam shook his head. "I don't know, May. It could be for any number of reasons."

May shook her head. "If things were going their way, they would not be reaching out. No, this has to be a way to get their plan back on track."

"By doing what?"

May's eyes got teary. "I don't know. But . . . I wouldn't put anything past them."

Liam rubbed her upper arm. "Don't worry, May. The King has put limits on what they can actually do."

"I know. But Ya'akov . . . "

She saw Liam furrow his brow.

" . . . stated they know how to push the limit." She paused and turned her head. "What's wrong?"

Liam shook his head. "I know you're emotionally charged, but you have to keep your new persona. You can't try and pull strings because you used to be Royalty." He gave her a sympathetic look. "It is the consequence you agreed to."

May sighed. "I'm sorry, Liam. But I had to get someone to listen to me."

Liam nodded. "I know. I know. But from here on out, I'm here in an official capacity. It's—"

"Protocol." She shook her head and gave a small chuckle. "I can't seem to follow it no matter which side of it I'm on."

Liam grinned. "That's what makes you so special."

Elsbeth walked in. Both turned her way. "Me'ira . . . " She shook her head. "Sorry. May. I have some bad news."

May stood. "What is it?"

Elsbeth grimaced. "We couldn't find a teleporter signature.

Not for Galen. Not for his parents."

May looked from Elsbeth to Liam and back. "I . . . I don't understand. How is that possible?"

Elsbeth shook her head as she sat at her desk looking bewildered herself. "There were a series of teleports up to the time you stated, but not at the time you specified." She unclasped and clasped her hands. "I don't have anything to trace."

May sat down with a thud. "So, what do we do?"

Liam rubbed the back of his neck with his hand. "Well, let's think of where they would probably go."

May turned to him. "And that would be?"

"Well . . . " Liam stroked his chin. "We know he has a home in Naphtali as well as a museum in Ephraim."

May looked puzzled. "Do you really think that's where they would go? Isn't that a little too obvious?"

Liam raised his eyebrows. "I'm open to other ideas."

May shook her head and turned to Elsbeth.

Elsbeth shrugged. "Since we don't know, let me get my folks here to figure out why the teleporter seems to have malfunctioned. If we figure that out, then we can track them wherever they went."

May wanted to do *something* but didn't know what it could be. She turned back to Liam. "Do you agree?"

He lifted his arms with an exaggerated shrug. "We're stabbing in the dark right now. I don't want to deploy people on a whim and not be able to rally them quickly when we really need them."

May nodded. "Yeah, I guess so." Her eyes watered and a couple of tears formed. "I just feel so helpless."

Liam reached out and squeezed her shoulder lightly. She knew he was trying to be supportive.

Elsbeth stood. "Liam, put May up at the Guest House

around the corner from here. Let's all meet back here tomorrow at 10 in the morning." She put her hand on May's upper back. "And I'll be sure John knows you're on my calendar."

May smiled and nodded. "Thank you, Aunt— . . . I mean, Administrator. But I'm already staying at the Guest House in the city proper."

Elsbeth smiled and held up a finger. "Give me a second. Transferring reservations can be tricky. I'll simplify the process."

Elsbeth called the Guest House on her holo-com and placed the call on speaker only.

"Jerusalem Guest House, Temple Complex. Ovid speaking."

"Good evening, Ovid. This is Administrator Isakson."

"Yes, Administrator." The man's voice sounded like he had straightened to attention. May smiled. She could almost visualize the man saluting.

"There is a guest at the Guest House near the Prince's palace. I need her reservation, and her belongings, transferred to your Guest House for tonight. Can you do that?"

"Oh, absolutely, Administrator. What is the name of the guest?"

"May Shafir."

"Very good, Administrator." There was a pause, then the man spoke again. "It is done."

"Thank you, Ovid."

"My pleasure." The holo-com call ended.

Elsbeth smiled at May. "All done."

May smiled back. She knew that, for a regular person, such a transfer would have been a very time-consuming process. Elsbeth had saved her a great deal of hassle.

After she said goodnight to Elsbeth, Liam walked with May to the Guest House.

"I'm really sorry, Sis."

May glanced at him. "Aren't you forgetting protocol?"

Liam smiled. "No. Since no one is around, I don't think protocol is necessary between us. I owe you that."

May slowly shook her head. "You don't owe me anything. My choice—my consequences."

Liam put his arm around her shoulders for a few brief seconds. "There's enough consequences without adding more." He gave a smile. "We all feel that way."

She looked at him, eyes darting over his face to see what he meant. "All?"

Liam nodded. "When I told everyone you had left with Galen, most were furious. Yet when I told them why you did what you did, they came to realize, just as I did, that you are really a brave young woman."

May's eyes watered. This was more than she could have hoped for. She clutched his arm and put her head on his shoulder. "Thank you, Liam. That means more to me than you know."

Liam smiled and patted her hand. "Now, now. You can't make me the one who causes a woman to cry in public, now can you?"

May chuckled and let go of his arm. She sniffled back her tears. "No, I guess not."

Outside the Guest House, Liam said goodbye.

"Liam, I don't deserve your kindness, but I'm really grateful."

He kissed her hand. "Just doing my duty for a citizen of my King." He gave her a wink. "I'll see you in the morning."

She nodded and watched as he walked down the street to the local teleporter. Evidently, he was heading home and not to the Royal Palace. After he turned the corner, she sighed and entered the Guest House. Tomorrow, she prayed, would be a good day.

CHAPTER 42

May kept waking up wondering where Galen had been taken and if he was OK. She rose early after a long, fitful night.

After dressing, she went downstairs for breakfast and ate on the large patio, which had a great view of the city. Since the Guest House was situated high in the city, the view cascaded before her. She could see the Ezekiel River flowing from under the temple, over the escarpment, between the two Mounts of Olives, and out toward the Jordan River in the far distance. The lush green valley spread out toward the Chaya Sea, which was slightly visible from where she sat. Jerusalem would always have a place in her heart.

She thought about Jerusalem and her new home in Vancouver. They were so different, but she loved them both. Yet her heart now ached even more for her new home as her life as a princess was becoming a distant memory. Life with Galen was now her reality. That's what she wanted—more than anything. She had to get their life back to that point.

As she left the Guest House to head to the Science Center, she saw Liam heading up the street toward her. Evidently he had just come from the teleporter.

He gave a slight wave. "Well, isn't this timing? Or do great minds just think alike?"

May laughed. "I think it's called divine serendipity."

Liam raised his eyebrows. "That's an oxymoron now, isn't it?"

May smirked. "If anyone would recognize a moron, it would be you."

Liam bumped shoulders with her and laughed. "Oh, I've missed my sister."

May started to say something, but her throat constricted, and she found herself unable to; her emotions suddenly overwhelmed her. She smiled instead. She missed their banter as well.

Once in the Science Center, everyone paid deference to Liam. It was such a contrast to her visit the day before. When Elsbeth's assistant, John, looked up from his console, he bowed. "Your Highness, Mrs. Shafir, Administrator Isakson is waiting for you in her office."

May smiled and nodded. "Thank you." She wanted John to know there were no hard feelings.

John nodded and gave a slight smile.

As soon as they entered her office, Elsbeth gestured for both to have a seat.

May looked at Elsbeth. "You've discovered something?"

Elsbeth nodded. "About oh-four-hundred, their teleporter signals came online."

May looked from Elsbeth to Liam and back. "What do you mean? It just . . . showed up?"

Elsbeth nodded.

Liam scrunched his brow. "How is that possible? How could they delay their teleportation signature from registering their teleportation?"

Elsbeth shook her head. "We have no idea—yet. But at least now we have a lead to go on."

May leaned forward. "So where did they go?"

"The teleporter stated Naphtali, near Galen's home," Elsbeth said.

May looked at Liam. "So we should have gone last night."

"No," Elsbeth said. "I don't think you would have found them."

May turned back to Elsbeth. "Why do you say that?"

"Well, the delay had to be for a reason. It gives them time to teleport somewhere else. Anyone chasing them would be looking in the wrong place while they escaped to another location."

Liam nodded. "That makes sense. But where would they be now?"

"It would be Ephraim." Both May and Liam turned to Elsbeth. "I've heard Ya'akov talk about this man. He's arrogant. He wouldn't actually hide but flaunt himself to show his superiority," Elsbeth said.

Liam ran his hand over his mouth. "OK, but where in Ephraim. Their museum?"

May suddenly sat upright.

Liam raised his eyebrows. "May?"

"They'll be at the café on the waterfront in Tiberius."

Liam furrowed his brow. "How would you know that?"

She smiled. "Because that's where Galen would have them go. That's where he and I used to meet. He would want us to find him. So he would lead them to a place he knows I would know."

Liam looked at Elsbeth. She shrugged. "Sounds as good a start as any," she said.

"OK," Liam said. "I'll send some of my men to their museum anyway, just in case." He stood. "Let's go."

Elsbeth came from behind her desk. "You two go to

Tiberius. I'll meet you there. I'm going to teleport to the museum first and see for myself."

Liam nodded. "OK, we'll see you there."

Elsbeth nodded in return—and then vanished, which her glorified state allowed her to do.

Liam looked at May. "Wish we could do that."

She chuckled. "We have the next best thing. Let's go."

As they walked to the nearest teleporter, Liam made several calls to have others under his authority head to the Shafirs' museum in Ephraim.

"If they are there, Elsbeth will need some support," Liam said.

May nodded.

Once at the teleporter, Liam inputted his royal code, and this allowed him to choose the teleporter at their palace in Galilee just outside Tiberius. In a matter of seconds, they were back at the palace where her entire adventure had started. It felt strange to be in a familiar place where she was technically not allowed to be. May realized how much things could change in a short period of time.

They walked from the courtyard into the sitting area. She recalled the conversation with her mother about protocol. She shook her head. No need to dwell on that now. What was done was done. Still, she had no regrets—at least when she was with Galen.

They stepped onto the large patio that overlooked the Galilean Sea. It remained a picturesque view with its blue water and colorful sailboats. Yet there was no time to take all this in and reminisce. They quickly headed down the path to the seaside and then into the city itself.

As they approached the seaside café, they met Elsbeth coming from the opposite direction.

She shook her head. "Nothing." She looked at May. "Do you see Galen?"

May turned. And there, just as she thought, Galen was sitting at the same table where they had sat all that time ago. He was again looking out over the sea, looking at the terns as they flew by. The wind had pushed a curly swath of hair down onto his forehead. Her heart stirred now—just as it had that day. There was no doubt. Her love for him was even stronger than before.

She pointed. "There in the back—next to the water."

She headed toward Galen without waiting for their response. They followed. Before she arrived, she called his name. "Galen!"

He turned and those dimples smiled back at her. Oh, how she loved this man.

"May!" He stood and took her in his arms.

"Are you OK?" Liam asked.

Galen nodded. "Yes, they just wanted to talk."

"Which way did they go?" Elsbeth asked. "I would like to have a *talk* with them myself."

Looking at Liam and Elsbeth, he pointed. "You just missed them. They headed that way."

May turned. "Look for a woman with a scarf over her head." She looked at Galen.

He nodded. "And sunglasses."

Elsbeth and Liam took off in the direction Galen had indicated, walking at a fast gait.

May turned back to Galen and embraced him again, adding a kiss and another hug. "Oh, Galen. I was so worried about you."

He had her sit and held her hand. "I tried to think of how to contact you but had no way to." He then glanced in the direction Liam and Elsbeth went. "What do you think they'll do with them if they find them?"

May raised her eyebrows and gave a small shrug. "Question them for sure and find out what their agenda is really all about."

The waiter came by. Galen looked at May. "Care for some tea?"

She nodded. The waiter bowed slightly. "Very good, madam."

May squeezed Galen's hand. "So, what happened? What did they want?"

"Well, we first teleported to Naphtali, then to Caesarea Philippi, and then here. At first I didn't understand why, but he told me they had found a way to delay their teleportation signature, and this would allow them more time to get away."

May nodded. "Yeah, Aunt Elsbeth—I mean, Administrator Isakson—found that out."

Galen smiled. "Old habits die hard, huh?"

May chuckled. "Yeah. I can't seem to follow protocol as a Royal or as a commoner."

Galen kissed her hand. "I wouldn't want you any other way."

May smiled.

The waiter returned with her tea, poured a cup, and left the teapot on the table.

She took a sip. "Galen, you said, 'He told me.' Does that mean you saw him?"

Galen nodded.

May's eyes widened. "That's great! You can describe him to Liam."

Galen shook his head. "No, May. No, I can't."

May turned her head, completely confused. "Why not?"

Galen sighed. "In order to talk to him, Isabelle . . . " He shook his head. "If that's even her real name . . . well, she made

283

me promise I would never reveal his identity to anyone."

"But, Galen . . . "

Galen shook his head. "I promised, May. I promised. I can't go back on a promise. He's my father—a bad father—but I just had to see his face." His eyes began to water. "I . . . I just had to. Can you understand that?"

May nodded slowly. "Yes, Galen. Yes, I can." She stroked his hand. "I know it was something you had to do. Did he tell you his name?"

Galen sighed. "No, he only referred to himself as The Leader. He wanted me to call him that. But I just couldn't do it."

"So, what else did he say?"

"You were right, May. What you did surprised them. They never expected you to give up your Royal position for me."

May smiled. That made her feel justified in what she had done.

"But what did they want with you?" she asked.

He shook his head. "It wasn't for a happy reunion." Galen cleared his throat. "He, uh, wanted me to know we didn't thwart their plans. He said we actually cleared up the prophecy for them."

May squinted. "What do you mean?"

Galen's eyes widened and almost twinkled. "He had President Hatim's journal. May, can you believe it? The very journal in which the Pre-Refreshing World President recorded his personal entries." He smiled. "He let me hold it. That was the highlight . . . " His smile vanished. "And only highlight, of my visit with him."

May understood his reaction to seeing the journal. Being an antique junky, Galen loved anything Pre-Refreshing. Still, she decided not to tell Liam or Elsbeth about this. They might not understand. "How did he get that?"

Galen shook his head. "I'm not sure. But he found it when he was very young during the early days of the kingdom. I only got a chance to peruse it but didn't get to read any of it. Apparently, the journal told about the Prophecy Plaque and other stone steles the president planted around the globe. The more my father heard, the more convinced he became that he would be the one to make the world ready for his return. He referred to this returning one as the Overtaker."

"Return? What do you mean, 'return'?"

Galen shrugged. "The journal stated he would return and overcome the current King."

"As in, overthrow?"

"I guess. I . . . I don't know if it's a true prophecy or not. He sure believes it, though."

May drank more of her tea as she pondered Galen's statement. She looked back into his eyes. "Galen, what did your father mean when he said we surprised him, but that we had actually clarified the prophecy of the plaque?"

Galen shook his head. "All he said was that our actions clarified which of the two parts of the prophecy we would fulfill."

May thought about that. *What did he mean?* She scrunched her brow while trying to think. "So, if our actions surprised them, then they think we're fulfilling the second part rather than the first?"

"I . . . guess."

"So, I wasn't the one *near* the Prince, but the one 'through afar'?" She shook her head. "Galen, did we fall into their plans after all?"

CHAPTER 43

Elsbeth and Liam returned to their table without any good news.

May looked up. "Don't tell me. They got away."

Liam nodded. "We saw them once."

Elsbeth gave a slight shrug. "Or so we thought."

Liam nodded again. "They just seemed to disappear into the crowd."

Galen gestured for both to have a seat.

Liam and Elsbeth sat but declined the waiter's offer to bring them anything.

Liam looked at Galen. "Is there anything you can tell us before we head back? There's still a lot for us to follow up on."

Elsbeth nodded. "Galen, do you know why they took you?"

Galen shrugged. "I'm not completely sure. All I know is they said we surprised them with our actions. But that our actions actually clarified for them the meaning of the Prophecy Plaque."

"Do you know what they meant by that?" Elsbeth looked from Galen to Liam. Liam shook his head and shrugged.

Galen also shook his head. "May and I were just discussing that. We're not sure."

Liam put his hand on May's shoulder and gave a slight

squeeze. "It doesn't make me comfortable you are now so far away," he said.

May put her hand over his. "Don't worry about me. What can they do, anyway?"

Liam shook his head. "I don't know. They are one crafty couple. I don't trust them." He looked at Galen. "Sorry, Galen. No offense."

Galen held up his palms. "Hey, I don't trust them either. No offense taken."

Liam gave a small smile. "Well, with my new position, it may mean I have to check up on you two every once in a while."

For May, this was still another positive out of all the chaos. "Well, maybe that's for the best. We appreciate you taking your new position so seriously."

"If I hear from him again, or from Isabelle, I'll contact you," Galen said.

Liam looked at Galen. "Isabelle? The same woman we met in Australia?"

Galen shrugged. "Apparently they're one and the same. That's the name my mother went by."

"You think it's an alias?"

Galen shrugged again. "That would make the most sense."

Elsbeth nodded as she rubbed her chin. "In all likelihood, it is. It's at least a lead, though." She smiled. "Thanks, Galen."

He nodded as Liam stood. The others followed. Galen shook both Liam's and Elsbeth's hands. "Thank you both for everything." They smiled and nodded.

May shook Elsbeth's hand. "Thank you, Administrator Isakson."

Elsbeth pulled her in and gave her a tight hug and whispered in her ear. "You take care. You may be May Irena now, but you'll forever be Me'ira in my heart."

May's eyes watered. She nodded. "Thank you."

Liam looked at her and gave another warm smile. He held out his arms and she walked into them. Giving her a tight hug, he too whispered in her ear. "I have to follow protocol, but you are forever my little sister. I love you, Me'ira."

She whispered, "I love you, too." She tried to keep her tears at bay but failed. As she released her embrace, Liam wiped away her tears with his thumbs. "No tears, now. You have a wonderful life to live."

She smiled and nodded.

Elsbeth and Liam turned and walked away. Galen put his arm around May's shoulders. They stood and watched both leave the restaurant patio and head down the path toward the seashore. Before they got out of sight, May saw Elsbeth put her hand on Liam's shoulder—and both disappeared.

Galen kissed May on the cheek. "Are you ready to head home?"

She looked at him, smiled, and nodded. "Can we do one thing first?"

"Sure. What is it?"

She led him back along the path leading to the Royal Palace and picked a sprig of lemonwood. As they walked back to the city and took the tram up to the long-range teleporter, she inhaled the lemony fragrance. It brought back memories of her and Lydia playing hide-and-seek. It also reminded her of the time she snuck out to see Galen before he came to Jerusalem to meet her parents.

She held the sprig for Galen to smell. As he inhaled the fragrance, he smiled. "You know, that's the aroma I kept smelling every time I met you in Galilee. I never knew why. Now I do."

May smiled and gave him a quick kiss. "Maybe we can plant some lemonwood at home."

In only a short time, they were back in Vancouver. Galen had an AGA take them to their shop. Before stepping out, May paused and looked it over from a distance; this place now had a special place in her heart. After stepping out, Galen sent the AGA back, took her arm, and led her around the back to the stairs.

Miriam came out of her house in the back and waved. "Welcome home!"

May smiled and waved back. *Home. Yes, we are finally home.* She rubbed her belly and smiled. Soon, they would start a family. She looked at Galen as they climbed the stairs, pulled him into her, and planted a loving kiss.

Although she was no longer a princess, she very much had her prince.

EPILOGUE

Jubilee Calendar
18:2:2

Almost four centuries later

Miriam rocked the baby in her arms. Hearing the doorbell, she rose and walked over to answer as she kept bouncing the infant to keep her asleep.

Miriam's eyes widened. "Isabelle. I'm so glad you got my message."

Isabelle entered and smiled. "Well, I was somewhat surprised to hear from you in mid-America. I thought you were still in the Northwestern Territory."

"Well, I went from descendant to descendant to serve as the nanny for each, just as I did for Galen. I followed your instructions, just as you suggested."

"Yes, but who would have thought each and every Shafir would have boys and not any girls?"

Miriam smiled as she cooed the baby in her arms. "Well, that spell is now broken. William Shafir moved here about seventy-five years ago to escape the scandal of some of his relatives following the Overtaker. He had his surname legally changed to Singleton. This is William's little granddaughter. The first female descendant of Galen Shafir and Me'ira Ranz's union almost four centuries ago."

Isabelle nodded. "Yes, I wondered if we intervened too early with the Shafir family. Yet it seems to have worked to our advantage. The family is now more separated."

The infant gave a slight grunt and stretched. Isabelle and Miriam looked at each other and chuckled.

Isabelle gently put her index finger next to the infant's hand, and the little one wrapped her tiny fingers around Isabelle's. Isabelle smiled and looked back up at Miriam. "And where are Galen and Me'ira now?"

"Oh, they moved some time ago to Australia and gave their store to one of their descendants."

Isabelle nodded. "The farther away they are the better." She smiled as she looked back at the child. "I had almost given up hope. But now . . . now we have a female descendant of the Prince living outside Israel."

She held out her hands and Miriam placed the baby in her arms. Isabelle pulled back the blanket from the child's face. "Let me look at you. My, how cute you are." She hummed and rocked the baby in her arms.

Isabelle looked up. "What's her name?"

"Janet."

Isabelle smiled. "Hello, Janet Singleton. My 'one through afar.'"

I hope you've enjoyed this book. Letting others know your thoughts is a way to help them share your experience. Please consider posting an honest review. You can post a review at Amazon, Barnes & Noble, Goodreads, or other places you choose. Reviews can also be posted at more than one site! This author, and other readers, appreciate your engagement. Also, check out my next book coming soon!

—Randy Dockens

Come Experience Who the Prophecy Revealed!

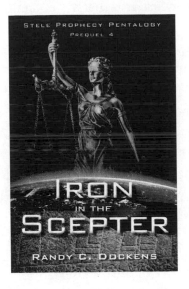

And tell us what you think at randydockens.com

**Advance orders available at
Amazon and Barnes & Noble
May 2020**

Submitting to authority sometimes seems just too difficult no matter the consequences.

That's how Janet feels. As a commodities analyst she has ideas for expanding teleporter efficiency that, to her, are logical and make sense. Still, these are rejected by the King. Janet is determined to not let anyone derail her plans. She develops a deep animosity for the King as she realizes her plans will never match those of the King or those who support him.

A coworker puts her on the path to a prophecy that supposedly states the King will one day be deposed by a coming Overtaker who will bring true freedom to everyone. Janet places her whole effort, and that of her family, into the fulfillment of this prophecy. She marries a man who is not necessarily against the King, but not necessarily for him either, and finds him supportive of her efforts.

She also sees having children as a means to a greater end. Will Janet's animosity for the King put them in harm's way—all to fulfill her desire to see the King deposed? Will her efforts, though detrimental to her family, make a path to fulfill this prophecy for the freedom she desperately desires? Will her coercive efforts propel her into a leadership position with a coming Overtaker?

Also, please check out:
https://randydockens.com/news/

IRON IN THE SCEPTER

CHAPTER 1

Look away, Janet. He's a farmer.

Janet tried to listen to her common sense. She focused on her three-cheese and spinach lasagna and took the last few bites. Studying her electronic tablet, she sipped her tea and tried to concentrate on a book she had started the night before. After reading the same paragraph for the third time, she sighed and put the tablet down. Why was something so engaging last night not able to keep her attention now?

The waiter came by. Dinner came with complementary cheesecake for guests with a birthday. How pathetic was it to spend her twenty-fifth birthday alone? Just like last year. Well, at least she was consistent. She stared at it. *Leave it, Janet. Walk out now.* She almost did. Instead, she picked up her fork.

She heard the man laugh. *Don't look over at him.* She glanced over. He had all the qualities in her "perfect man" list: square jaw, dimples, engaging smile, and, most importantly, muscles. He was wearing a long-sleeved shirt, but when he bent his arm it looked as if the fabric would burst. His hair had strong red highlights, somewhat disheveled, but that made him all the more intriguing in her eyes.

She looked away and shook her head. *Why did I look? I should leave.* Still, she didn't. She sat there taking a few more bites of the cheesecake. *You're a loner, Janet.* That's the way she had always worked. That's why she became a commodities analyst. She avoided entanglements. She should leave this farmer to his wheat and antigravity harvester. That's the way it has to be. But, against her better judgment, she glanced at him again.

This time he glanced back. Their eyes made contact. The glance was brief—but not so brief—before he smiled at her. She tried to act nonchalant, picked up her tablet again, and pretended to read. His glancing rate increased, and soon he was looking at her nonstop, even when talking to his friends.

They stood. *Are they leaving? Good.* She would soon put all of this behind her.

The man patted the shoulder of one of the others and headed her way. She now tried to ignore him completely.

That became impossible when he stood next to her table.

She repressed the urge to look up. "Can I help you?"

"That depends." He sat down across from her.

She took a glance. He had his chin in his palm with an arm propped on the table, donning an adorable smile.

She put down her tablet and forced herself to remain expressionless. "Upon what?"

"Whether you go out with me or not."

"And why would I do that?" Janet tried to keep her remark stern, even cold.

He shifted in his seat, let go of his chin, placed both elbows on the table, and leaned forward, dimples now in full force.

"Let's turn this into a challenge," he said.

Janet's eyebrows shot up. She didn't say anything. The guy's smile broadened, if that was even possible.

"If I get you to smile in, say, the next three minutes, you go out with me."

"Oh, that's the challenge, is it?" Janet kept her matter-of-fact tone.

The man nodded.

"I must warn you. Better men have tried."

"Other."

Janet scrunched her brow. "Excuse me?"

"*Other* men. Other men have tried. Not *better*."

Janet set back. "Oh, confident are we?" She nodded toward a table on the other side of the restaurant. "See that lady over there?"

The man turned his head and looked to where Janet nodded. The woman sitting there quickly diverted her attention back to her salad.

"She's been staring at you the whole time, eating her salad very slowly, trying to get your eye," Janet said, as coldly as she could. "Maybe you'd have better luck with her."

The man shook his head. "I'm more of a three-cheese lasagna guy myself."

Janet almost smiled—but she caught herself. *Careful, Janet. If you let him win it will only complicate things.*

The man's eyebrows raised, but she ignored him.

Janet looked at her T-band, a thin bracelet around her wrist displaying the time when touched, and then back at the man. "I believe you have only two more minutes."

"All right, then." He cleared his throat. "Four men walked into a restaurant. Which one left with the prettiest lady there?"

Janet rolled her eyes and crossed her arms. "That's it? That's the puzzle you want me to solve?"

The man nodded, dimples now seemingly glaring at Janet.

"Well. Let me ponder this a moment. The depth of this puzzle is so vast."

"Yes, but your pondering is eating away my two minutes."

Janet unfolded her arms and put her hand to her chest. "Oh, sorry. Yes, I wouldn't want to win on a technicality." Janet thought for a moment. "I'm going to assume this a hypothetical question and not what is currently happening. OK?"

The man shrugged. "Sure. OK."

Janet squinted, mostly with her eyebrows. *What is this guy up to?* She really had no idea how to answer his riddle. There was no information to come up with a logical solution, so there probably wasn't one.

"Sorry," she answered after a few more seconds went by. "I have no idea how to answer that."

The man leaned in. "The one who asked her."

Their eyes met for several seconds. His had a twinkle. Hers? She was trying not to give in to his. In spite of herself, and against all internal reservations, a smile swept across her face. She shook her head and chuckled. "That has to be the stupidest question and answer in the world."

The man sat up and laughed along with her. "Yes, but effective." He held out his hand. "Hi. I'm Bruce. Bruce O'Brien. It's my honor to meet the most beautiful woman here."

Janet took his hand. "Hi, Bruce. I'm Janet." She was hesitant to give out her last name. While he was adorable, if this didn't work out—or she didn't want it to work out—she didn't want him knowing how to reach her.

"Janet." The way he said her name made it sound like it was the most beautiful name he had ever heard. He held her

298

hand a couple seconds longer before letting it go.

He is certainly the smooth operator. Stay on your guard, Janet. But if he would hug me with those arms, I might just melt into the floor. Without meaning to, she was now staring at his biceps.

"Shall I pick you up at nineteen hundred tomorrow evening?"

"What?" She shook her head lightly and started to come out of her trance. "Oh, yes. That will be fine. I admit my defeat and accept the consequences."

Bruce held his head back and let out a laugh. "I certainly hope you find our time together to be one of good consequences."

Janet smiled. "We shall see."

Bruce smiled, displaying those dimples again. He stood, took her hand, and planted a kiss on the back of it. "Until tomorrow night, Janet. Shall I meet you in the hotel lobby over here?"

Janet nodded.

Bruce turned and walked back to his friends who had waited to see if he would be successful. They each patted him on his shoulder or back as they left the restaurant and headed toward the hotel.

Janet leaned back and let out a long breath. She took her napkin and fanned herself. *That was quite the experience.* She smiled. Her smile slowly faded. *What did you do, Janet? What can a city girl and a farmer find in common? After all, you came from farming territory to Chicago vowing never to return. Can any good come from this? Come on, Janet. It's a date, not a life-long commitment.* Her smile returned. Maybe it would be a good consequence after all.

She validated the check to her hotel room with her thumb-print, gathered her things, and headed back to her room.

Either sleep would be hard to come by or she'd have very pleasant dreams.

THE STELE PENTALOGY

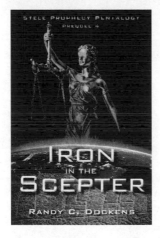

The next book in this exciting series, *Iron in the Scepter*, from Randy C. Dockens, will be available June 2020.

THE CODED MESSAGE TRILOGY

Come read this fast-paced trilogy, where an astrophysicist accidently stumbles upon a world secret that plunges him and his friends into an adventure of discovery and intrigue . . .

What Luke Loughton and his friends discover could possibly be the answer to a question you've been wondering all along.

Available Now